WINNING WAYS

A NOVEL

Toni Leland

Parallel Press

Winning Ways
©2004 Toni Leland

ISBN 1-887932-23-2
Library of Congress Catalog Number: 2004092285

First Edition

Printed in U.S.A.

This story is a work of fiction. Any resemblence to places, events, or persons, living or dead, is coincidental.

"Romancing the Horse"
http://www.tonileland.com

Parallel Press is an imprint of the Equine Graphics Publishing Group

Acknowledgments

Without the support and help of many people, this book would never have seen ink. Deepest appreciation to my critique partner, Janet, for her thoughtful and inspiring comments; horselover and fellow writer, Rebecca, for setting me on course; Bob, plotting partner and devil's advocate; John G. Lengel at U.S. Equestrian, Equine Drugs & Medications Program. Love and thanks to Mitzi and Katie, my first readers; Art & Holly for unlimited moral support. Special gratitude to Beth, Priscilla, and Charla–horse-women who reviewed the story from "inside the ring."

Cover

Arabian Filly, photograph by Diane Horton
Woodbury, Connecticut ©1990
Used with permission

*For Bob,
whose winning ways
kept me on track.*

One

Terrified whinnies echoed through the cavernous rafters of the huge show barn. Liz Barnett leapt to her feet and listened intently, trying to determine the location of the cries that could be nothing other than a horse in pain. She hurried toward the sound and, a moment later, cautiously lifted the latch on the heavy wooden stall door. She moved slowly toward a panic-stricken young horse in the corner.

Offering her hand, she kept her tone soft. "Easy...Whoa."

The wild-eyed filly nickered nervously, then resumed struggling to free her foreleg trapped between the thick bars of an old-fashioned iron hayrack mounted high on the wall.

Liz frowned at the ancient contraption.

"I can't believe anyone still uses these damned things."

Placing her right hand on the horse's slender back, she inched her left hand toward the head. *Thank God, she's wearing a halter.* Seeming to sense that help had arrived, the filly stopped thrashing for a moment. Liz lightly stroked the sleek neck and considered the situation. The horse wouldn't be able to free herself without rotating her hoof sideways into an unnatural position. Looking closer, Liz saw blood pulsing through a deep gash in the tender flesh across the top of the foot.

I can't let go of the halter. How'm I going to do this with one hand? She quickly reached through the bars, grasped the small foot, and then twisted it sideways just as the horse pulled back. The trim hoof slipped through the narrow opening.

The adrenaline crashing through Liz's body began to subside, making her legs weak and shaky. Ignoring the uncomfortable feeling, she concentrated on the filly's gushing wound. She needed to stop the bleeding–quickly.

She spotted a tack room across the aisle, and darted into it, thinking about what she might use as a tourniquet. A shirt and tie hung on a hook in the corner. She snatched the tie, grabbed a towel from a stack by the door, then sprinted back across the aisle.

The little mare trembled visibly, and Liz knew time would be critical. A glaze began to move over the filly's dark eyes, as her blood flowed into the straw bedding.

Liz stroked the smooth neck, murmuring, "It's okay, baby...it's okay."

Liz kneeled beside the injured leg, winding the tie twice around the fetlock joint, then securing it tightly just above the cut. The bleeding dwindled, and then stopped. Liz examined the deep laceration. *This'll need stitching. I'd better go find the show vet.*

"What the hell are you doing in here?"

Liz gasped, nearly toppling into the straw at the unexpected nearness of the angry voice. She scrambled to her feet, and whirled around. A dark, scowling man towered over her.

"Answer me!"

He stepped forward, and Liz automatically moved back, her breath coming in short puffs as she attempted to gain control of her thoughts and explain her presence. A second later, indignation bubbled up and she returned his hostile frown.

"Your horse's leg was wedged in that old hayrack, and–"

The man stepped past, brushing her off like a bothersome fly. Her skin prickled with anger and she glared at his back.

You arrogant jerk! A nasty comment formed on her lips, then she took a deep breath. *No. This isn't the way.* Her professional persona took over.

"The wound is deep, but I don't think the artery was damaged." She drew herself up to her full five feet. "And, by the way, you don't need to come barging in here acting as though I'm doing something wrong."

The man didn't respond to her challenge. He tenderly smoothed his hand over the animal's neck, murmuring reassurances to her. An instant later, he looked down.

"Damn! You used my best tie."

Liz blinked. *He's worried about the tie?*

He dropped to one knee. The filly stood quietly, her muscles quivering beneath her satiny coat, her breathing shallow, as he probed her injury. A minute later, he shook his head and stood up, turning to pin Liz with the darkest eyes she'd ever seen.

Her heart stumbled in its path at his exotic appearance. Skin the color of olivewood kissed by the Mediterranean sun. Gleaming blue-black hair sculpted against his skull, accentuating strong cheekbones and a wide forehead. An elegant moustache shadowed an aristocratic mouth. She took a deep breath, now aware of a new, stirring odor in the close quarters–the scent of a male ready to do battle for his territory.

His jaw relaxed, and he spoke gruffly. "Okay, thanks for your help. I need to get a vet."

A flash of heat warmed Liz's neck. "I *am* a vet." She looked him directly in the eye, her tone patronizing. "Now...would you like me to go find the show vet while you stay here with the horse?"

The hard lines on his face softened a little, the corners of his moustache twitched with the beginnings of a smile. His eyes dropped to her chest, and Liz's heart thumped behind her ribs, a surprising and infuriating reaction.

The moustache curled enticingly around a charming smile.

"Nah, she'll be fine. I'll keep an eye on her for awhile, then get her stitched up."

Liz said nothing, but turned and walked quickly away from the man that was making her pulse jump with something other than irritation.

The sounds and smells faded into the background as Liz strode down the aisle, consumed with shadowy feelings and confusion. Her skin tingled and she couldn't seem to breath normally. Who needed a battle with a cowboy in the middle of caring for an injured horse?

Absolutely nothing has gone right since I moved here. What's wrong with me? Liz dropped down onto a bale of hay in her tack stall and stared at the dusty toes of her paddock boots. *Why do I have such a negative effect on these damned Californians?* She replayed the stall scene again, and warmth crawled across her chest.

Heaving a sigh, she rose, and started down the aisle toward a brilliant square of sunshine framing the world outside the now-busy barn. Early spring sun warmed the top of her head, and glancing up at the vast, cloudless sky, Liz felt some of her tension fade. In retrospect, *she* definitely wouldn't appreciate finding a stranger messing with her horse. On the other hand, he could have been a little more gracious about her help, especially after he saw the wound.

I could have stood up for myself a little better. Why didn't I tell him right away that I'm a vet? Maybe I could have diffused the situation. She pursed her lips. Lately, her track record with surly cowboys hadn't given her much confidence. But then, she hadn't met any that looked like this one.

The handsome horseman's face flashed through her mind, provoking a distressing flutter in the pit of her stomach. Exhaling sharply, she shook off the sensation, and opened the show-office door.

An icy blast of air-conditioning peeled away the sun's delicious warmth from her bare arms, and an involuntary shudder shook her shoulders as she closed the door behind her.

"May I help you?"

"I want to settle my account for Legacy Arabians. I'm leaving early in the morning."

The woman behind the counter smiled brightly.

"Okey-doke. Just give me a minute."

While the show secretary pawed through the files, Liz reflected on the past four days. She'd spent a lot of money on the show, money she wasn't earning fast enough. *But I think I've done pretty well for the new kid on the block.*

The woman rattled a sheaf of papers. "Here, got 'em. Looks like three hundred dollars even." She leaned her elbows on the counter. "You new? I've never seen your name on any of our exhibitor lists."

"Yes, I moved here from Kentucky about six months ago. Takes some time to get organized."

Liz handed her a check, and the secretary lifted her chin and peered at it through her bifocals.

"A horse doctor, huh? How do you have time to show horses and be a busy vet at the same time?"

Yeah, right! Liz attempted to keep the sarcasm from her voice.

"It's a struggle, believe me."

On her way back to the barn, the woman's question needled her. *I'm anything but busy, thanks to the rural mentality of the locals.* The clash with Mr. Cowboy simply emphasized that her efforts to establish an equine practice in northern California were doomed. *What the hell am I going to do? It cost me a fortune to move the horses out here. I don't have a prayer of being able to go back home.*

A familiar voice interrupted her brooding.

"Liz! Wait up!"

Colleen O'Hearn jogged up, a smile brightening her pixy face. The petite blonde was the breeding manager at Fairhill Arabians, about a mile down the road from Legacy. The first time they'd met, Liz had been charmed by Colleen's feisty, take-no-stuff attitude, probably because her personality was so different from Liz's. *If I had just one-tenth of Colleen's determination to have things the way she wants them, I wouldn't be in this mess.*

Colleen's green eyes twinkled with genuine friendship.

"Congratulations! Great show!"

"Thanks. And Fairhill?"

The tiny woman's western twang rambled over her words. "Can't complain. Hey, I'm goin' to watch a coupla classes. C'mon over when ya get packed up."

Tossing a wave, she crossed the gravel drive, and disappeared into the arena building. Liz headed for her own stalls.

She packed everything except what she'd need the next morning, then took a moment to think. Looking at the seven colorful rosette ribbons pinned to the wall, pride and love swept through her chest. Five months of hard work had paid off. Her gaze swept over the elegant heads turned her way. *Having outstanding horses doesn't hurt anything either.*

Her focus stopped first on two-year-old Legacy Ashiiqah, a stunning rose-gray Polish-Egyptian mare who'd pranced her way to first place in the Two-Year-Old Mare Halter class, then on to claim the Champion Two-Year-Old Mare trophy. *Not bad for her first show season.* Liz's attention moved to the next stall, where Legacy Karma peered back at her from between the bars. The pure Polish bay colt had earned second place in the Yearling Stallion class, competing against twenty other horses. *Rather extraordinary for just a baby.* In the last stall stood Liz's favorite mare, Double B Amy's Pride, one of the original five foundation mares from her father's famous herd. A seasoned show-horse, the white mare had trotted away with the Over-Five championship.

Liz cocked her head and smiled at the large, dark eyes watching expectantly. "You were wonderful, Amykins."

These mares are the future of Legacy Arabians, the foundation of a great breeding program. And if Karma matures as perfectly as I think he will, he'll command some pricey stud fees in a year or two. For the moment, Liz forgot that her original plan had been to work her way gradually into showing her animals, fine-tuning them when she had the time. Thoughts about the future sent her spirits on a downward spiral again. Never in her wildest imaginings had she dreamed it would be so difficult to set up her veterinary practice in Gold Rush country, or that she'd have so much free time on her hands, as a result.

She moved back toward her packing, hearing the echo of old Doc Sams' crusty voice cajoling her over the telephone, describing the abundant opportunities she'd have if she joined his practice. It had seemed almost too good to be true, but her desire to start over in a new and interesting place had hampered her customary good judgment. How could she have foreseen the obstacles? Her shoulders slumped. Since moving to California, she'd woefully acknowledged, many times, the foolhardiness of accepting the position without thoroughly researching the area.

She examined her situation for what was probably the twentieth time that month. She had excellent credentials. Graduate of Tufts University Veterinary School. A specialty in equine reproduction. Top of her class. *That's not it. I'm overlooking something, but what?*

Her mood saddened further at the memory of the exciting two

years she'd spent as the resident veterinarian at a large Thorough-bred farm in Kentucky–the job she'd given up when her invalid father had died unexpectedly. Her throat tightened painfully. She knew now that she'd made decisions while the pain of his death was still a shroud over her heart. Made the wrong decision, and now didn't know how to reverse it.

Determined to shake off the hurtful memories, she packed the ribbons into the trunk, and snapped the latch.

"Dammit! I'm here now, and I don't intend to let a bunch of opinionated old ranchers decide my future!"

Two

Liz stepped through the entrance of the arena building and blinked. After the brilliant midday sunshine, the softer light inside made everything appear dark and dreamy for a few moments. When her eyes adjusted, she scanned the rows of seats ringing the center arena. Few spectators attended this last day of the show, but small pockets of exhibitors peppered the grandstand, unwinding after a long week of classes. Colleen's blonde head was not amongst them, but Liz sat down anyway, grateful for a chance to relax. A youth driving class entered the ring, and she watched with little interest.

Five minutes later, Colleen scooted into a seat, and took a long swig of soda. "You all packed?"

"Yeah...I could take off now, but I'd get home late, and still have to unload the horses and feed them. I'll stay here and try for a decent night's sleep."

"Ain't you goin' to the celebration tonight?"

"I'm not much for parties."

"Aw, come on. You could go for just a little while. These shindigs are fun. And besides, you'll meet lots of people from your area. You could hand out business cards." She grinned. "You can't ever have too many customers, huh?"

Little do you know. Colleen's comment was a keen-edged reminder that Liz needed clients, or she'd soon be in *real* trouble. Rather than a social event, she'd have to regard the get-together as a business necessity.

"Okay, but only for a while."

The music floating through the arena stopped abruptly as the last horse and cart left the ring. The loudspeaker blared the name of an exhibitor, the gate opened, and a tall woman led a beautiful chestnut stallion into the ring.

Colleen nudged Liz. "Liberty class. This is such a hoot."

Liz shook her head. "I haven't figured out the purpose of this class, but everyone seems to enjoy it."

The heavy bass thump of rock music filled the air, and the woman in the ring unhooked the lead rope. The horse whirled on his hind legs, and raced along the length of the arena, tail flagged and mane flying. The handler started after him, barking commands, and urging him on by snapping a long driving whip.

Liz watched with amusement as the woman positioned herself to catch the horse within the required two minutes. The animal danced away, tossing his head and staying just out of reach until the buzzer sounded, signaling the end of the time limit. Another three minutes passed before the woman and two helpers cornered the playful stallion.

Colleen chuckled. "She can never catch her horses. I don't know why she enters these classes."

Seconds later, a throbbing melody pulsed through the arena, the theme from *Bolero* charging the atmosphere with exotic promise.

Colleen gasped. "Oh, Gawd, there's Kurt! Ain't he the most gorgeous hunk you ever saw?"

Liz was already focused on the swarthy man in the ring. *Mr. Cowboy. Yes, he's most definitely gorgeous. Too bad that's where the attraction ends.*

She tried to keep her tone light. "What's his name?"

Colleen's eyebrows wiggled lecherously. "Kurt DeVallio. He's Italian or something. Mostly *something*!"

Liz glanced back at the arena and huffed. "Mostly jerk, I'd say."

She felt Colleen's inquiring gaze, but carefully ignored it, concentrating instead on Kurt. He reached out, and unhooked the lead rope from a small bay stallion with long legs and an exquisite head.

Liz's sharp eye for pedigree drove her thoughts. *That horse has to be straight Egyptian.*

The animal pranced away, his neck arched and tail up. He skimmed over the soft dirt, his finely boned legs moving in what seemed to be slow motion. Enchanted, Liz watched the horse dance in almost flawless rhythm to the music. *My God, how did he teach him to do that?*

Colleen spoke as though she'd read Liz's mind.

"That man has some really spooky, mystical powers over horses. It's almost like he's one of them, instead of one of us."

Liz wrested her gaze from the stallion and looked back to where Kurt stood motionless in the center of the arena, watching every move of the spectacular creature floating around the perimeter.

In the uncomfortably close quarters of the stall that morning, the man had seemed bulky and intimidating, but from this distance, Liz admired his tall stature, trim frame, well-developed muscles, and fluid movements. A now-familiar flutter started in the pit of her stomach, and warmth crawled up her neck. Audacious men usually didn't impress her, but this one absolutely had her attention.

The passionate swell of the music grew, and Kurt took two steps, holding out his right hand. The stallion ceased his performance and trotted straight over to Kurt. The lead rope snapped into place as the buzzer sounded and the audience went crazy. Liz exhaled slowly, unaware she'd been holding her breath.

Colleen nudged her arm. "Are ya gonna tell me about it?"

Liz blushed, wondering how many of her thoughts had been obvious.

"I had a little run-in with him this morning."

Colleen leaned forward eagerly, her eyes sparkling with curiosity. "Good or bad?"

"Definitely not good. Let's just say Mr. Cowboy is short on couth."

Colleen chuckled. "Yeah, I've heard he can be moody, but *I* wouldn't throw him away!"

Liz smiled wryly. "He's all yours."

❧

Three

L aughter and music drifted through the doors of the recreation hall. Inside, horse owners, trainers, and grooms partied, celebrating the end of a rigorous week. Liz took a deep breath and tried to relax. *I hate this!* She hesitated, trying to calm her thoughts. A glance down at her teal silk pantsuit sent doubt crawling through her head. *I'm probably over-dressed. Maybe I should have worn jeans.* She started thinking up reasons to avoid the festivities. She was tired...tomorrow would be a long, busy day...she needed her rest.

She sighed. Colleen was right. It was important to get out and meet other people in the industry, but Liz's quiet nature turned social gatherings into bad dreams. The last thing she wanted to do was pretend to have a good time. Before Liz could escape, Colleen appeared, her keen expression confirming there'd be no weaseling out of the evening.

The two women bumped their way through the crowd, inch by inch. The music was too loud, and people shouted over the ever-increasing din. Peals of unfettered laughter ricocheted around the room, and Liz's head began to swim. *Why did I let her talk me into this?*

They battled their way to the front of a small bar in the corner, and Liz ordered white wine. Glass in hand, she turned to watch the people. A few familiar faces, but mostly strangers. Mindlessly, she slipped her hand into her pocket, and fingered the hard edge of the business cards.

Many of the women in the crowd were well-dressed, wealthy owners whose designer clothes and stunning, one-of-a-kind jewelry generated a glamorous testament to the financial health of the Arabian horse industry. Liz relaxed a little, relieved that she *hadn't* worn jeans, but a tiny shiver of apprehension rolled across her shoulders anyway.

Colleen interrupted the fashion critique.

"That bartender is the cutest thing I've ever seen. I'll have to see if I can rattle his cage for later."

She caught Liz's expression, and a wicked smile sneaked across her face. "What? You think I'm a nun?"

Liz reddened, uncomfortable with Colleen's frank sexuality. As a girl, Liz's only female role model had been an aged maiden aunt in Connecticut, with whom she'd spent little time. Aunt Grace would *never* have revealed her interest in a man. By choice, Liz had limited experience with men, having always preferred to stay immersed safely in her studies, her veterinary practice and, more recently, her horses.

An urgent whisper tickled her ear. "Look who just walked in." Liz had already spotted Kurt. Her brain absorbed every detail of the impressive man moving through the merrymakers.

She shook her head. "Too bad his personality doesn't match his looks."

Colleen giggled. "Why don'tcha see if you can get him for a client?" Her tone became suggestive. "Or something?"

Liz shook her head vigorously and frowned. "Not a chance!"

Colleen gave her a pitying smile, then returned to the bar, intent on her mission to snare the bartender.

Liz looked back at the crowd, her eyes searching for Kurt. From her invisible spot amongst the mass of horse folk, she focused on the man who sent her pulse skipping through her veins. His outward appearance seemed warm and approachable, and he appeared to be popular with everyone, but something else enhanced his allure. Liz remembered the almost intimate interchange that morning, surrounded by wooden walls and iron bars, the air humming with repressed hostility and sensual tension.

She exhaled slowly, remembering how seamlessly his angry

face had smoothed into undisguised interest, and her surprising reaction to the change. Just thinking about it brought the same feelings flooding back into her chest.

Irritated that the memory held her so firmly, she redirected her
thoughts. *I might as well get some work done.* She reached for the
lump of cards in her pocket. As she worked through the crowd,
introducing herself to several horse owners, she advanced steadily
toward the door and her escape. She hated making small talk, but
she gave it her best shot, subconsciously marking time until she'd
be able to slip away.

A statuesque woman stood alone in the corner, and Liz saw
her chance.

"Hi, I'm Liz Barnett, Legacy Arabians in Garden Valley."

They shook hands and the woman smiled, visibly pleased to
have company.

"Annie Brown. I'm from Placerville."

"Yes, I saw you in the liberty class this afternoon."

"I can *never* catch that rascal. I don't know why I keep entering those classes, except they're so much fun."

"Isn't that what it's all about? Fun?"

"Here and now, yes. But get in there with the big boys, and
you spend a lot of time watching your back. What a crazy business!"

Liz nodded solemnly, then extended a business card.

Annie's face lit up. "A vet! Great! Doc Sams is always so busy
you can't get him when you need him. Everyone in these parts will
be glad he's found himself a partner."

Like I ever get called. Liz peeked at her watch, and then
searched the far corner to find Colleen, who was still optimisti-
cally chatting up the bartender. *I'll just slip out of here, then apologize later.*

She said goodbye to Annie, turned to leave, and collided with
a substantial body. Large hands grasped her shoulders firmly to
keep her from stumbling.

A velvety voice kissed the air. "Whoa, Girl."

Liz's gaze moved up the ladder of pearl buttons on a pale blue
shirt, and met the smoky gaze of Kurt DeVallio. Her heart thudded,

her senses sharpened by his nearness. Beneath the silk blouse, her shoulders burned under his firm touch, the sensation creeping downward like a slow trickle of warm honey. Her breath caught as amusement flooded into his dark, captivating eyes. His jaw was shadowed with a charcoal dusting of five-o'clock, and his moustache twitched as though he held back a smile.

Embarrassed by her thoughts, she dropped her eyes, her heart pounding so hard she feared he would hear it.

She stepped back from his grasp, and turned to leave.

"Sorry," she mumbled.

"Wait a minute."

She stopped, bracing herself for a tirade, though his voice held none of the aggression she'd heard that morning. She looked up, noticing his lips as he talked, and how his moustache rippled invitingly with the shape of each word.

"I want to apologize for this morning. I shouldn't have been so rude."

"I understand. I'm sure you were startled to find a stranger in your horse's stall."

He didn't reply, but a contemplative expression softened his strong features. The silence hanging between them felt uncomfortable, and Liz turned to leave. Kurt's hand settled on her arm, and a volley of tingles raced across her skin.

"Would you like to dance?"

She swallowed hard. She couldn't imagine getting close enough to this man to feel his arms around her.

She glanced up apologetically. "I really need to go. I'm leaving early in the morning."

His rich laugh swirled around them.

"One dance won't make you late."

Smiling wickedly, he reached down and took her hand. Unable to protest, she followed him onto the dance floor, the warmth of his strong fingers sending tiny electric shocks through her body, and waves of delighted terror through her mind. She slipped into his arms and let herself be swept away by the music and the man.

One spin later, his velvety voice broke into her tumbling thoughts.

"Let's start over. I'm Kurt DeVallio."

She tipped her head back to look at him. "Liz Barnett."

"I don't believe I've seen you here before."

"That's because I've never been here before."

Oh yeah, Liz... that was profound!

He pulled her close against him, guiding her effortlessly around the jammed dance floor. His warmth pervaded her clothing, taking her breath away. The soft surface of his chambray shirt brushed against her cheek, and a tantalizing whiff of spicy aftershave teased her nose. The music faded, and Liz stepped back, surprised and disappointed that the dance had ended. Kurt stood motionless, looking down into her eyes, his expression oozing self-confidence. Slowly, the sensual rhythm of *Bolero* filtered into Liz's head for the second time that day. With a smoldering look, Kurt roughly took her back into his arms, and began to move to the exotic beat of the music, his body brushing against her suggestively, his gaze never leaving her face. Courage rose in her chest and she held his eyes with her own, savoring the indescribable feelings that coursed through her body. The last strains of the song died, and Kurt stepped back, still holding her arms as he stared straight into her soul. Her chest felt as though it might cave in, excitement surging through her in reply to his unspoken message. A speculative smile spread slowly across his face. His voice hummed on the air between them.

"So, Liz Barnett. Where are you from?"

Relieved for the distraction, she relaxed. "Garden Valley. I've joined a veterinary practice there."

"Oh, yeah, Doc Sams. I heard he had a new partner, but nobody told me he'd wimped out 'n' hired a *fee*-male."

Like a bucket of ice water, the remark drenched Liz's warm feelings. She jerked her arms from his grasp, and stepped back.

"And what possible difference could *that* make?"

The deep frustrations of the past few months leapt up, and adrenaline flooded through her. She couldn't deal with one more insult that day. Without waiting for an answer, she left the dancefloor, headed for the exit.

Outside, Colleen snagged her arm. "Well, you two certainly hit it off."

Liz glowered. "I don't *think* so!"

She glanced back over her shoulder. Through the open door, Kurt remained exactly where she'd left him, his arms casually folded across his chest, a sexy smile lighting his extraordinary face. Dark eyes challenged her to come back.

She met his gaze. *No way, Cowboy!*

Kurt's attention lingered on Liz's firm behind, rippling innocently beneath the slinky fabric of her pants as she stalked away. *Man, she is some classy filly!* The opulent color and sheen of her clothing complemented her smooth olive skin and enhanced her deep blue eyes. Raven-colored hair, thick and shiny, brushed her shoulders. *If I had to guess, I'd say the lady has some Italian blood flowing through those hot veins.* He grinned, remembering her feisty manner in the stall that morning. He'd also felt her tense eagerness on the dance floor. The memory stimulated his thoughts toward finding a way to get her into his bed.

Four

The rising sun sparkled through the branches of the massive oaks towering over the exercise paddock. The air felt crisp and cool, but the promise of a sweltering day whispered on the breeze ruffling through Liz's hair. The muted, waking-up sounds of morning were a joyous melody to her ears. *I'm so glad to be home.*

The blacked-legged, chocolate brown colt at the end of the lunge-line slowed his pace, sensing that Liz's attention had wandered. Clucking her tongue, she snapped the whip and encouraged him to stay on the outer edges of the circle he trotted.

"Good boy, Karma."

Liz appreciated the horse's immediate obedience. In another six months, her little boy would start to mature into a breeding stallion and, when that happened, it would be difficult to keep his attention on such mundane things as trotting in a circle.

She considered her ambitious dreams. Qualifying her horses at a regional show meant they would be eligible for the national competition in Albuquerque, where she'd show them against some of the toughest trainers and fanciest horses in the industry. Walking back to the barn, she squared her shoulders and lifted her chin. *Why not? My horses are as good as any out there.*

A moment later, Kurt DeVallio's face wormed its way into her thoughts again. *I don't need that kind of attention. I don't know who he thinks he is, but I'm not buying it.* Lost in thoughts about the dark cowboy's intrusion into her life, Liz closed the stall door so hard the latch snapped loudly, startling Karma. The giddy colt leapt about his stall as though bogey-men were after him.

Liz stepped back inside, and reached for his shoulder. "Oh, Sweetie, I'm sorry."

She moved closer, stroking his neck, murmuring reassurances to him until his quivering nostrils and wild eyes returned to their normal state. A few minutes later, soothed by the familiar smells of fresh hay, sweet oats laced with molasses, and the unique odor of warm horseflesh, she turned her thoughts to the future and what she needed to do to salvage it.

Later that morning, Liz stood at her desk, looking around the office she'd set up in her study. The rambling old farmhouse had been added to over the decades, and that room had been one of the newer additions. Warm oak paneling absorbed the morning sun, casting a glow over the floor-to-ceiling bookshelves that filled one wall. The array of well-worn book-spines looked like a colorful miniature skyline on each shelf. Interspersed here and there were several photographs of her father with his champion horses. The wall behind her small desk was filled with framed diplomas, awards for excellence, and her veterinary licenses.

How excited she'd been, arranging furniture, organizing the filing cabinet, recording a crisp, professional message on the answering machine. Her dreams had seemed fulfilled–associate status with an established veterinary practice. How much better could it get? Her throat tightened and tears prickled her eyes. *How much worse might it get?*

The telephone jarred her from the clutch of dismal thoughts, and Colleen's bright voice chirped over the line.

"Hi, you busy? I thought I'd stop by."

Liz's mood brightened. "Hey, that'd be great. I want to talk to you about a couple of things."

While she waited, Liz made some notes. Colleen had lived in the area for a long time. Surely, she'd have some insights that would help solve Liz's problem.

A few minutes later, the crunch of tires on gravel was followed by the creak of the screen door. Colleen appeared at the study door, looking a little like a western Barbie doll in tight jeans and a denim shirt with fringe dangling saucily across her chest. Pristine red snakeskin cowboy boots looked as though they'd never seen a stirrup.

She dropped into a chair. "How's business?"

Liz grimaced. "Don't ask."

Colleen leaned forward, her tone sincere. "What's going on? Maybe I can help."

Liz plunged in, frustration coloring every word.

"I was such a fool to make this move without checking it out. Hell, I've researched vacations more thoroughly than I did this job!"

"What do you mean? You *are* an associate, aren't ya?"

Liz snorted. "Oh, yeah, but only on paper. I *never* get called. Doc Sams takes all the farm calls, and I end up writing prescriptions for Mrs. Long's neurotic parakeet."

Liz heard her own whiney, cry-baby tone, and shook her head.

"Colleen, in the last six months, I've been called on one emergency, and that was only because Doc Sams was already taking care of two others." She rose from her chair, and paced. "Lord knows, I have the credentials to handle anything that comes my way, but nobody will give me a chance and, since I don't know what the problem is, I can't fix it."

Colleen sat back in the chair, crossed her legs, and cocked her head. Her tone was sympathetic, but firm.

"I can't believe you haven't figured it out. The problem is, you haven't been in practice very long, and you're a woman–a young one, to boot...You're in ranchin' country, Honey, and these guys ain't gonna fall all over ya just 'cause you were a hotshot back East. In fact, that probably works *against* ya."

Liz's brief wave of self-pity disappeared. She'd already suspected that her problem might have something to do with her age and gender, but the idea that the locals considered her inexperienced and incapable *really* stung. Her own confidence in her skills had apparently blinded her to the essence of the problem.

Colleen's tone softened a little. "You'll just have to prove yourself, whatever it takes. Doc Sams is long past retirement, an' he knows it. He wouldn't have offered you the job if he didn't plan to step down at some point, but maybe he's startin' to resist the idea of retiring, so he's still tryin' to handle everything. His long-time clients want his attention as long as they can have it. And you're playin' the prima donna, waitin' to be invited. I think you'll need to do some active marketing if you want to get these old geezers on board."

Liz sighed. "You're right, of course. I just needed someone to kick me in the butt." She brightened. "Well, at least I've had plenty of time to work with my show horses."

Her optimism disappeared with the shadow that crossed Colleen's features.

"Liz, I hate to be the one to tell ya this, but you're gonna run into the same thing in the show ring. Not the small shows, but the big ones, the ones that count. I know you're trying for Nationals, but it's a long, political road to get there, and you ain't paid your dues yet."

Liz had finally had enough. "You know...this is the modern world. Women have been accomplishing wonderful things for a long time, and I don't intend to let a bunch of time-warped cow-boys send me running!"

Colleen applauded, her face breaking into a sunny smile.

"All *right*! That's more like it. Now, tell me what I can do to help."

An hour later, Liz had a list of over a dozen potential clients within a thirty-mile radius–all women who owned horses.

Colleen's approach to the problem was a clever one.

"Why not fight fire with fire? Let Doc *Sams* take care of the tough old boys." She chuckled wickedly. "And *you* concentrate on the *real* horse people."

Liz had to admit the plan made sense. After all, if the men supported each other and stuck together, why wouldn't the women welcome the same option? At least it was a place to start her sal-vage operation.

Over lunch on the screen porch, the conversation moved to a more personal level. Colleen took a long swallow of iced tea, then thoughtfully set down her glass.

"You've never told me why you decided to move out here in the first place, other than the job."

Liz shook her head dejectedly. "I've wondered that myself lately." She sat back in the comfortable wicker chair. "My dad was a famous horse-trainer. My mother died when I was four, and Dad retired from the ring to raise me. We lived on a small farm in Kentucky, where he started breeding Arabians. He ended up with one of the most popular bloodlines in the industry, Double B."

"Oh, Lordy, I *guess*! That was *your* dad?"

Liz nodded, feeling the familiar pain begin in her chest. "I was in my last year at vet school when he suffered a mild stroke. By graduation, he'd mostly recovered, but couldn't continue working with the horses. He became very depressed. I took a job at a large Thoroughbred farm nearby, and things were fine for awhile. Then he had another stroke, and I had to juggle work and looking after him."

The painful memories flooded through Liz's head, images as clear as if they'd been yesterday.

"Then, one morning he didn't wake up..."

The pain in her chest was now so intense she couldn't breathe. Her father's death still affected her deeply, even after almost three years. She struggled on with her story.

"It took me over two years to settle the estate and disperse sixty head of horses. I'd been on emergency leave from the Thoroughbred farm, but they finally had to replace me."

Colleen's face reflected her regret at starting the conversation. "Liz, I'm so sorry. I didn't know–"

"No, it's okay. Anyway, I decided a change of scenery would do me good, and I thought I'd like to try my hand at showing horses, since I had some really good ones. Then this job jumped up and bit me." She smiled without mirth. "Figuratively speaking."

"Liz, you're gonna do fine. You just need to work at it."

The intense atmosphere began to dissipate, and Colleen took the opportunity to leave. On the way out to her truck, she snapped her fingers and stopped.

"Oh! Are you still interested in buyin' more mares?"

"Yeah, but with my current career slump, my bank account probably isn't."

Colleen climbed up into the driver's seat, then rolled down the window.

"Go see Marilyn Cook over in Placerville. She's on your new list of prospects. She's gettin' on, and has lots of horses. I think she has some pretty good lines, but I don't remember which ones." The truck engine coughed, then started. "And don't forget to give her a business card. Ya might get lucky."

As Colleen's taillights disappeared down the driveway, Liz's thoughts were skeptical. *I need more than luck right now.* Sadness crept into her heart, followed by an overwhelming urge to go home. Even if she did, would she be able to pick up the pieces, go on with her life as before? She blinked back the tears. *No. That was then, and this is now. I can't look back.*

Five

The twenty-five-minute drive from Garden Valley to Placerville allowed Liz plenty of time to think about her precarious financial position. *Colleen's right. I can't sit back and wait for something to happen.* She flushed, embarrassed by Colleen's candid comment about over-confidence.

An instant later, she bristled. "Well, I *am* good! What's wrong with believing in yourself?"

Can't see the forest for the trees, that's what.

Another troubling thought intruded, and her shoulders slumped. She'd assumed that winning enough points at the regional show would assure her chances to compete at the Nationals. Apparently, she had *another* obstacle to worry about.

Ahead, a dilapidated wooden sign leaned at an angle, the white paint peeling, the black letters faded. *Cook's Arabians.* Liz left her problems behind and followed the dirt road, stopping in front of a small house flanked by an old barn. Three small, scruffy dogs barreled out from behind the building, barking wildly. A short, sturdy woman opened the screen door and hollered at them. The dogs quieted at once, and ran to sit at her feet.

Liz glanced down at three pair of watchful eyes.

"Quite the security crew you have there."

The older woman grinned. "Oh, them. They're harmless. I think they'd probably share the loot with a burglar. I'm Marilyn. C'mon in."

Liz stepped into the dim house, wrinkling her nose at the stale odor of cigarettes and animals permeating the air. Beyond the kitchen, a tiny sitting area overflowed with horse tack, magazines, dog beds, and a dingy overstuffed couch where several cats dozed.

Marilyn dropped into a worn recliner, and Liz eased onto a bare spot on the couch next to a fat tabby that angrily twitched its tail at being disturbed. While Marilyn sifted through large piles of papers on the coffee table, Liz's gaze moved around the room. One wall displayed dozens of photographs of horses at shows, horses in pastures, horses with riders or being driven. Dusty trophies, platters, bowls, and loving cups covered the surface of a card table in the corner–a lifetime of accomplishment.

"It looks like you were pretty successful in the ring."

Marilyn glanced up and waved her cigarette dismissively.

"Oh, that stuff. Did that when I was young and had some help. Now I don't even polish 'em." She shoved a folder across the table. "Here's some snapshots of the horses I have for sale. I hate to get rid of 'em, but I gotta...I'm too old, they're too much work."

Liz looked through the photographs, disappointment filling her thoughts as she glanced at the pedigrees. *Good, but not spectacular. Nuts! How can I diplomatically tell her that the horses aren't good enough, then turn around and ask for her vet custom?*

"Uh, Marilyn, they're very nice, but, you know, I don't think photographs do a horse justice. Could I take a look at the mares?" *Dammit! Quit beating around the bush. The pedigrees won't improve by the time you get to the barn.*

"Sure, honey. Mind the dogs, they'll go off again."

Following Marilyn, and trying to dodge the clouds of cigarette smoke that trailed behind, Liz pondered a way to get to the main reason for the visit. *Maybe I can take a quick look to be polite, and then tell her I'm not quite ready, that I'm still in the browsing stage.*

When they reached the barn door, Liz pulled out a business card and plunged in.

"How many horses do you have?"

"Nine...about eight too many."

Liz offered the card. "I'd like the chance to care for your stock."

Marilyn dropped the cigarette, and ground it out, then looked at the card.

"So *you're* the new doc. Nobody told me it was a gal, but that's even better. It's about time the old coot got some *real* help!"

The inside of the barn was as messy as the house. Neglect and carelessness. A disaster waiting to happen. The floor hadn't been swept in at least a week. Two broken bales of straw littered the aisle, aided by the draft that swirled through the barn from open doors and windows. Liz glimpsed masses of cobwebs draped through the rafters, frosted with dust and speckled with pieces of straw. A serious fire hazard. Her heart thudded and she pushed the horrible thought away.

Marilyn opened a stall door at the end of the aisle.

"Come on down here. This here's my pride and joy, Miss Marcy." Marilyn smiled proudly as she pointed at the animal. "She's half Egyptian an' half Polish. That's a very popular combination, y'know."

Liz stepped forward to get a better look into the dimly lit stall. Her heart sank. At least nineteen years old, Miss Marcy had seen better days. Significantly underweight, the mare's hip bones stuck out and her ribs were visible beneath a dull, white coat. Her eyes held no luster or fire, and her ears drooped. The poor old thing looked as though she hadn't been groomed in months. Liz's eyes burned. *How can anyone treat these animals this way?*

"Her sway-back is 'cause she's had eleven foals. Did you look at her pedigree?"

Liz smothered a sigh. "Marilyn, she's nice, but too old for my herd. I need young broodmares."

She started edging toward the door and her freedom.

Marilyn's tone sounded cross. "Well, you could go on down the road to Aliqua Arabians. They've got dozens of horses–not all that great, but they're *young*."

Liz was dismayed at how badly she'd botched the visit. As they walked toward the house, Marilyn hurried to end the visit.

"They're in El Dorado, not far. Owner's name is Eve." She opened the screen door and looked back.

"I'll give a holler if I need ya."

Back home, the light glowed steadily on the answering machine in Liz's office. Disgusted, but not surprised, she headed for the barn to clean stalls and set up the evening feed.

Nine stalls later, she climbed wearily up the stairs to the hayloft. A shaft of late afternoon sun slanted through the single window. Hay dust danced in the beam, reminding her of smoke, followed by a mental picture of Marilyn's firetrap barn. Liz's skin crawled with horror. Nothing was more terrifying to a horse owner than the possibility of a barn fire. She'd had one experience with a fire in Kentucky, for which all of her medical training had been useless. Four horses, overcome by smoke, had perished while Liz and others had helplessly stood by, unable to enter the blazing barn.

Shaking off the ghastly memory, she began tossing flakes of hay into the stalls below. Finally, hot and tired, she dropped into a pile of straw, and closed her eyes.

Unbidden, Kurt's face appeared in her mind, and a shiver of delight moved across her damp skin. How wonderful she'd felt in his arms, traveling around the dance floor. Immersing herself in the daydream, she heard his soft voice, felt the texture of his shirt, smelled his male scent. Nestling deeper into the straw, she abandoned herself to dreams of how his arms might feel embracing her in the heat of passion. Her body tingled and arousal seethed through her.

Stunned by her response to the sexy daydream, she scrambled to her feet. *This is ridiculous. I'm acting like a lovesick teenager. I'll probably never even see him again.* Angrily brushing the hay dust from her jeans, she took a deep breath and tried to will away her tension. Moving toward the stairs, she glanced back at the bed of straw, feeling the uneasy burn of desire that would haunt her for hours.

Six

Abandoning herself to thoughts of Kurt had been an unfortunate mistake, and Liz's restlessness threaded through the remainder of the day. In the study, she looked at her empty schedule book, and thought again about Colleen's plan, and her own good intentions. She pulled out the list of prospects, and reached for the phone.

A woman answered, her voice lilting with a hint of accent.

"Aliqua Arabians, Eve speaking."

"Hi, this is Dr. Liz Barnett in Garden Valley. Marilyn Cook gave me your name."

"...Yes?"

Liz gulped at the frosty tone of voice. *Perhaps mentioning Marilyn wasn't such a good idea.*

"She said you have horses for sale, and I'm looking for Arabian breeding stock. Specifically, mares."

The woman's tone didn't sound friendly. "Oh. And who are you again?"

"Liz Barnett. I'm the new vet at Doc Sams' practice, and I own Legacy Arabians in Garden Valley. I've been here about six months."

Eve's tone warmed considerably at the prospect of a real sale. "Well, I do have some mares for sale. I breed predominantly Polish, some Egyptian. Would you care to look at the stock I have available?"

"I could come by tomorrow." *Or any day, for that matter.*

"Fine. My trainer's away at an auction, but I can show you what I have."

Liz put the phone down and took a deep breath. *Here I am again, shopping for horses when I should be chasing customers.*

The next afternoon, Liz again cruised along the road to Placerville. The ever-present Sierras reigned over the valley like ermine-mantled monarchs. The magnificence and desolation of northern California energized her, and filled her with optimism that goals could be accomplished on a grand scale.

South of Placerville, Liz quickly came upon El Dorado, a quaint town in the heart of gold country. Following Eve's directions, Liz pulled into an enormous gated entrance of white marble and ornate wrought-iron. An elegantly-lettered sign hung over the drive. The paved road climbed gradually through a huge stand of ancient pine trees. Emerging from the green canopy, Liz gasped. On the hillside sat an incredibly large house, obviously brand new and custom-built. Beautiful landscaping framed the building against the evergreens on the mountain behind it. A garden area, stone benches, gazebo, and large deck filled one entire side of the property.

She drove past the front, and pulled in next to a late-model Corvette parked beside a new Lincoln Navigator. A luxury six-horse trailer sat alongside the barn. *That cost an easy fifty-grand.* The traditional New England style barn was gorgeous, complete with cupola and antique weathervane. Behind the building, white-fenced pastures spread in every direction.

Walking along the stepping stone path to the front door, Liz promised herself she wouldn't leave that farm without Eve's business.

Before she could lift the knocker, a small, shapely woman in her mid-fifties opened the door. Eve Aliqua was every inch Irish: vibrant green eyes, a ruddy complexion sprinkled with tiny freckles, and flaming red hair pulled back in a ponytail.

She smiled and gestured toward the living room. In person, her accent was more noticeable.

"I made some iced tea. I'll be right back."

Liz examined the surroundings while she waited. Spacious

rooms were illuminated by floor-to-ceiling picture windows, providing a panoramic view of the surrounding foothills and valleys, the mountains standing guard on the horizon. Lustrous oak beams and paneling glowed in the reflection of carefully designed lighting in each area. Comfortable, unpretentious leather sofas and chairs huddled around a tile-topped Spanish-style coffee table.

Eve certainly had money, but from where? Selling horses? Surely not. More likely an inheritance or a lucrative divorce. A moment later, Eve returned with a tray.

Liz wasted no time in offering her a business card.

"I'm in the process of setting up my equine practice. Are you a client of Doc Sams?"

Eve rolled her eyes and shook her head. "When he can work me in. I usually have to get the vets to come over from Cameron Park. Not for emergencies, of course. It's too far." She looked at the card. "But now that *you're* available, I can call you."

Liz beamed, her stomach doing a somersault. *This isn't so hard.*

Eve moved to a glass-fronted barrister's bookcase by the fireplace, and pulled out a thick notebook.

"You can look through the pedigree book, see if anything matches up with your breeding program."

"Eve, I feel really peculiar calling you out of the blue, like this."

"Oh, that's all right. I will say, it rather threw me when you mentioned Marilyn. We've had some problems in the past, and I wondered just what she'd thrown my way this time."

Liz paged through the binder, bewitched by the extraordinary bloodlines. Any horse that had ever been anything was included in the first three generations of every pedigree. She could barely contain her excitement. *What a gene pool! Here's a chance to bring some outstanding blood into my herd, if I can just afford it...*

Eve's lightly clipped words penetrated Liz's thoughts.

"We can go up to the barn whenever you're ready. I think the grooms have everyone cleaned up."

As they walked across the gravel toward the impressive building, Eve apologized.

"I'm not very good at showing off the horses to prospective

buyers, and I can't demonstrate their riding or driving capabilities. But if you see something you like, perhaps you could come back when the trainer is here."

Liz's stomach fluttered with anticipation of seeing the mares that matched those incredible pedigrees.

The interior of the barn was finished in solid oak, smooth and lustrous. Liz looked down the length of the immaculate aisle. When the lights came on, inquisitive faces appeared over stall doors, and Liz didn't breathe for a moment. The heads were exquisite, as Arabian heads *should* be. She walked slowly down the aisle, stopping at each stall for a closer look, understanding that they were some of the finest horses she'd ever seen. Her heart sank. *I'll never be able to afford any of these mares.*

Eve opened a stall door. "This mare is a Polish-Russian cross. You can see that her conformation is a little different than the others. That's the Russian influence. They prefer strong, athletic horses. She's in foal to our straight Egyptian stallion, and due in January."

Liz assessed the dark gray mare. The horse's features were heavier than Liz preferred, but the conformation was excellent and the animal had a regal, almost distant bearing.

"Why are you selling her?"

Eve closed the stall door. "Actually, I just don't like her very much." She shrugged. "Her personality isn't as friendly as the rest of my mares."

Liz nodded, but said nothing. *You're not exactly out-going yourself. Horses are very tuned-in to human body language.*

Following Eve down the aisle, Liz seriously considered the gray mare. *A real possibility...introduce some diversified blood into my herd. Plus, the foal she's carrying could be really outstanding.*

Eve stopped beside another stall door and waited for Liz's reaction. Inside the twelve-by-twelve enclosure filled with mounds of straw, a magnificent white mare watched the two women. Her large, dark eyes held a soft luminosity. Her statuesque body was strong, yet delicate, with superb bone structure and faultless conformation. The horse had a magical effect on Liz. *All she needs is a unicorn horn.*

"Fair Lady's a ten-year-old Polish-Egyptian cross. I've had six beautiful foals out of her."

As if summoned, a tiny head peeked around Fair Lady's chest. The foal was an exquisite replica of her mother. Fair Lady lowered her head and, chuckling in her throat, nudged the little one back.

Eve laughed. "As you can see, she's a very good mother."

They moved on down the aisle, and Liz looked at other horses, but couldn't shake the image of the white mare.

Abruptly, Eve turned, brushing past Liz. "Well, it's about time you showed up!"

She walked rapidly toward a tall silhouette in the open barn door. Liz turned her thoughts to how she could manage to buy the gray mare *and* Fair Lady.

Seven

W ell, well. If it isn't *Doctor* Barnett!"
Liz's heart froze at the sound of the familiar voice behind her. *What's he doing here?* Hayloft fantasies rushed into her head, but she quickly pushed them aside. She turned, and met Kurt's gaze.

"Hi...I'm sorry, what was your name again?"

The flicker of a smile beneath his moustache implied that her impudence had been wasted.

Confused, Eve stared at Liz. "This is my trainer, Kurt DeVallio. Have you two met?"

Liz struggled to keep her expression neutral. "Yes, we were introduced at the Sacramento show." *If you could call it an introduction.*

Kurt cleared his throat. "I'll go unload my gear and let you two get on with whatever you're doing." He threw Liz a veiled look. "Nice to see you again."

She nodded, but said nothing as he sauntered away. *Unbelievable! Of all the bad luck.*

Eve's voice brought Liz back to the business at hand.

"Did you see any mares you're interested in?"

"Actually, I'm considering the gray Russian, and I love that white mare with the foal. Would you consider a package price?"

Eve grinned. "I'm in the horse business. *Anything's* possible."

On the drive home, Liz pondered the sticky turn of events. *I suppose Mr. Cowboy would have something to say about a lady vet working at Aliqua.* His attitude concerning women had come across loud and clear at the show, but there'd been no hint of it there in the barn. He might have his opinions, but probably wouldn't buck the boss. Eve didn't appear to be a woman who would put up with chauvinistic behavior. Following that thought, Liz decided her biggest challenge would be to keep Kurt from influencing *her*.

A minute later, the prospect of new horses at Legacy sent a jolt of excitement through her. Muscala, the Russian mare, had never been shown. Eve had acquired her strictly for bloodlines. Fair Lady had been retired from showing years before, and enjoyed the pampered life of a top-producing broodmare. The only negative aspect of the deal was that Fair Lady's beautiful filly foal was not part of it. Eve had adamantly refused to sell her.

Even without the baby, Liz's "package deal" had ended up costing eighty thousand dollars–more than she'd anticipated, but a reasonable price for such excellent bloodstock. She knew she probably shouldn't be dipping into the savings account, but she was beginning to have a much better feeling about the future. *Once I have some cash flow, I can replace what I borrow.*

The following morning, she returned to Aliqua to sign the sales contract and drop off a deposit check.

Eve smiled brightly as she handed over the paperwork.

"Congratulations, and welcome to the area. We're about due for vaccinations and foal check-ups, so I'll definitely be giving you a call."

A cloak of security settled around Liz's shoulders. Things were definitely looking brighter. Giddy thoughts filled her head as she took everything out to the truck. *I can't believe I actually own Fair Lady.* She rolled down the window to release the heat in the cab, then headed toward the barn for one last peek at her fairy tale horse. At the door, she heard angry words echoing inside.

Kurt's voice rang sharp with irritation. "I'm telling you, you're making a mistake. That mare is one of the best horses you've got."

Liz stood outside the door, not meaning to eavesdrop, but also reluctant to get involved in an argument that sounded as though it might concern *her*. Then her true feelings edged in. What she *really*

didn't want was to face Kurt again–an upsetting thought. Her career–
no, her very existence–depended upon her profession. She could
not afford to be distracted or deterred by anyone or anything.

She stepped inside the door, pausing for a minute to let her
eyes adjust to the dim light. Kurt stood with his back to the door,
Eve in front of him, her face flushed with anger.

Kurt's voice rumbled. "And why you'd even consider selling
her that–"

Eve spotted Liz, and quickly shook her head at him. An overly
bright smile masked her ruddy face as she strode toward Liz.

"I'm going to turn Fair Lady and her baby out for awhile. Since
you own her now, would you like to lead her? The baby will just
follow...Oh!" She laughed. "I guess I don't have to tell *you* that."

From the corner of her eye, Liz saw Kurt move to the other
side of the aisle. Her thoughts churned as she haltered Fair Lady,
then led her out of the barn. *Why is he being so standoffish? He
didn't even say hello.* Recalling the heated argument she'd overheard, a chill ran across her neck. *I wonder what that was all about.*

From the murky depths of the stall, Kurt watched her, letting
his gaze roam boldly over her body, licking his lips at the way her
shirt caressed her breasts, then tapered softly into her trim waist-
band. His gaze drifted to her tight rear-end, and a stir moved beneath his belt buckle. *What that woman does for blue jeans is a
crime!*

His delicious discomfort painted all sorts of erotic images into
his brain. He remembered how good she'd felt in his arms, and he
teased himself with the vision of seducing her on a bed of straw.

Exhaling sharply, he directed his thoughts back to his task.
*Not now. There's only one thing I should be thinking about, and I
don't need any distractions.* He watched Liz and the horses disappear through the barn door. *Maybe later.*

After returning home, Liz tried, without success, to figure out
Kurt's puzzling behavior. *I guess I'm a little short in the experi-
ence-with-men department.* She giggled out loud at the understate-
ment. Who did she think she was kidding? Kurt DeVallio wasn't

like any man she'd ever met. Fascinating. A little frightening. His take-charge attitude irritated the hell out of her, but in spite of everything, she felt deeply attracted to him. *And now I'll have to work with him. Why can't my life be simple?*

She telephoned Aliqua later that evening.

"Hi, Eve. I forgot to ask you when I could pick up the mares."

"I can't let Fair Lady go until the filly is weaned, but you can pick up Muscala any time...Actually, I guess I could just have Kurt deliver her to you."

Liz had conflicting emotions about the idea, and her heart skipped a beat.

"Okay, that'll be fine. Let me know."

If she had the chance to talk to him alone, he might act differently...maybe she'd even find out what the argument was about.

Eight

E ve stuck her head through the tack room door.
"When you're finished there, come up to the office. I need to talk to you."

Kurt nodded, then turned his attention back to a set of tangled reins. *Yes, Ma'am!* He clenched his jaw, resisting the urge to bark a retort that would get him into trouble.

I wonder what she wants now. He shook his head. Eve was a difficult woman to work for. *Hell, any woman is difficult to work for. They throw their weight around, acting like men should agree with them just because they're females.*

Kurt's attitude had gotten him into trouble before, but he'd come by it naturally. His father had immigrated to America as a young man to seek his fortune, bringing a timid new bride with him. Kurt and his three sisters had grown up under their father's ruthless thumb, as the elder DeVallio had struggled to keep his neighborhood grocery store alive in an era of flourishing super-markets and greater customer mobility. The deep cultural influences of Kurt's old-country upbringing were firmly ingrained and, while some of his opinions reflected his father's, modern times had tempered them somewhat.

Papa DeVallio had believed that women belonged at home, bearing the children and caring for the men–period. Kurt's over-bearing sisters had given him a small insight into what made women tick, but not enough to keep him out of trouble. He still firmly resisted being bossed around by any female.

Eve was hanging up the phone when Kurt came into the office. She glanced up and pointed to a chair by the desk.

"We need to talk about the next few shows."

Kurt bristled, but sat down. He didn't appreciate being told how to manage his show schedule. He'd been showing horses for a long time. Very successfully...until New Mexico.

He composed himself. "What's up?"

His boss's expression was one of guarded excitement.

"I have a buyer for Ebony. Billy Benton has made an offer..." She paused for effect. "A hundred-and-seventy-five thousand."

Kurt whistled. "Holy Moley!"

Eve's tone sobered. "But there's a catch. The offer only stands if the horse wins the regional championship in San Francisco."

Kurt's eyes narrowed into slits. "So? The horse is national material. What's the problem?"

"You *have* to win. I need this deal, Kurt. Billy wants to show Ebony at the Nationals himself. I don't have to tell you, a national championship and a major sale would put my breeding program on the map." She looked directly into his eyes, her tone menacing. "I *want* to be on the map, and it's *your* responsibility to see that it happens. You owe me."

Rage billowed inside Kurt's head. *These damned rich owners! They think they can buy their wins, get what they want just by snapping their fingers.* His gut instinct about the young stallion told him that the horse could win any competition he entered. Kurt just didn't like being told that he *had* to do it.

Further infuriated by the prospect of turning over a "made horse" so that someone else could have the glory, Kurt felt like a prisoner. Worse, Eve was right...he *did* owe her. She'd hired him when no one else would take a chance. Sadness speared his heart. It hadn't always been thus. There'd been a time when he'd been at the top, been in control, a time when.... By habit, he forced himself away from that line of thought.

Before he had time to say something he'd regret, Eve's voice broke in.

"If you can pull this off, I'll double your commission on the sale."

Eve was talking about a lot of money. Enough money to round

out a savings account sitting idly in New Mexico. Money he could earn by simply doing what he loved most.

He stood up, drenching her with his most dazzling smile.

"Consider it done."

Nine

Not-so-distant thunder grumbled through the quiet afternoon, and the atmosphere in the barn became expectantly still. Liz set the manure rake aside, and moved to the window. An ominous sky pressed down on the landscape, and strong gusts whipped a row of graceful cedars into a frenzied dance. As Nature played out its awe-inspiring scene, Liz suddenly had the feeling she wasn't alone. Holding her breath, she turned slowly, and moved silently toward the stall door.

Directly across the aisle, Kurt lounged against the wall, his eyes twinkling, a dimple punctuating one corner of his smile. Liz's heart banged against her ribs, a flood of anger spurring the crazy rhythm as she stormed out of the stall, and up to within a foot of his tall frame.

"Just what the hell do you think you're doing, sneaking in here?"

He grinned and shrugged away from the wall.

"You look gorgeous when you're mad." He reached out, laying his hand on her shoulder. "I'm sorry, I didn't mean to scare you. I started to say something, but you seemed so deep in thought, and you looked so pretty in there, shoveling that stuff...well, I just stood here and enjoyed the scenery."

She stared at the man she'd been trying not to think about for the past three weeks. Her pulse slowed a little, but her knees felt weak. The warmth of his fingers seeped through her shirt, and she suddenly imagined how they would feel on her bare skin. Slipping from beneath his touch, she stepped back.

"What are you doing here?"

"I brought your mare over. Didn't Eve call you?"

"Oh. Maybe she did. I've been out here most of the day."

Her tension quickly faded, but she needed a minute to regroup. Without a word, she moved down the aisle to the wash rack. Kurt's voice followed close behind her.

"Are you excited about your new mares?"

She rinsed her hands, and reached past him for a towel. "Oh, yes! I can hardly believe–"

Her breast touched his arm, sending electric shocks through her body. Embarrassed, she jumped back, chancing a quick look at his face. The fire smoldering in his dark eyes sent a river of warmth crawling between her thighs and confusion fluttering through her head.

His voice was husky. "I'd better go get that mare before the sky opens up."

A second later, she exhaled and leaned her back against the wall, closing her eyes and willing her pounding heart to quiet. Outside, a trailer ramp clanged heavily into the gravel, followed by the sharp tap-dance of hooves. Rousing herself from the delicious cloud that enveloped her, she crossed the aisle to join Kurt and the gray mare. He handed her the lead rope, then gazed around appreciatively. "This is a nice little barn. Just right for a one-person enterprise."

"Yes, it's perfect. I need a streamlined operation when I'm busy with the clinic." *Hah! Right now, I could have forty stalls and still have time to take care of them.* "Would you like a tour?"

His expression added subtle meaning to his response.

"Yeah. I'd like to see what *else* Legacy Arabians has to offer."

His cunning smile sent shivers of excitement across her shoulders. His effect on her body was as disconcerting as his hold on her thoughts.

As they walked the aisle, she watched his reaction to each horse. Proud of her small herd, she delighted in showing off her horses to a professional trainer. A loud crack of thunder echoed through the barn, and lightning flashed its eerie light across the open door, just as Kurt stopped in front of Karma's stall.

"Whoa! Who's this? Did you show him at Sacramento?"

"Yes, indeed. He won the yearling stallion championship." She grinned mischievously. "You're telling me you don't remember?"

A strange flicker moved across his features, then disappeared. He turned back to the stall, and leaned on the edge of the Dutch door. Karma immediately came over, and Kurt murmured something under his breath. The colt listened intently, his ears pricked forward, his eyes bright with interest.

Liz couldn't hide her surprise. "I'm impressed. He usually stays in the farthest corner of his stall and has to be trapped before I can get a halter on him. It's one of his little-boy games."

A few minutes later, Kurt moved away from the stall, trying to keep his expression neutral.

"He's an outstanding colt. What are your plans for him?"

His casual tone belied his churning thoughts. The horse could give Ebony a run for the money. *My money, dammit!* He hadn't shown Ebony at Sacramento, so he hadn't paid attention to that class–a poor move on his part. He didn't like surprises.

He listened politely while Liz told him of her plans to use Karma as the herd sire when he matured. As she talked about her national show goals, a knot grew in his stomach. *This is not good news.*

He switched off the negative thoughts and smiled. "So, was that the full barn tour?"

She was openly pleased by his interest. "Well, I do have a unique feeding system, one of the main reasons I bought this place." She nodded her head toward the far end of the barn. "C'mon, I'll show you."

The ingenuity of the barn builder showed in the carefully planned and well-organized feed room. Built-in grain bins with tight-fitting, hinged lids were situated against two walls.

Liz lifted a cover, and pointed inside. "Each one is lined with tin to keep rodents out." She pointed toward the baseboards. "The builder even put a metal liner around the bottom of the walls. Pretty neat, huh?"

Kurt watched her mouth as she talked. His recent erotic thoughts lurked just beneath his consciousness, and the earlier accidental touch of her breast had stirred them up again. It required tremendous will power to keep himself from hauling her into his arms. Even in work-stained barn clothes, she was attractive. Her full lips were pink without the benefit of lipstick, and her blue eyes sparkled as she showed off the special features of the room. Another strong stir ran through his gut and, as she turned away, his gaze drifted to the front of her shirt. A second later, she turned back to say something, and he caught a tiny glimpse of pale skin above white lace, sending him over the edge. *The woman has no idea how sexy she is.*

Her foot rested on the bottom tread of a steep staircase that rose through a dark hole in the ceiling.

"The best part is up here."

As he followed her into the dim hayloft, he couldn't tear his attention from her tight butt. His breath quickened and his jeans strained against his arousal.

Liz pointed to the evenly spaced trap doors in the floor. "There's a hatch over every stall. Takes me five minutes to throw hay into twelve stalls."

She searched his face to see what he thought of the innovation. The desire in his eyes sent a jolt through her stomach, and her head suddenly swam with the erotic daydreams she'd enjoyed in that very hayloft, in the pile of straw directly behind her. She stared into Kurt's eyes as he moved toward her. Anticipating what might happen next, her breath stilled. Lightning flared again through the window, sharpening every angle of his strong face and accentuating the electricity crackling between them.

In one swift move, he wrapped his arms around her, and pulled her close. She closed her eyes, feeling his heat, inhaling his unique scent. In all her fantasies, she'd fallen short of how wonderful he *really* felt. She slipped her arms around his back, her fingers traveling over the firm muscles beneath his shirt. She tipped her head back and shivered as his bristly moustache brushed against her skin and his lips caressed her neck. His arms vised her body, forcing her belly against his hardness.

His urgency jolted her from the euphoric state. *My God! What am I thinking?* She wrenched free, and stepped back. Her face burned and her breath came in short gasps.

Kurt lifted her hand to his mouth, and caressed her fingers with soft kisses that threatened to invade her resolve. A bold smile sharpened his handsome features.

"Come on, Liz. I *know* you're attracted to me. Don't play games."

Mortified, and feeling vulnerable, she snatched her hand back. Outside, the storm unleashed its fury, and the hammering rain and her clattering pulse accompanied her brusque words.

"In your dreams! You don't *know* anything about me. But I can tell you *this*. Mixing business with "games," as you put it, doesn't work, and I won't jeopardize *my* business of caring for Eve's horses."

His expression showed that his boss hadn't mentioned it. An instant later, his cocksure manner returned, and a sneer colored his words.

"We'll see about *that*."

His boots thumped as he stormed across the loft and disappeared down the stairs.

Ten

Liz trembled with anger, but her skin still hummed from his touch. She closed her eyes and summoned Kurt's face, wanting to relive the sensation of his breath against her neck, the feel of his body. She'd desperately wanted to step back into his arms and let go, wanted to sink into the fragrant straw and abandon herself to her fantasies.

She opened her eyes and shook off the visions. If she ever took that step, there'd be no one to blame but herself if she got burned. *Can't happen. My whole existence depends on proving myself and keeping my career on track. I can't risk my future for a roll in the hay.* She laughed out loud at the pun, and her spirits lifted a little as she descended to the main part of the barn. The thunderclouds had moved on, and the late afternoon sun slanted through the dripping trees that lined the front pasture. Kurt's face wormed its way into her mind's eye again. *I have to stop this. I can't afford to think about a relationship with him, no matter how sexy he is.*

Contented animal sounds drifted from the stalls, a reminder of her beautiful horses. Pushing away thoughts of Kurt, she gazed around her small kingdom. *This is the only love affair I need.*

Kurt pulled the truck up in front of his quarters at Aliqua, and killed the engine. He stared thoughtfully across the pale green fields dappled with late afternoon sunlight. *Crap! This is not going well. That colt of hers is really good. I'm gonna have to work my butt off to beat him.*

Liz's image danced into his thoughts. Desire still simmered in his belly, even though her revelation had ticked him off royally. *That's all I need...a hands-off policy on a woman who'll be hanging around here all the time.* His irritation grew. Eve had no business leaving him in the dark about *any* aspect of the barn. Changing vets on a whim? Just like a woman–they all stick together. He slid out of the truck, and slammed the door. *Well, these two aren't going to get in my way.*

She listened to the steady drone of the dial tone. The call couldn't be put off any longer. Doc mustn't hear about her plans from someone else.

She flinched a little at his polite tone.

"Well, hello, Elizabeth. What can I do for you?"

"Hi, Doc. I just wanted to check in, see if anything's going on that I need to know about."

"Things are pretty quiet, now that calving and foaling season is over. It was pretty hectic there for awhile."

Her courage faded. "Yeah." *Not that I had any part in the frenzy.*

"Well, anything else? The wife just called me to dinner."

She hesitated, tempted to put the conversation off until later. It wouldn't be any easier. Swallowing hard, she plunged in.

"I've met with two farm owners, and they'll probably use my–er, our services. I just wanted to let you know, in case they called the office."

The old vet's gravelly voice brightened. "Really? Who'd you meet?"

"Marilyn Cook and Eve Aliqua."

"Hah! You can *have* Marilyn. What a pain in the neck *she* is! Eve Aliqua's been a client for years, but I haven't seen her horses in a long time."

Liz's brain numbed–maybe her plan wouldn't work.

The old man's tone became friendlier. "Well, good for you. You'll probably get along better with the women-folk in these parts than I do. In fact, if you want to go through the files, you could pick out a few more, and just make 'em your own."

Relief bloomed. "That's a great idea. I'll come by tomorrow."

Doc's voice softened a little. "You know, Elizabeth, I feel bad that the ranchers around here aren't more receptive to you...I guess I can't blame 'em, though. Their animals are their livelihood, and they just don't want to take any chances on a newcomer. Maybe once you get going, get a reputation in these parts, things'll change."

Later that week, Eve called.

"I've decided to wean Fair Lady's foal a little early. You can pick the mare up in two weeks. How does that sound?"

Liz made some quick calculations, not liking the results. In two weeks, the foal would be less than three months old.

"Sure, Eve, that's fine with me. Mind if I ask why you're weaning her so early?"

"Kurt wants to show her in the weanling class at Stockton next month. Are you going to that show?"

"No, I'm going to the show in Tahoe. I couldn't manage both."

Liz frowned. Weaning a foal early to take it to a show wasn't good animal management. Mares naturally weaned their foals at about six months. Occasionally, for convenience, breeders made the separation at four months, but Eve's reason wasn't sound. Fair Lady would be a nervous wreck when Liz picked her up.

I'm glad I don't have to deal with that poor little baby, crying for her mother and crashing around her lonely stall. I guess when breeders are only interested in money, they do things the way they want to, regardless of what's best for the horses.

On Saturday morning, the telephone chimed, and Liz fumbled for it, her fingers not fully awake or functional.

Kurt's soft voice came through the receiver like a caress.

"Good morning. Did I wake you?"

She squinted at the large six on the digital clock and groaned.

"Ah, yes, matter of fact." Fully awake now, she felt her heart thudding beneath her silky nightgown. She rolled onto her back, then snuggled under the quilt, cradling the phone against her neck. "It's all right. I'm usually up by now."

"I wondered if you'd like to go out for dinner tonight. There's a little rib joint here in El Dorado. The atmosphere's kind of down homey, but the food's great."

She didn't answer, torn between wanting to be with him again, and worrying that she'd get sidetracked from her goals if she let him into her life for even an instant.

"Liz? You there? It's no big deal. We've sort of been at logger-heads, and I thought maybe we could spend some time together, so you can see that I don't bite."

An intriguing image of him, taking little bites out of her, sent a shiver of delight across her shoulders.

"What time?"

After hanging up, she slid farther down into her bed, thinking about an evening alone with the intriguing cowboy. *I can handle this...I really can.*

Eleven

Pete's Barbeque was an interesting little hole-in-the-wall with sawdust on the floor, plank tables, and cheap plastic chairs. The heady aroma of an open fire mingled with that of juicy meat simmering in pungent barbecue sauce.

Kurt held Liz's elbow, guiding her through the mob of customers to a table in the back. He glanced down at her as they walked, dazzled by how attractive she looked. The memory of someone from his past sent a stab of sadness through his heart, and he raised his defenses against the emotions threatening to intrude. He was playing with fire–he had a new job, a demanding boss, and some scores to settle. *I can't afford to get involved with anyone.*

They settled at a table, and he furtively binged on the way her dark blue silk blouse clung to her, enhancing every feminine curve. A pulse of desire welled up deep inside, and he turned his attention to the menu, relieved that his arousal was hidden from view.

Through dinner, he talked about his early days showing horses, describing some of the blunders he'd made as a very young trainer. Liz laughed at his stories, and it pleased him that she'd relaxed. In the time he'd known her, he hadn't seen her smile even once.

She laughed and dropped a rib bone onto the growing pile in front of her, then licked her fingers.

"What a delicious mess!"

He squirmed, watching her small pink tongue remove the last drop of barbeque sauce from her thumb. *She's oblivious to what she's doing to me!* Tender thoughts moved in. Untouched, modest, genuine. All the words that jumped to mind described the woman he watched through lowered lids. *Like someone else in my life.*

Liz sat back and smiled. "When I was a kid, my dad always took me to Louisville for ribs after a big win at the nationals."

Kurt's brain made a sudden connect. "You're Ben Barnett's daughter? I never made the connection. Now *there* was a horse trainer."

A wistful smile shadowed her features. "Yes, I learned a lot from him."

Kurt leaned across the table and gave her a teasing look.

"I guess I better worry about facing you in the ring."

She giggled. "I hardly think so...I'm still pretty new at this."

He sat back and narrowed his eyes. "We'll be at the regional together...*That* should be interesting."

He saw the apprehension move into her eyes. He wouldn't need to worry about her skill as a trainer...before they competed against each other at a show, he'd make damned sure she was a nervous wreck.

Though the hour was late, the evening air remained warm. The scent of jasmine drifted through the open windows as the truck wound along the curved highway toward Placerville. Kurt was quiet, apparently lost in his own thoughts, and Liz felt content to gaze out the window at the blue-black sky peppered with stars. A large, yellow half-moon hung just at the top of the hills to the east.

Kurt's hand slipped onto her knee and she smiled, relishing the warmth and soft pressure of his fingers, and the prickles of excitement that rushed up her thighs. She placed her own hand over his, and they traveled through the night in comfortable silence.

Kurt's banter during dinner had been about his career, but he'd revealed little about his personal life. Finally, Liz's curiosity got the best of her.

"Where did you work before you came to Aliqua?"

He glanced at her, his expression suddenly wary. "A farm in New Mexico."

"Why did you leave there, and come to work for Aliqua?"

He didn't say anything for a few moments, then shrugged.

"Simple. Better horses. Better pay. More responsibility."

"Eve has wonderful horses. You must be thrilled to be working with them."

"Yeah. Poor old Eve's been struggling for a long time to make a name for herself, but just hasn't been able to pull it off."

Liz patted his hand. "That must be why she hired *you*."

Scorn edged his reply. "I guess."

Suddenly, his head snapped forward, his attention riveted on the horizon. "Oh, God."

Liz followed his gaze. The night sky over Placerville was filled with an eerie, pale-orange glow.

Kurt pushed the gas pedal flat against the floorboard, his expression grim as he navigated the narrow highway toward the light. Liz held her breath as they came into the outskirts of town, wondering what nightmare awaited them. As they rolled through the deserted streets, her heart moved into her throat. The glow had changed to deep orange with a halo of dark yellow, and the odor of burning wood lay heavily on the night air. Kurt turned the truck into the dirt lane that led to Marilyn Cook's farm, and Liz shut her eyes tightly, fighting the wave of fear that threatened to overpower her.

The equipment shed behind the barn was engulfed in flames. Against the orange blaze that roared through the small building, Liz saw the black silhouette of a tractor. She gasped as her attention snapped to a corner of the horse barn, where flames worked their way along the edge of the roof.

The truck slammed to a stop, and Kurt hit the ground at a dead run. Liz jumped down, and started after him, praying there would be enough time to get the horses out before tons of hay in the loft exploded into flames. A pumper truck was on the scene, and firemen were frantically hauling a huge siphon hose down to the pond below the house. Two sheriff's cars were there, and several people stood around watching the frightening spectacle.

Liz sprinted toward the barn doors and into darkness that echoed with the terrified cries of the horses. The smoke was beginning to filter in, and breathing would be impossible in another few minutes. She stopped for a second, looked around to get her bearings, then dashed over to the wash rack. A stack of towels caught her eye. She tied one around her face, bandit-style to cover her nose and mouth, then snatched up another, and headed for the nearest stall.

The frightened neighs tore at her sanity, echoes of another fire in the past. *Please, please, let us get them all.* Grabbing a halter and lead rope from a hook on the stall door, she entered. The animal inside cowered in the corner, eyes wild with terror. Liz quickly slipped the halter over the horse's head, then wrapped the towel around its face.

Kurt came running into the barn as she emerged from the stall with the struggling horse.

"Take them down by the pond," he shouted over the din. "It's fenced!"

He disappeared into the dark recesses of the barn. Two men came running up to help.

"Halters are hanging next to the doors!" she shouted. "Try to cover their eyes with something!"

The horse beside her pulled and reared, trying to turn back. Yanking hard on the lead rope, she brought him back to all fours, then started down the slope toward the pond. The terrified animal fought her, crazed by his strong instinct to get back to the only safe place he knew–his stall.

A few minutes later, Liz released the horse into the small pasture, turned, and sprinted back up the hill. Fire-hoses pumped long jets of water over the barn roof, the fire fighters desperately trying to smother the flames before the hay ignited. From the corner of her eye, Liz saw a figure standing next to the house. Marilyn stood like a statue, huddled in her robe and slippers, her arms hugged tightly against her body, her gaze glued to the inferno. *What's wrong with her? Why is she just standing there?*

Kurt ran past, leading two horses toward the pond. Another man followed close behind, trying to control a young horse that reared and bucked at every step. Liz refocused on the emergency and did a mental head count. *Three more and we've made it.* She dashed back into the murky depths of the barn. *The old mare–Miss Marcy–where's her stall?* Liz stopped a second to let her eyes adjust to the darkness, then headed toward the far corner.

The elderly mare whinnied loudly as Liz opened the stall door. The horse weaved back and forth, her eyes dark with terror, her nostrils flared, as she fought to breathe in the acrid atmosphere.

"Easy, Girl. It's okay."

Talking constantly to the mare, Liz tied the blindfold. A loud crack overhead startled them both. The fire had reached the hayloft, and tiny snake-tongues of flame licked between the boards above the stall, intent on eating their way through. Smoke filtered through every crack and knothole, the wisps swirling in elegant, deadly patterns against the ceiling, waiting for a gust of air to carry them downward to snuff out their victims.

Liz's eyes burned and tears streamed down her face as she led the mare out of the stall. *Two more and we'll be okay.*

One of the other men suddenly appeared, and Liz thrust Marcy's lead-rope at him.

"Here, take her down. I'll get the other two."

The old mare obediently followed the tug of the lead-rope and left the barn. Liz tried to figure out how to get the last two horses out of the barn at the same time. Kurt materialized out of the smoke and grabbed a halter. He looked up at the flames dancing across the ceiling of Miss Marcy's stall, and threw Liz a grim look.

"Hurry!"

As she pulled the horse out of the stall, a deafening noise like a freight train roared through the building. The hay in the loft exploded, and the already-scorched and brittle wood splintered. The ceiling in the corner disintegrated, and the animal reared, squealing with terror. Liz squeezed her eyes against the thick smoke, tears pouring down her cheeks. Voices shouted from outside, urging her to run. Another explosion, and the ceiling directly overhead started to groan. Liz frantically pulled on the rope, but the terrified animal wouldn't budge.

Suddenly, a blast of icy-cold water hit her, and the tension in the lead-rope relaxed. Spinning around to look, she saw that the horse had also been drenched, and the shock of the water had momentarily distracted him. She started to run, the horse right behind her. As she leapt through the door, another loud explosion sent debris slamming into her back.

The dazed horse followed Liz down the hill. When she reached the gate, Kurt stepped forward to help her.

His voice was tight. "I think we got 'em all. I count nine. Is that right?"

She nodded numbly. Adrenaline crashed through her system, her breath came in ragged snatches, and hot tears burned her cheeks. Without a word, Kurt reached out, and pulled her to him. Two hearts thundered against each other, separated only by heaving rib cages. In the safety of his arms, the terror of the ordeal began to fade.

A moment later, the horse at the end of the lead-rope nickered, and Liz smiled foolishly. Kurt wiped the tears from her face, a tender look passing over his features, and Liz's pulse jumped at the tiny glimpse of the *real* man inside "Kurt DeVallio–Tough Guy."

As she reached for the gate, a flash of red caught her eye. A long gash angled across the animal's shoulder, the edges of the wound filled with splinters of wood. Blood ran steadily down his foreleg.

"He must have been hit by flying wood in that last blast. I need to clean him up and take a look. See if the firetruck has a first-aid kit."

While she waited, Liz inspected the injury, a superficial laceration that wouldn't require stitching. She pressed her fingers firmly over the area that bled the hardest. Within minutes, the rivulets slowed, then stopped. Kurt returned, lugging a large, red box. He dropped it on the ground, exhaling sharply. A moment later, she brandished a bottle of sterile water.

"You'll need to hold him. He won't like this."

Kurt stepped up to the horse's head and murmured something as he grasped the halter. The animal's body relaxed, and Liz started cleansing the wound, a part of her brain focused on Kurt's magic.

Thirty minutes later, the injured horse was inside the pasture, quietly grazing with his herd mates, the nightmare forgotten. Liz dropped onto the grass, her knees finally too weak to hold her up any longer. Kurt eased down beside her, and slipped his arm around her shoulders.

In somber silence, they watched the old barn burn to the ground.

Twelve

B y the time Liz and Kurt trudged up the hill, the firemen had
rolled up the hoses, and were peeling off their heavy suits.
The sodden, smoldering ruins permeated the air with an acrid odor.
Liz walked toward the spot where Marilyn sat on the ground, her
back against the house.

Squatting down, Liz lightly touched her arm. "Marilyn, let's
go inside."

The old woman slowly turned her head, following the sound
of Liz's voice and trying to focus vacant eyes. Her lips moved, but
no words came out. She tried again, her voice but a whisper.

"It's gone."

Liz felt deep sympathy for the poor soul who'd just lost so
much, but seconds later, a positive attitude tempered Liz's pity. *It
could have been worse–at least we saved the horses.*

When Marilyn was inside and settled into her chair, Liz moved
into the kitchen to make some tea, staring with distaste at the sink
piled with dirty dishes filled with scummy water and moldy bits of
food. As she poked through cupboards looking for a kettle, Marilyn's
rocky condition worried her. *She might be in mild shock, or need to
be hospitalized. I'll have to watch her closely for a while.* Reaching into a small cupboard to retrieve a teakettle, Liz spotted a small
glass vial and metal box. She threw a quick look toward the sitting
room, then picked up the vial. A second later, she understood
Marilyn's confused state. *Insulin. She's diabetic.*

The labor of the night's drama screamed through every aching muscle, as Liz washed the greasy, black soot from her hands and arms. Her thoughts returned to the fire. *How did it start? And how did it get so far out of hand before the fire department showed up?*

Kurt appeared beside her. "Find a kettle?"

She nodded. It felt so good to have him near. She resisted the powerful urge to lean against him and close her eyes for just a minute. Glancing toward the sitting room, she lowered her voice.

"How do you think the fire started?"

Kurt shook his head. "I dunno. Maybe smoker's carelessness."

"But, Kurt, the woman's been in the business for *years*. Surely she wouldn't smoke in the barn!"

He shrugged. "Folks get worn out in this rat-race, get careless. I really don't know much about her."

Liz remained silent, unable to deal with the notion of setting one's own barn on fire.

A few minutes later, Marilyn sipped the tea, but still seemed dazed. Liz grasped her arm.

"Marilyn, do you need your insulin?"

The woman looked baffled, then shook her head and spoke haltingly.

"No...I took my shot at dinnertime...I'm just tired."

Liz rose from the couch, motioning for Kurt to follow her to the kitchen.

"I think I'd better stay with her the rest of the night. She's diabetic, and seems a little shocky. If she needs medical attention, someone should be here to take her to the hospital."

"I'll stay, too. You might need help."

She searched his face, warming to the sincerity written on his weary features. Gratitude swelled in her chest, followed by another unfamiliar feeling where Kurt was concerned–trust.

Marilyn finally drifted into a deep sleep, and Kurt went down to the pond pasture to check on the horses, leaving Liz alone with her thoughts. She was sticky and dirty, but didn't have the strength to let it bother her. Leaning her head back on the couch, her heavy, burning eyelids closed. Immediately, against the dark backdrop of her brain, flames licked around the corners of the barn and into stalls filled with screaming horses. Her eyes flew open, her heart thundering. *How many times will I have to live this night again?*

As the urgency of the disaster began to fade, her thoughts centered on the teamwork she and Kurt had shared in order to save nine horses from death. Kurt had plunged into the dangerous situation without hesitation, confident of his skill in getting the terrified animals to obey him.

Her own courage had been bolstered by his presence, and the certainty that he would help her if she needed him. The memory of his protective, tender embrace warmed her heart. *There's a lot more to this man than he wants me to see.*

Kurt returned, and settled down next to her, intruding on her musings and bringing her back to the reality of the present.

"The horses are fine for tonight. I'll pick up some feed and hay in the morning." His gaze drifted to Marilyn's sleeping figure. "I wonder what she'll do with 'em, now that she doesn't have a barn."

Liz's analytical mind switched on. "That's a legitimate question. Nine horses can't live in that tiny pond pasture for more than a day or two. We can talk to her when she wakes up, see what she wants to do." She thought for a minute. "I have two empty stalls in the barn, and my run-in shed is pretty large, but I don't have room for all of them. Could you take a couple back to Aliqua?"

He shook his head. "I doubt that Eve would be agreeable. She and Marilyn have never gotten along."

Liz bristled. "Well, this isn't exactly a social event we're talking about! Doesn't she have any feelings for other people?"

Kurt's crooked smile emphasized his words. "Not much, Lovey. She's a one-woman woman."

Liz fumed for a minute, then decided not to waste time and energy thinking about Eve Aliqua.

"I'll call Colleen. Fairhill might have some room."

As she outlined a plan from beginning to end, she was aware of Kurt's indulgent smile. A minute later, he slipped his arm around her shoulder and pulled her close, resting his cheek on top of her head.

"You are *somethin'*, you know that?"

She laid her head on his shoulder, loving the protective feel of his arm, the soft pressure of his face against her hair, his heart beating strong and steady beneath his shirt. They cuddled quietly for a few minutes, then Kurt lifted her chin and gazed at her without speaking. She looked into his eyes, saw the desire, and spiraled into a whirlpool of her own longing. The spin ended as his lips covered hers, melting her against his body and capturing her in the kiss she'd dreamed about for so long.

When their lips parted, a flash of courage surprised her.

"You're not too bad yourself," she whispered, breathless from the sexual energy coursing through her body. "I think we're pretty good together."

Kurt pulled her closer, his hand quickly moving to her breast, his voice husky with need.

"Let's find out."

Marilyn sat straight up in her recliner.

"What's goin' on? What're *you* doin' here?"

Liz leapt up from the couch, embarrassed at having been caught in Kurt's arms, and struggling to control the emotions raging through her head.

She moved to the chair. "How are you feeling?"

Marilyn looked confused, then indignant. "I'm fine. Now, what the hell are *you* doin' here?"

Liz laid her hand lightly on the woman's arm. "Do you remember the fire?"

A brief silence, then recognition flashed across Marilyn's lined face. Her worn features crumpled with the reality that the fire hadn't been a bad dream. She started to weep and keen, rocking back and forth in her dingy chair. Liz felt helpless, watching pain rack the old woman's body and mind.

Marilyn's tears finally subsided, and she turned her misery-ravaged gaze toward Kurt. "Are they all gone?"

"No, they're all okay. We put them down by the pond."

The old woman began to weep again, this time, with relief.

After about an hour, Marilyn had regained her composure. Liz took charge and the conversation turned to the fate of the horses.

"I can take three or four to my place. We'll find temporary

homes for the rest while you rebuild the barn."

Marilyn's red eyes brimmed with tears again. "I can't rebuild. I don't have no insurance...I couldn't pay the premiums."

Kurt hadn't said much, but now he spoke up.

"How about we get them settled somewhere, then help you sell them?"

Marilyn looked defeated. "Yeah, I guess that'd be okay. I really *can't* take care of 'em anymore. I'm too old, and I can't afford their upkeep. Sellin' 'em's the best thing to do."

The outlines of the trees were barely visible against the dawn sky when Kurt and Liz silently climbed into the truck. As they headed down the lane, Liz looked back once more at the blackened rubble, and shuddered.

Kurt remained quiet during the drive. Liz glanced at him several times, wondering what he was thinking. Her own thoughts were filled with the embrace on the couch. *God, I have never felt so wonderful in my life!* The skin on her breast tightened with the memory of his caress, and she felt a stir deep inside. Her breath quickened. In moments, they'd be able to pick up where they'd left off.

The truck eased to a stop by her back door.

Kurt's expression was serious. "Listen, I'm sorry about last night. I got a little carried away–tired from all the excitement, I guess." He hesitated. "Truth is, I just don't have any room in my life for a relationship. You really turn me on, but as *you* pointed out, we shouldn't mix business with our personal lives."

The words stung like a slap, and Liz's thoughts hardened. *You arrogant son-of-a-bitch!* Without a word, she opened the door, and jumped to the ground.

His voice followed her. "I'll probably see you around."

Looking back at him, she saw a hint of sadness cross his features. Her heart bumped painfully, but her voice was without emotion.

"Not if I can help it."

Kurt drove through the early morning mist, a cold lump in the pit of his stomach. Liz Barnett had wormed her way into his life, and he'd found himself thinking of her as the most fascinating women he'd ever met. She always seemed to be in control of what she wanted. Smart. Professional. Successful. Sexy. He wanted to be with her in the worst way, but now she'd be the Aliqua vet, *and* she owned a colt that might derail his own plans. He had to consider her as nothing more than competition in the show ring.

As he watched the narrow road ahead, her face floated through his thoughts, the taste of her willing mouth still on his lips, the memory of her firm breast beneath his hand. The jarring events of the previous six hours had shown Liz's courage in the face of danger, and it was proving to be even more exciting than her physical appeal. Her self-confidence gave her the strength to take charge when needed. He cringed, recalling what a jerk he'd been the morning they'd met in the stall. It had only taken her a moment to put him in his place. *And I've been right there ever since.*

He slipped back into the memory of their embrace on Marilyn's couch. *What was I thinking, kissing her like that?* Taking a deep breath, he shook off the thoughts and switched on the radio. The country-western strains of "Achy, Breaky Heart" drifted through the cab, a fitting tribute to his life.

Thirteen

L iz was trembling by the time she reached her bedroom. A rush of emotional choices swept through her: cry, scream, throw something. She stood beneath the pounding heat of the shower, hugging her arms tightly, fighting the urge to let herself go. The silky water flowed down her shoulders and over her breasts, a sensuous reminder of Kurt's intimate caress. She'd wanted him, desperately wanted him, but bad timing had interfered, and he'd panicked. Now, her own fear loomed as a reminder of her vulnerability.

Twenty minutes later, she fell into a deep sleep, free of the filthy reminders of the night, but not the pain. When she awoke, the bright sunlight streaming through the window confused her. Immediately, the inferno burned its way into her conscious, a memory of the living nightmare. She slid out of bed, her body protesting as painful muscles begged her to crawl back under the covers.

Lulled by the gurgle-hiss-plunk of the coffeepot, she thought about Kurt: his confidence during the fire, the tender moment on Marilyn's couch. These facets made him seem real and vulnerable, even likeable. His awkward apology had embarrassed her at the time, but now it simply puzzled her. *I can accept the business-pleasure conflict, but what's really bothering him?*

A minute later, she knew she couldn't spend any more emotional energy on it. She had to concentrate on her own, very real problems–which now included the fate of nine horses.

She slipped on her boots, then headed up the drive toward the barn, her brain replaying the horror of the fire. She tried to block out the image, unable to even *think* about a disaster in her own barn. A second later, her mood lightened as heads appeared over stall doors and eager whinnies warmed her heart.

Dishing out the morning grain, she mentally reorganized the stalls. *Miss Marcy will definitely be in the barn. At her age, she deserves all the comfort she can get.*

Muscala stared at Liz from the back of the stall.

"Hi, Sweetie. Ready for breakfast?"

As Liz opened the latch, the gray mare abruptly turned away, retreating to the farthest corner of the stall, and swinging her rump toward her owner.

"Hey! That's not very nice."

Surprised by the display of bad attitude, Liz hesitated outside the door and watched the horse for a minute, then slipped in, and poured grain into the feed tub. Something about Muscala's bearing put Liz on edge. *I hope it's just the new surroundings, or her pregnancy. I'd better keep an eye on her.*

Colleen gasped several times as Liz related the saga of the fire.

"If we'd been thirty minutes later..." She stopped, unable to think about the consequences of bad timing. "Colleen, do you have room for a couple of extra horses until we find buyers for them?"

"We have four empty stalls right now. I'll ask Effie, and call ya back."

Liz hung up, and did the math. Three horses would have to stay outside, but that wouldn't be a problem. The weather was good, and the run-in shed would provide some protection if they needed it. She sighed deeply. Five extra horses would put a strain on her, especially with Fair Lady arriving the following week, and a horse show at the end of the month. *Well, can't be helped. I'll just have to deal with it.*

As she approached the dirt lane to Marilyn's farm, Liz felt a rush of anxiety. Rounding the curve, she choked back the hard lump that rose in her throat as the black pile of cold rubble came into view.

She knocked on the door, then pushed it open, calling out. Marilyn's voice answered from somewhere at the back of the house. Liz stood awkwardly in the middle of the room where she'd spent the better part of the night. She looked everywhere but at the couch where she and Kurt had shared their tender moment. One of the cats rubbed against her leg and mewed pitifully.

Marilyn appeared, waving a cigarette. "These cats are drivin' me crazy."

Liz got right down to business. "I've made room at my place for five of your horses, and Colleen at Fairhill will take four. They'll be well cared for until we can find buyers for them. How does that sound?"

Marilyn stubbed out the cigarette, and threw Liz a withering look. "That sounds just dandy. What do you want me to do? Applaud?"

Liz's anger rose quickly. "Hold on just a minute. I don't think you fully understand your situation. The horses can't live on their own, and you said yourself that you couldn't take care of them any more. I thought we agreed about what needs to be done."

Marilyn's face crumpled, and she slumped into one of the kitchen chairs.

"I know. I'm sorry. I can't believe this is happening. My life has been just one big downhill slide."

Willing away her anger, Liz picked up the dish of cat-food that Marilyn had filled, and placed it on the floor.

"I know it's been horrible, but we need to think about the horses. *And* you. I can pick them up tomorrow afternoon, and then you can concentrate on whatever you have to do about the barn."

The old woman nodded in defeat. She lit another cigarette, and inhaled deeply.

"Sorry. I just need time to get adjusted."

Liz headed toward the door. "I'm going to check on the horses."

Walking briskly down the hill toward the pond, her anger faded as nine heads swung toward her. Miss Marcy offered a long greeting, then returned to her patch of grass. Liz smiled wryly. *At least someone appreciates my efforts.*

Kurt had already been there. A large bale of hay lay open, and the horses had scattered most of it over the ground. She located the horse with the wound, and examined her work of the night before. *Looks pretty good, but twenty-four hours will tell the tale.* Holding the horse's halter tightly, she injected an antibiotic into the soft flesh at the base of his neck. *That should do it, but I'd better ask about tetanus shots.* Marilyn's lax barn maintenance probably also meant that vaccinations weren't up to date. *One more thing to worry about.*

Marilyn came out of the house as Liz climbed into the truck.

"Liz, I'm really sorry about the way I acted. I do appreciate everything you're doing for me...I'll help...I promise."

"Good. That'll make things easier." Liz hesitated, considering what she wanted to say. "Marilyn, were you smoking in the barn yesterday?"

The woman looked stunned. "Are you *kidding?* Do you think I'm an idiot?"

"No, I don't...but, *something* started the fire. When were you out there last?"

Marilyn thought for a moment. "I fed around six o'clock." Suddenly, her eyes narrowed and her voice became hard. "I had a guy working on the tractor out in the shed. He didn't leave until after dark."

Liz climbed into her truck. "You'd better call the fire marshal, and give him that information."

That evening, Kurt phoned, and Liz took the call cautiously, not eager for another disastrous conversation.

His voice sounded subdued. "I was wondering if you need any help collecting those horses."

Her first impulse was to say yes, just to see if anything had changed, then self-preservation kicked in.

"No, I can handle it. I have a large trailer, and Colleen is taking the rest. But, thanks anyway."

There seemed to be nothing more to say, and the line remained silent for a very long moment.

Kurt spoke first. "Liz, about what I said last–"

"No, Kurt. Don't say anything more. You've let me know how you feel. Let's leave it at that."

Fourteen

L iz's new charges settled in comfortably over the next few days. Except Miss Marcy. The poor old girl weaved back and forth at the stall door, confused at being uprooted from her familiar sur-roundings, and loudly whinnying her distress to anyone who'd lis-ten. The plight of the elderly mare touched Liz's heart. How well she knew the feelings of isolation and loneliness. Her head danced with images of home, and sadness filled her thoughts. Would she find peace and happiness here in the rough grandeur of California? Would she ever find common ground with the ranchers and farm-ers that called this place home? And how long would it be before she'd have answers to those questions?

The fire and its aftermath had consumed several days, putting Liz behind in her training schedule and her plans to call on poten-tial clients. For the next week, she pushed her timetable, working horses from sunrise until two o'clock, then spending the rest of the afternoon trying to set up appointments. Besides advancing toward her goals, the rigorous schedule also kept her mind busy and away from thoughts of Kurt.

The afternoon temperature had spiked, and the large chestnut horse sweated heavily, white froth accumulating on his neck where the reins touched. Kurt took another turn around the practice ring. Why Eve wanted to put the mediocre gelding into the country plea-sure class was a mystery–the horse was anything but a pleasure to ride. The animal stopped and pawed the ground impatiently. Kurt's own patience evaporated into the hot, heavy air. Nudging the horse forward, he started back to the barn, catching sight of his boss headed in the same direction. *Oh, great, now what does she want?*

He rode into the cool interior of the barn, and dismounted.

Eve's tone was light. "How'd he do?"

"Okay, I guess. I just don't think he's saddle horse material. I've already told you that. You'd better not count on any great wins with him at this show."

He began toweling the sweat from the horse's neck.

Eve stepped up close, placing her hand on his arm. "Kurt? What's wrong? You've been so cranky late–"

He stepped away from her touch, his tone sharp.

"I'm just trying to get into the swing of things. It's show season, and that's what I'm here to do. Show your horses. Right?"

He gave her a hard look. Her pale skin colored slightly, and a flash of anger momentarily sharpened her green eyes. Just as quickly, it disappeared and she smiled sweetly.

"Of course it is. And I know you'll do a fabulous job. You're the best."

"Sorry. I'm always edgy during show season."

Eve gently stroked the gelding's face. "I really love this horse. He was one of my first foals. Are you sure he's not show material?"

Kurt picked up a brush. "I think he'd make a great driving horse. His conformation is correct, and he has a nice way of going, but a saddle horse he isn't."

She gave the gelding a motherly pat on the shoulder. "Then you just turn him into a driving horse, and we'll scratch him from the riding classes."

"Okey-dokey." Kurt unsnapped the crossties. "C'mon, Bud. You just got a reprieve."

As he led the horse away, Eve's voice drifted after him.

"Oh, by the way, you'll need to stick around Monday morning. Liz Barnett is picking up Fair Lady about ten."

He slammed the stall door. *Like Hell! Monday's my day off. I'm not hanging around here to baby-sit these women. Liz can load the horse by herself. She sure didn't need my help collecting Marilyn's horses.* His bruised ego shouldered its way into his thoughts, expanding his irritation. Liz's brush-off had been uncalled for–he'd only been trying to help.

Shrugging off his self-indulgent thoughts, he started after Eve, his long legs quickly closing the distance between them.

"I need my days off to take care of my personal affairs. That Barnett woman has been in the horse business a long time. She can manage the mare by herself."

Eve stopped abruptly, and turned, a frown knitting her pale eyebrows together.

"You *know* my policy. I always have the trainer present when a horse is delivered. She'll be here early, then you'll have the rest of the day to yourself."

Kurt glowered at the small figure. God, he hated being controlled, especially by a woman. Irritation crawled over his neck, and he fought to suppress his aggression. Eve wrote the paychecks, and he couldn't afford to be on her bad side.

"Okay, but I wish you'd–" Her challenging look stopped him in mid-sentence. "Never mind."

"How would *you* know she's been in the horse business a long time?"

He swallowed, perturbed by the direction the conversation had taken.

"I heard she's Ben Barnett's daughter, and she's been around horses all her life. Plus being the new vet in town." He narrowed his eyes and gave his boss a meaningful look. "*Our* new vet, I've just learned."

Eve didn't take up the gauntlet. A second later, she changed the subject again.

"Did you hear about the fire at Marilyn Cook's?"

Kurt struggled to keep his expression neutral. Did she know about his involvement in the disaster?

"Yeah, I heard all the horses were saved. Pretty lucky, huh?"

She nodded slowly. "Yes. That's lucky."

She gave him one more thoughtful look, then headed toward the house, leaving him to wonder.

Fifteen

E arly on Monday, Kurt prepared Fair Lady for the trip to Legacy, still irritated about wasting part of his precious day-off coddling Eve's ego. Show season was unbelievably hectic, and there were times when Mondays were his only chance to catch up on sleep, a commodity in short supply at a horse show.

Fair Lady stood quietly in the crossties while he brushed her with firm, practiced strokes that brought up the highlights of her white coat, the rhythmic movement soothing his own unsettled thoughts. The mare turned her head, and nuzzled his shoulder gently, chuckling deep in her throat. He smoothed his hand across her shoulder and thought about the past.

His father had always teased him about his "magic" with horses. Kurt never thought of it as magic, rather as an invisible bond he made with the creatures. Even when he'd been a young boy, the large, flighty animals had always responded to his touch as though they were kindred spirits. He'd never wanted to do anything with his life but work with horses, and those dreams had been a reality until New Mexico. *The only time I ever allowed my personal life to interfere with my work.*

Disturbed by the intrusion of old memories, he turned his attention to what still needed to be done before Liz arrived. Earlier, he'd prepared a stall at the back of the barn, where the soon-to-be-weanling would be held while her dam was loaded onto the trailer. He gazed down at the tiny, frisky baby playing peek-a-boo through her mother's long, silvery tail, oblivious to the imminent disruption of her world. He didn't approve of Eve's abrupt method of weaning, but she'd been determined that he would show the foal at the Stockton show in two weeks. And Eve *always* got her way.

Draping his lean body over the stall door, he watched the two horses share their last hours together. Unbidden, thoughts of Liz crept into his head–how she tasted, the feel of her skin, the scent of her hair. A sharp rush of desire ran through him. The woman was irresistible, and he wanted another chance to hold her in his arms.

Exhaling slowly, he recognized his choices: stay on track to pursue his independence, or take a chance on a serious relationship with Liz.

Liz's truck moved slowly along the winding highway, as she checked the trailer in the rear view mirror. Giddy excitement rippled through her stomach at the prospect of having Fair Lady all to herself, despite the fact that the next few days would be difficult for both of them. She'd prepared the stall next to Muscala, thinking familiar company might keep the mother's mind off her baby. Hopefully, the arrangement would also help Muscala's attitude, a situation that deeply concerned Liz.

She pulled up in front of Fairhill, and Colleen climbed into the truck, grinning brightly.

"Ain't this fun? I've been lookin' forward to it all weekend."

Liz smiled grimly. "It might not be as much fun as you think. I didn't tell you that Eve is weaning Fair Lady's filly today. We'll have a hysterical mommy on our hands."

"Today? Good grief! Well, I guess selling the mare off is *one* way to separate 'em."

"That's not the worst of it. The filly's not even three months old, and Kurt's taking her to a show in two weeks."

Indignation tightened Colleen's features. "You have to be kidding!"

"I wish I were."

Fifteen minutes later, Liz parked the rig next to the Aliqua barn. Following Eve down the aisle, Liz suppressed a grin, noticing Colleen's unabashed scrutiny of the elegant interior. Horse owners with lots of money turned their barns into elegant showplaces, a practice that seemed silly to ordinary horse-folk. But who knew what drove these people? For sure, the horses didn't care whether they had chandeliers in the barn.

"Mornin', Liz. Your mare's ready to load."

The familiar voice sent a collection of butterflies through her stomach. Kurt's manner was wary, and Eve peered at him intently, as though trying to read his mind.

Liz's voice felt wooden. "Thanks."

Eve excused herself and hurried off to collect the paperwork from the office. Kurt turned to Colleen, making small talk and carefully avoiding eye contact with Liz. Alone with her thoughts, she moved to Fair Lady's stall, and watched the tiny filly nurse. Images of the little creature's impending terror and confusion sent a painful ache through her chest.

A moment later, a musky scent caused an eddy of excitement in the pit of her stomach. Kurt stood next to her, his arm lightly touching hers, his warmth seeping through her sleeve.

He gazed at the mare and foal, his voice soft and husky. "Seems like a shame to break up such a beautiful pair, doesn't it?"

Liz looked up at him, confused by the tone of his voice and the compassion on his strong face. *If it's such a shame, why is he determined to show her so soon? It's all a charade. He couldn't care less about this baby.* She moved away from him without answering.

Eve returned, waving a sheaf of papers in the air. Liz took them, and walked out to the truck, trying to sort out her conflicting thoughts. Her brain had already firmly imprinted the way Kurt's arms felt, so her body tingled from his brief nearness. However, those feelings had nothing to do with her opinion of him as a horseman, and his blatant disregard for the foal's mental well-being.

She dropped the trailer ramp, checked inside, then held her breath and watched the barn door. Within seconds, terrified squeals rang out from inside the barn, and Kurt emerged, his eyes dark, his features rigid. Fair Lady danced alongside him, twisting her head back, trying to see her baby.

Once inside the trailer, the agitated mare called out, answering each cry from her terrified foal. The pitch of the abandoned filly's screams was heartbreaking. Liz looked at Colleen, whose face reflected her utter contempt for the situation.

Eve saw the exchanged looks, and spoke up, her tone menacingly sweet. "Is something wrong?"

Liz hesitated. *Should I stand up for what I believe? If I'm going to care for her horses, she needs to know how I feel.* Briefly, the fear of messing up a chance to have Aliqua's business immobilized her. A second later, the paralysis disappeared, and Liz's professional integrity prevailed.

"I just think she's too young to wean."

Eve's eyes narrowed, and she stepped closer.

"Oh, really? And just what makes *you* such an expert on weaning?"

The woman's face had taken on an ugly red flush, giving her green eyes an otherworldly appearance. Liz hesitated, then tilted her head and looked directly at her challenger.

"In addition to being a vet, I've been the breeding manager for a large Thoroughbred farm in Kentucky, *and* I grew up on a breeding farm."

A heavy silence hung between them, but the atmosphere around them was filled with the cacophony of the filly's frantic cries and Fair Lady's hysterical answers.

Eve stepped back. "Well, that's very impressive, but this isn't Kentucky. If you want to work for me, you'll do it *my* way."

She turned, and stalked off toward the house. Liz felt sick, positive she'd just signed her walking papers with Aliqua Arabians.

Kurt watched Eve's retreating figure, then looked at Liz, and nodded. "Well, good luck."

He turned on his heel, and strode back into the barn.

Once they were on the road, Fair Lady quieted down somewhat, although Liz felt the trailer rocking with the mare's agitated movements.

Colleen leaned across the seat, and patted her arm.

"It'll be all right...they adapt pretty fast. But that was *really* awful."

Liz felt the tears, knew she couldn't contain them, and pulled over to the side of the road. Colleen didn't say anything, but continued to stroke Liz's arm.

A few minutes later, Liz regained her composure, and eased the truck back onto the highway. They rode in silence for about ten miles before Colleen spoke.

"It ain't just about the weaning, is it?"

Sixteen

L iz's concern for Fair Lady's mental state disappeared within the first twenty-four hours. The mature mare had been through the weaning process many times in her life, and seemed to accept the separation quickly. By the day before Liz would leave for Tahoe, the mare was eating heartily, getting acquainted with her barn-mates, and offering friendly nickers when Liz approached.

However, the biggest surprise was Miss Marcy. The elderly mare had instantly bonded with her new barn-mate and, as long as Fair Lady was across the aisle from her, Marcy remained quiet and content. She'd found a friend.

Liz led the two mares up the slope to the pasture, thinking about her conversation with Colleen on the return trip from Aliqua. Liz had desperately needed someone to talk to, and had finally opened up, admitting her deep attraction for Kurt. When describing the all-night vigil with Marilyn, Liz had left out the ending to the story, too embarrassed to admit she'd been cast aside.

Inside the gate, Fair Lady took off at a gallop across the pasture, Miss Marcy close behind her. Liz watched with delight as the horses flew over the ground, as though they had wings. They were true "Drinkers of the Wind," epitomizing the Bedouin description of Arabian horses. Fair Lady made another pass, tail flagged, head up, nostrils flared. The beautiful mare wheeled and came to an abrupt stop, snorting and shaking her head. She nickered softly, then dropped her head and started nibbling grass.

While she cleaned stalls, Liz recalled the rest of the conversation with Colleen. Liz hadn't wanted to hear her friend's comments, but Colleen had insisted that Liz keep her eyes wide open if she planned to flirt with the unknown. She'd also reminded Liz of the tough road that lay ahead, if she planned to continue her veterinary career in the region.

Colleen had been direct. "Ya don't know anything about Kurt DeVallio. No one does. Why ask for trouble?" She'd rolled her eyes. "God, Liz, he'd be a great hobby, but ya wouldn't want to keep him!"

Liz's reaction had been almost defensive. "Colleen, I don't plan to get serious. I have to concentrate on my practice, but, there's something different about him..."

"He's different, all right."

The warning edge to Colleen's tone had caused Liz's own apprehension to grow.

"Do you know something you're not telling me?"

Colleen's face had shown a trace of indecision.

"I heard he was involved in some kind of scandal in New Mexico, but I don't know any details...Just be careful."

Immersed in the reflection, Liz spread the last wheelbarrow load of wood shavings around the stall floor. *What could the scandal be? Something really horrible? If it were so terrible, wouldn't everyone know about it?*

It was clear that if *she* wanted to know, the story would have to come directly from Kurt. Finding a way to accomplish that would be the trick.

Eve telephoned shortly after Liz returned to the house.

"Liz, I need to get some shots, and an ultrasound on one of my mares. When can you do that?"

Liz thought quickly. Should she try to squeeze a farm call into an already horrendous afternoon? *No, I can't set a precedent like that, especially with Miss Aggressive.*

"I'm leaving for Tahoe in the morning, but I could see you early on Monday."

Eve agreed, then her tone changed. "About the other day–sorry

I was so touchy. It probably *is* a little early to wean the filly, but I'm in the horse business, and there's simply no room for sentimentality. I do appreciate your concern, though. It tells me a lot about you."

The compliment pleased Liz. Eve probably wasn't generous with such things. After hanging up, she mulled over the brief conversation. There was a lot to be learned from the episode. Where business was concerned, the degree of success was based solely on one's determination to have it. *Here I've been standing around, feeling sorry for myself 'cause those big ol' bad men wouldn't let me play. Time to get real. Working harder to prove myself is the answer, and I'd better start with Eve Aliqua.*

Seventeen

The drive up to Lake Tahoe energized Liz, as she soaked up the deep green serenity of the mountains. The unreal topaz color of the lake contrasted with the dark shades of towering pines and Douglas fir that blanketed the surrounding slopes. A cloudless blue sky polished the scene to a breathtaking picture-postcard effect, and her problems seemed to shrink into miniature proportions in the presence of such magnificence.

By late afternoon, she'd settled the horses, unpacked her gear, and returned to her motel. Karma's yearling class would be the first one the following day. The colt could be a real handful early in the morning, and she'd have to get up with the sun in order to have time to work the kinks out of him.

The next morning, she had Karma at the end of the lunge-line by five o'clock. He wouldn't behave, and her nervousness grew. The colt class was important–it would give him the final qualifying points for the regional show. If she didn't get him into the regional, she could forget the nationals.

She snapped the whip and barked a command at the prancing bay, but he was too wound up from the excitement and stimulation of all the new sounds and smells. He ignored her, crow-hopping for a few feet before moving back into an animated trot. Liz gave up and returned to her stabling area. She glanced at her watch and panic careened through her chest. The class would start in two hours. Karma peering impudently from his stall, as if to ask, *"What's next?"*

A little while later, she led him across the road to the wash racks, mentally checking her prep list again. Attention to detail and constant work with the horses was an absolute requirement for success. The eager youngster reared, and Liz shook her head. *Talk about needing to pay attention.* Karma tossed his head and skittered around, anticipating the splash of water on his back. Liz soaped, then rinsed, the chore made more difficult by having to chase him around the enclosure. Once the ordeal was over, his energy level skyrocketed, and Liz had to yank hard on his nose-chain to keep him on the ground. Two minutes later, he reared, then walked on his hind legs for about four feet before she snapped him back under control. *Oh, please, not today!*

"Having a little trouble, Missy?"

Liz whirled to see who taunted her. A short, vaguely-familiar man led a beautiful mare. He threw her a sly look, then continued on his way toward the barns.

She took a deep breath. Sometimes, it just felt like she was in over her head.

She checked her reflection in the travel mirror on the wall, brushing a light film of perspiration from her forehead. Her cheeks were flushed with anticipation, and anxiety rolled through her stomach. Her hair wouldn't stay in the small, neat bun she'd fashioned, and a second later, her small bowtie came loose. Her hands shook as she fixed the renegade accessory.

"Dammit! What is the matter with me?"

Karma had quieted down a little by the time she took him out of the stall to finish preparing him for the class. The first call came over the loudspeaker as she buckled the fine cord show-halter. She drew a deep breath, made a quick check to see that her exhibitor's number was still pinned to her back, then headed toward the arena. Rounding the corner, she stopped in her tracks, her self-confidence vanishing into the cool morning air. A crowd of about thirty horses and handlers milled around the in-gate. There'd be no chance for a win in *that* crowd.

As soon as he saw the other horses, Karma's obedient attitude disappeared. Once inside the arena, he danced around, spring-loaded, and Liz knew she'd be exhausted by the time it was her turn in front of the judge. Her stomach did somersaults, and the colt responded to her nervousness.

Struggling to relax, she tried to evaluate the competition. Though the Tahoe show was a small event, it attracted exhibitors from the surrounding states, all fighting for the same qualifying points that Liz sought. The horses entered in Karma's class were some of the highest quality animals in the industry. Liz recognized several trainers who'd been stars in the business for years. She grinned with amusement as they postured and posed, attempting to keep their horses' attention. Hollywood had nothing on these guys.

Her turn came, and she walked her horse toward the judge. Karma obeyed her commands without a hitch, stretching his swan-like neck to its fullest, and showing off his beautiful flat back and level croup. He flagged his tail, taking on the look of a sculptor's creation. Liz's chest swelled with pride. The colt was magnificent, every bit as beautiful as any of the others in the ring. Maybe even more.

She glanced surreptitiously at the judge, trying to read his body language. He walked a complete circle around them, scrutinizing the colt from every angle, then nodded and told her to trot the horse away. Karma stepped out briskly, lifting his front legs high and fairly floating over the ground. Liz's pulse quickened. *Perfect! Maybe we do have a chance.*

The judge nodded and scribbled something on a clipboard, then turned to the next exhibitor. Karma continued to prance as Liz led him back to their position in the line. She stood him up and kept him alert, remembering her father's wisdom. *"The class is important from the in-gate to the results."* Her eyes misted at the memory. *I wish he were here to see me now.* She swallowed the lump in her throat. If he were still alive, she'd be in Kentucky, working at her profession, not standing in a show ring out West.

The loudspeaker crackled and the crowd grew quiet.

"Ladies and Gentlemen, the judge has made his decisions."

Liz's heartbeat thudded as the announcer started with eighth place and worked his way up the list.

"Your second place winner is FSF Kahiil bin Samaar, owned by Fire Stone Farms and shown by Bill Benton."

Liz sized up the handler accepting the red ribbon. With chagrin, she recognized him as the man who'd commented on Karma's unruly behavior at the wash rack. She'd seen Benton's picture in the breed magazines, where he was touted as the reigning king of the halter classes. Rumor had it that he was a millionaire. *Great, now I've made a fool of myself in front of one of the big boys.*

"And Ladies and Gentlemen, first place goes to...Legacy Karma, owned and shown by Elizabeth Barnett!"

Liz's mouth fell open, her brain unable to grasp the reality of the announcement. A second later, she leapt into the air, letting out a whoop. The colt danced and pranced, and shook his beautiful head as though to admonish her: *"You thought there was any question?"*

By the time she returned to the stalls, her knees had stopped wobbling, but her heart still thundered with excitement. She threw her arms around Karma's neck, and hugged him tightly, feeling the dampness of his coat against her cheek.

"You are *such* a good boy!" she exclaimed, scratching behind his ears. "You are going to be the star of Legacy. I can feel it in my bones!"

Eighteen

L iz found a seat in the grandstand, and settled down to watch some of the remaining stallion classes. She spotted a tall, dark man in the ring and, thinking it was Kurt, she let out a little gasp. She leaned forward, trying to get a better look. He turned around, and she relaxed. While similar in height and build, the man's bearing was far different than Kurt's self-confident demeanor.

Her mind wandered through the qualities she liked about Kurt. His gentleness with Fair Lady. His calm determination to save every horse on the night of the fire. His strong hands holding the injured horse while she ministered to it. The passionate kiss. She closed her eyes, feeling his arms holding her tightly, tasting his urgent lips, and delighting in the touch of his hand on her breast.

A loud cheer jolted her back to reality. The class had ended, and the man who'd triggered her thoughts loped around the arena on a victory lap. She left the grandstand, flustered by her sensual images of Kurt, and perturbed by how easily they intruded.

Legacy Arabians was stabled in a far corner of the show barn, a location that Liz had requested, preferring to be off by herself, rather than in the midst of the chaos. At that mid-morning hour, most of the exhibitors were either in the ring, waiting to enter the arena, or watching classes. She took advantage of the quiet time to contemplate the future.

Her plans were right on target. If Karma continued to win his classes, by the time he turned four, she would start using him as the herd sire. Once he'd proven his potency, his Double B bloodlines would attract outside mares, and the future of Legacy Arabians would be bright.

"Congratulations. Great performance."

The familiar husky voice sent a shock wave through Liz's chest. She turned to look at the face that had filled her earlier daydreams, a flutter moving through her stomach.

"Kurt! What are *you* doing here? Aren't you getting ready for the Stockton show?"

His mustache curled enticingly at the corners of his full mouth. "Not for a few days yet. Eve changed her mind about showing that weanling, so I decided to run up here and see how you were doing."

"*Eve* changed her mind? I thought *you* were the one who was so hot to show that baby."

Kurt's smile faded abruptly. "Not me. I'd never wean a foal so early...I don't believe in it. 'Course, that opinion could cause me problems with Eve down the road." He grinned wickedly. "But, I'll take my cues from you."

Liz flushed at the reference to her dispute over the weaning.

He leaned his shoulder against the stall door and cocked his head. "Why did you think *I* wanted to show her?"

"Eve told me I needed to pick up Fair Lady because you wanted to take the foal to Stockton. I wondered about that–you don't appear to be so uncaring about the horses' welfare."

Disgust darkened his features and he shook his head.

"Eve's just playin' games with me to see how far she can go. I also told her she shouldn't have sold Fair Lady. That mare was one of the best in the barn. But, no, Eve's gonna do as she damned well pleases. Then, the next thing I know, she's got this ridiculous idea of weaning that baby, then showing her in a class two weeks later." He shook his head in pure wonderment. "I don't know what's the matter with the woman...she's probably just been in the horse business too long."

"I'm glad it wasn't your idea. That whole scene just about broke my heart."

He looked at her thoughtfully, then cleared his throat.

"Liz, I want to–"

Uncomfortable with the prospect of a serious conversation, Liz reached for a halter. "I have to work Ashiiqah. Her class is right after lunch."

Kurt nodded and stepped back. As Liz entered the stall, she felt him watching her, and a now familiar, delicious feeling crept through her. Though thrilled to learn that he'd come to the show specifically to see her, it frightened her to think about opening up another opportunity to be embarrassed. *Why do I turn into such a wimp every time he's around? I need to get a grip. Mr. Cowboy will have to redeem himself before I'll fall into another one of his tender traps.*

She emerged from the stall, and Kurt took the lunge-line from her other hand.

"Mind if I come along?"

Kurt leaned on the rail and watched Liz work the beautiful mare. Much as he'd tried to convince himself that his only interest was checking on the competition, he knew his desire to see Liz again was the real reason he'd come to Tahoe. She'd been on his mind constantly since she'd picked up Fair Lady. On that day, he'd wanted nothing more than to sweep her into his arms and tell her how badly he felt about his behavior after their kiss, that he hadn't meant a word of what he'd said.

He grinned, thinking about her feisty manner when she'd stood up to Eve to defend her opinion. *Her self-confidence is what makes her so successful. I'll bet she's got the ranchers eating out of her hand by now.*

As he watched her lunge the horse, his thoughts changed from personal to practical, and a frown creased his forehead. *I can't let her influence me like this. I have too much at stake.*

Liz felt Kurt's gaze boring into her back, feeling as though he were mentally undressing her. *Hmm...Not an altogether unpleasant idea.* However, within a few minutes, she pushed the sensual thoughts from her head, and concentrated on exercising Ashiiqah.

On the way back to the barn, Kurt was openly enthusiastic.

"Beautiful mare. What are her bloodlines?"

Liz loved to talk pedigrees with anyone knowledgeable, and she spent the next fifteen minutes chronicling the Polish and Egyptian bloodlines of the herd, delighted by Kurt's obvious appreciation.

He held the stall door open as Liz put the mare away.

"You planning to work that colt again today? I'd like to watch, if you don't mind."

"My pleasure."

She watched him saunter down the aisle, his jeans sculpted around his tight butt and muscular thighs. *My pleasure, indeed!* Her heart quickened at the prospect of being with him again. Learning that he hadn't been the one who'd insisted on the early weaning had altered her attitude. On two separate occasions now, she'd seen a gentleness peek from beneath his tough, professional exterior. She wanted to see more of that softer side of him, and swore to find a way.

At the edge of the arena, Liz waited nervously for the results of Ashiiqah's class. The mare had performed beautifully, as usual, but Liz never took anything for granted. A magnificent bay mare caught her attention. The horse's body looked as though it had been carved by an artist's hands: extremely fine legs, sharp facial bones, shapely ears with tips that almost touched. *Has to be straight Egyptian.* Bill Benton held the mare's rapt attention, and Liz shook her head. *I guess if I'm going to lose, I'd just as soon lose to a really perfect horse.*

Keeping her head lowered, she scanned the grandstand, looking for Kurt. There weren't many spectators, and it was easy to see that he wasn't there. Sharp disappointment surprised her. *I guess whatever he had to do earlier was more important than watching my class.* Brushing away the petulant thought, she returned her attention to the blaring loudspeaker.

"Second place goes to...FSF Egyptian Lady, owned by Fire Stone Farms and shown by Bill Benton!"

Liz blinked. *Good grief! If he's on second, who's on first?*

In the next instant, Ashiiqah's name echoed through the arena. Liz's thoughts raced as she trotted the lovely young mare toward the ring steward. *We're certainly making a name for ourselves at this show! Now, if I can just win like this at the regional.*

As she left the ring, Kurt fell into step beside her.

"Boy, that was something! I was *sure* Benton's Egyptian horse would take it."

Liz laughed. "I figured Benton would win just because he's Benton."

Kurt didn't respond, but nodded thoughtfully as they walked toward Liz's stalls. While she removed the mare's halter, Kurt grabbed a soft cloth, and began wiping down the damp coat. Liz watched secretly as he went about the work he obviously loved, relaxed and absorbed in his task. Surprisingly, she enjoyed seeing him with her horses–she usually disliked anyone else handling them. *What a team we'd make. The two of us could take Legacy Arabians to the top.* The bold thought shocked her. *Whoa! There's no team here. And I don't need anyone to help me succeed...especially someone who distracts me the way he does.* Her pulse jumped. *Maybe I just need someone for me.*

She sighed and leaned her forehead against the mare's neck, exhausted from the excitement of a strenuous and emotional day. Kurt stepped up beside her and rested his hand on her shoulder, his smile making her heart do its gymnastic thing again.

"Get yourself together, and we'll go grab a bite to eat. There's a good steakhouse over on the lake."

Peeling off her show clothes, she assessed the changes in Kurt's manner. It seemed as though he wanted to make amends for his behavior on the night of the fire. Her heart thumped at the memory. *Am I setting myself up for another experience just like it?* A second later, a surge of excitement blurred her fears. *This will be my chance to find out who he really is.* A stab of apprehension. *And his secret.*

Nineteen

The late afternoon sun slanted through the giant pines along the highway that circled the rim of South Tahoe Lake. Liz felt as though she were in another world, far away from the dust and chaos of the show. Shivers of delight coursed through her body as she relived the victories of the day.

Kurt sat relaxed in the seat, his arm draped nonchalantly over the steering wheel. "Penny for your thoughts."

"Just revisiting today's classes. I can't believe we won. There were some *very* good horses in the ring."

He laughed sharply. "I *guess*! And some of them just happened to be *yours*! Why are you so surprised? If you have excellent stock, and you've trained them right, they *always* have a chance to win."

She valued the compliment. "But I have a lot to learn."

The truck rolled into the gravel parking lot beside an ordinary-looking, flat-roofed building. Pocketing the keys, he turned to her, his tone sincere.

"You had a good teacher. You picked up more from your father than you think."

The exterior of the cinderblock building was stark and unappealing, marked by a single, dark door with an oval window and a small sign that read, "The Place." Kurt pulled the door open and a delectable aroma wafted out. Inside, old-fashioned chandeliers cast dim light over a long room, and ceiling fans kept the wonderful smells moving through the air. A huge mirror covered the wall behind a solid oak bar that had been burnished to a soft gleam by decades of elbows. Dozens of liquor and wine bottles, glasses, and mugs sparkled in the reflection of the soft lights. He took her hand, leading her to the end of the bar, then down a short hallway to a heavy door.

The sharp contrast between the lounge and the dining room amazed her. Dark mahogany woodwork and ceiling cornices framed deep burgundy walls, and soft light spilled from bronze sconces, darkened with the patina of time. White cloths draped the tables, and fresh flower arrangements graced each one. Soft music played in the background.

His tone was tentative. "Like it?"

"It's wonderful! Who would know, looking at the outside?"

"That's the way they want it. You can't get near this place at dinnertime."

She felt a small twinge of jealousy at the idea of Kurt enjoying the cozy restaurant with someone else.

"Do you come here often?"

He chuckled and squeezed her hand. "Lizzie-Liz! Why are you so interested in my past?"

Embarrassed and annoyed, she snatched her hand away. "Don't call me Lizzie!"

Instantly, she realized that she teetered on the verge of spoiling what might be a nice evening. Reaching for his hand, she gave him a contrite look.

"I'm sorry. I didn't mean to snap. My father used to call me that."

"No problem. So, tell me what Legacy Arabians is up to these days, besides winning everything in sight."

His smile tranquilized her wound-up brain and body, and she settled back into the comfortable captain's chair. The late afternoon drifted into twilight as they sipped wine, enjoyed a quiet meal, and discussed all the leading Arabian farms, the hot trainers, the major shows and, in general, life with horses.

Kurt sneaked his spoon across the table and stole a bite of her chocolate mousse. He rolled the creamy delight around in his mouth, then seductively licked his lips. Struggling with lustful thoughts, she looked away from his suggestive expression, tightening her thighs against the rising heat. *I wish he wouldn't look at me that way. I don't think I could resist him right now. Do I even want to?*

He smiled knowingly, his expression hinting that he recognized her discomfort. She blanched and looked away, trying to compose her thoughts.

He changed the subject. "What are your plans for the rest of the season?"

Relieved to focus her thoughts on something less stimulating, she answered quickly. "Karma and Ashiiqah are both qualified for the regional show in September."

He nodded, but his expression held a shadow of tension. She moved past the brief distraction.

"If I do well at the regional show, I'll take them to the Nationals in Albuquerque. I need some serious wins on these horses–especially Karma–if I want to build name recognition for the farm. Otherwise, I'll be just another breeder."

Kurt signaled the waiter for the check, then sat back in his chair and gave her a quizzical look, as though analyzing her words.

"You'll probably do okay at regional, even though there'll be some pretty big-name trainers there. But don't get your hopes up for the nationals. That's big business. A loss at that show can put your farm *off* the map just as quickly as a win can put it *on*."

She straightened up, her indignation rising quickly.

"What do you mean, big names? Names don't have anything to do with winning."

He snorted. "Boy, you really *are* naïve! At a certain level in the horse business, money talks–whether it's Arabians or Quarter Horses or Thoroughbreds. Money makes the really big decisions. It's a fight-for-blood environment."

Bristling at his patronizing attitude, she snapped, "That's not true. My father *never* paid to win a class."

She pushed away from the table and stood up, ready to walk out of the restaurant. *God, I can't stand this man!*

"Whoa, Liz, hear me out." He took her hand, looking at her sympathetically. "Please, sit down and let me explain, okay?"

Grudgingly, she returned to her seat, not feeling receptive to whatever he planned to say.

"Things were different when your father showed his horses. That was the 'real' horse business. So much has changed over the last twenty-some years. The breed has become a commodity, an investment. The reality, now, is that there are some heavy-hitters in the Arabian industry, people who have more money than you or I could possibly imagine. People who have no real interest in the horses themselves. Business tycoons. Royalty from other countries. Mafia-types. They can pay anyone to do anything."

He watched her for a moment, then continued.

"Some of the big-name trainers are paid so much money, and have such free rein, that they become celebrities in the show world, and *that* generates even more power. Some of the horses that pull off big wins don't have a fraction of the outstanding bloodlines that yours have. But enough under-the-table payoffs, plenty of slick advertising, a big enough trainer name...it makes a difference in the ring."

"What are you getting at? I just beat Bill Benton *twice!*"

"That won't be your only problem."

She stared into dark brown eyes that seemed to reflect sincerity and apology for his comments. Remembering Colleen's warning, Liz intuitively knew what he wanted to say.

She looked him straight in the eye. "I'm a woman, right? That's what will keep me from reaching the top with my horses?"

The expression on his face told her she'd hit the bullseye.

The effects of the wine meshed with Liz's anger, confusion, and the deep weariness of a very long day. She wanted to fall into bed and lose herself in sleep, but still had work to do at the stalls. Karma's championship class would be the next afternoon, and she *had* to be ready.

Stepping up into the truck, her thoughts were on the tense conversation. Why had he brought up the subject of show politics? They rode along for a few miles, wrapped in uneasy silence, Liz still mulling over his views on the business of showing horses. Finally, she decided to pursue it.

"Tell me why you think I can't succeed as a woman in the

show ring."

Kurt squeezed his eyes shut for a second, then glanced over at her. "Have you ever looked around at the exhibitors in a class? Do you see many women?"

She gave him a blank look. "Of course. There are *lots* of women showing Arabians at most of the shows I attend."

He snorted. "That's right. And most of the shows you attend are small, local shows. And most of those women are owners showing in the amateur classes. C'mon, Liz, how many big-time, *really* successful female professional trainers have you seen?"

She couldn't answer him. She'd never paid any attention to the *people* in the ring, only the horses. The silence grew around them. *What is he trying to prove? There must be a reason he's trying to discourage me from showing my horses, and I don't think it's because he's afraid I'll lose, or have my feelings hurt.* Her misgivings started to mount.

Kurt's tone became a little less patronizing. "I'm not saying you can't ever win some classes as a woman, or without buying your way into the ribbons. I'm just saying the odds are tough. You need to be aware of it going in. Don't be surprised by *anything* that happens at the big shows that really count."

He patted her hand like a father consoling a child who'd lost a toy. Liz pulled her hand away, crossed her arms, and stared out the window.

Why am I being so obstinate? He's been around this business a lot longer than I have. He's bound to have some insights. Another minute passed in silence. *Here I am, finally with the man I've been daydreaming about, and I'm spoiling it.*

"Kurt, I understand you are only trying to help. I'm sorry I acted so cranky about it. You just don't know what I've been going through since I moved to California."

He didn't respond, and she continued.

"I've been beating my head against the wall, trying to establish my practice here. I can't seem to break through the good-ol-boy barrier, no matter how good I am at what I do. And now, you're telling me the problem extends into the only joy I have–showing my horses. Can you blame me for being upset?"

His hand covered hers again, his voice sincere.

"I know, Hon, but sometimes there are things so far out of your control, that it makes more sense to find another way to make a mark on the world."

Liz gazed at his shadowed profile. *I wonder how you would know something like that. What is your secret, Mr. Cowboy?*

Twenty

L iz's earlier fatigue had disappeared by the time they returned to the show grounds.

"Kurt, you don't have to stay while I work Karma. Don't you have a long drive back?"

He grinned. "I'm not driving back tonight. I want to stay and see the fireworks tomorrow." His expression turned serious. "Besides, you shouldn't be down here at the barns alone late at night. You don't even have anyone watching the horses when you're not here."

"What are you saying? About the horses, I mean."

He gave her a solemn look and reached for a lunge-line hanging on the wall.

"Just be aware that there are folks out there who would do bad things to keep a good horse from winning. You should always have someone at your stalls, especially at the big shows."

"You *are* kidding, aren't you?"

One look at his face told her he wasn't.

She pressed the issue. "Is that why you got so upset when you found me in your mare's stall that morning?"

"Something like that."

He turned and entered Karma's stall. She started to pursue the conversation, but was immediately distracted by her colt's meek attitude as Kurt haltered him.

"How did you *do* that? He acts like you've hypnotized him."

"Actually, I don't know." He grinned. "I guess I'm part horse."

More than ever, she wanted to know more about the real Kurt.

"Y'know...*you* know a lot about *me*, and I know *nothing* about you."

"One of these days, we'll play true confessions, but for now, shouldn't you work your champion yearling?"

She recognized the put-off. *There's something he doesn't want me to know, but I* want *to understand him. I'll just have to find out on my own.*

Still under Kurt's magical influence, Karma stood quietly while Liz attached the lead rope. *Having a professional like him around could sure make my life easier.* The thought zapped her brain like a cattle prod, and she glanced sideways at Kurt's firm body, instantly feeling the stir of excitement again. *And definitely more interesting.*

Together, they walked through the night to the lighted exercise paddock, and Liz went to the center. Karma remained the picture of obedience, although he looked back twice to locate Kurt. The colt's good behavior was short-lived. Once he started around the circle, Liz felt his tension in the line, and tried to communicate to him through the lead. He bucked and jumped and walked on his hind legs. He stopped and wouldn't go forward. *Oh, no, don't do this now, not when I have an audience that just told me I couldn't succeed because I'm a woman. Let me at least look like I have* some *control!*

Kurt materialized at her side. "Mind if I give you a couple of tips?"

"Wouldn't you know he'd act up when someone's watching?"

"Well, if he misbehaves tomorrow, you can kiss your championship good-bye."

She handed him the lunge-line and stepped back. Karma had stopped prancing and stood quietly, his attention locked on his new handler. Kurt clucked softly and stepped toward the colt, who immediately trotted perfectly around the circle, head held high.

Liz watched, admiring the way Kurt handled her "bad boy" with a skill acquired through years of experience, and some other mysterious craft.

Kurt commanded the horse to halt, and Karma stopped in his tracks. Transferring the whip to the other hand, Kurt gave it one small snap at ground level, and Karma pivoted on his hind legs, and trotted in the opposite direction. Liz shook her head. *He makes it look so easy. I spend hours fighting this colt, and along comes a cowboy who can make the horse stand on its head if he asks it to.*

Kurt nodded toward Amy's stall. "You showing that bay mare tomorrow?"

Liz stopped picking Karma's hooves and looked up. "Yes, but I can work her in the morning."

She unhooked the colt and put him into his stall, then tossed in a flake of hay. When she returned to the aisle, a mischievous grin rippled across Kurt's face.

"I want to show you something."

She laughed. "You've already impressed me. What *else* can you do?"

A seductive look slipped into his eyes, and she immediately regretted her choice of words.

His voice deepened suggestively. "Come over here and I'll show you."

She giggled nervously, her cheeks burning. "Ahhh, I mean with horses."

Beckoning her to follow, he walked over to Amy's stall. The elegant mare stood motionless, watching him with interest. He stepped inside the door, talking softly, then moved to her head and turned to face the same direction as the horse. Bringing his right hand up beneath her chin, he snapped his fingers loudly and stepped toward the open stall door. Amy moved forward with him, staying exactly at his shoulder. Kurt "led" the horse out of the stall and into the aisle. When he stopped, she stopped. He started forward again, and the mare followed.

Astonished, Liz watched Amy walk freely down the aisle beside the handsome cowboy. He brought the horse back to where she stood, and reached for the halter hanging on the wall.

He grinned. "She hears the snap and thinks she's attached to the lead line."

"Doesn't say much for being very bright, does it?"

"Doesn't have anything to do with being smart. Horses are

creatures of habit and response. She's well trained, so it works."
He grabbed a brush and started smoothing it over the mare's sleek
coat. "Just don't try it with a green horse."

At that moment, Liz knew she'd fallen under the same spell as
her animals.

A quick glance at her watch jarred her. "Oh, man, it's mid-
night. I have to go. I didn't realize it had gotten so late."

A self-conscious smile played at the corners of his mustache.
"Sorry. I lose track of time when I'm working with horses. Come
on, I'll walk you out to the truck."

The night was quiet as they moved across the parking lot. At
Liz's truck, he stepped up close and gently grasped her shoulders.

"You get some rest. You're gonna clean house tomorrow."

He kissed her softly on the forehead, then waited while she
climbed into the truck.

"Lock your doors."

Liz watched him disappear into the darkness, her heart thump-
ing, her shoulders tingling where his hands had rested, her guard
completely down.

The scent of Liz's perfume still lingered inside Kurt's truck.
How many lady trainers wore perfume? As he'd watched her work
with the colt, his thoughts had raced, knowing he shouldn't be helping her, that he was just digging himself in deeper. He knew he
shouldn't have given her such a hard time about the pitfalls of showing horses. *Well, dammit, it's true! She'll find out for herself soon
enough, and there's nothing I can do to save her.*

The charitable thought surprised him. He'd never considered
another trainer's feelings or goals. Extremely competitive, he'd lived
his life to win with his horses and make a name for himself. He
shook off thoughts of the past, focusing instead on Eve's "incen-
tive plan" and his own future. His life held no room for sentimentality, romance, or sympathy. On this trip, he'd learned what he
needed to know. Now, he had to figure out what to do with it.

Twenty-One

The next morning, Liz glanced up and down the aisle frequently as she prepared Amy for her class. By gate call, Kurt still hadn't shown, and Liz's distraction puddled into disappointment.

Only four exhibitors waited by the in-gate. Few owners bothered to show older mares in halter classes, concentrating instead on their younger broodmare prospects. A quick assessment of the competition convinced Liz that her chances of a blue ribbon were excellent.

The class went flawlessly, and Liz observed how quickly the judge assessed the other entrants. *He made his decision as soon as he saw Amy.* Feeling almost smug, Liz ran beside her mare on yet another victory lap and grinned, recalling Kurt's comment about "cleaning house." Another quick look at the grandstand, and disappointment edged into her happy thoughts. His absence dampened her elation, and *that* irritated her. *Why should I let anything detract from the excitement of this win?*

As she left the ring, a short man approached her, his even white teeth sparkling through a crooked smile.

"Congratulations. Nice mare. Is she for sale?"

Liz stopped and looked closer at the familiar tanned face.

He offered his hand. "Bill Benton. Fire Stone Farms."

"Liz Barnett. Legacy Arabians."

He grinned. "I know who you are. So, is the mare for sale?"

At close range, Benton was nice-looking, but his arrogant, almost condescending attitude detracted from his physical appearance.

"No, this is one of my best broodmares. She produced the colt I showed yesterday in the yearling class."

Liz felt a tiny thrill as she zapped the "big-name" trainer.

"Huh. If she's already one of your best broodmares, why are you showing her? Is she in foal?"

Liz's hackles rose. *Another guy trying to tell me what to do.*

"I'm showing her to promote my farm name. She's open this year. I'm giving her a rest."

Benton rolled his eyes and sighed. "Oh, I see. Being a good mommy, are we?"

A snarling response snapped into Liz's thoughts, but Benton stepped back and tossed out a limp wave.

"If you change your mind, give us a call. We're in the book."

He swaggered off, leaving Liz feeling ridiculous and very much like an amateur.

Kurt stood in the shadows by the arena entrance, his jaw tightening with concern as he watched Liz talking to Bill Benton at the rail. *If I know Benton, he's trying to buy something.* Kurt's stomach pitched at the possibility that the sale on Ebony might fall through if the trainer took a notion that Karma was a better stallion. Benton walked off and, even from a distance, Kurt saw that the conversation had upset Liz.

He pasted a smile on his face as she approached.

"Hey, congratulations, again. I see you had a little visit from Billy-Boy."

"What a nasty man! He wanted to buy Amy."

Kurt felt a rush of relief, then laughed. "He's nasty for wanting to buy your horse? I'd say that's a real compliment. Fire Stone touches nothing that isn't first-class."

Liz frowned. "No, I mean he's just obnoxious. He started giving me a hard time for showing a broodmare, then made snide comments about the fact I didn't breed her this season."

Kurt softened his tone. "That nasty man is a steam-roller in the ring, and the more important the show, the nastier he gets. Better to have him for a friend than an enemy." He hesitated. "Are you going to sell her?"

Liz's scowl deepened across her features.

"Why would I do that? She's part of my breeding plan."

Kurt waded in, knowing the water was deep and treacherous.

"Isn't money part of your plan, too? I'd say a chance to sell a horse for a good price is pretty critical to expanding a breeding farm. Having your breeder prefix integrated into the Fire Stone herd wouldn't hurt you much, either."

Liz's voice rose with irritation. "I've had just about enough of know-it-all men telling me what they think I'm doing wrong. This horse is one of my father's last foals. She's special to me. She produces excellent babies. And I'm keeping her!"

Snapping Amy's lead rope a little too hard, Liz strode forward, followed by the surprised mare, who tossed her head and danced sideways. Kurt caught up with her.

"Easy, Liz. I'm only pointing out the obvious. If you have personal reasons for keeping the mare, that's fine—we all have our favorites. Just don't jeopardize your breeding program with sentimental decisions. Remember, you recently added a truly outstanding mare to your barn, one that cost you a *lot* of money. No offense to your father, but Fair Lady is three times the horse Amy is. The name of the game in breeding is to keep the best, and cull the rest."

His inner voice goaded him. *Like Eve did with Muscala.*

Liz heard everything he said, and knew in her heart that he spoke the truth, but her anger overruled her common sense. In the past twenty-four hours, Kurt had brought up obstacle after obstacle to her plans for Legacy. She was sick of it and wanted to be left alone.

Kurt took her silent cue. "Well, I'm gonna scoot. Good luck this afternoon."

She started to reply, but he was striding away. *Fine. Go sulk. You can't always be right.* Her thoughts turned to the championship class scheduled for that afternoon, and her stomach flip-flopped in anticipation of what she hoped would be the win of the weekend.

Kurt walked toward his truck. He should really head back to

El Dorado. He had a lot of work to do, and he was sure Eve wouldn't appreciate his extended absence. Irritation crawled across his shoulders. *To hell with her.* He wanted to see the outcome of the championship colt class. Karma might win, and that could prove to be a monkey wrench in Kurt's plans. The last thing he wanted was to show against Liz at the regional show, especially if Bill Benton started shopping around.

Liz's soft voice startled him.

"I owe you an apology. I shouldn't have been so snippy."

"It's okay. I'm used to being chewed out by beautiful women."
Like hell, I am—just this one.

"No, seriously. I know you just want to help, but I *have* to try to do this, or I'll always feel like a quitter."

Her eyes held an emotion he couldn't quite read. Anticipation? Fear of rejection? He wanted to step down and pull her close to him, touch her hair, smell her perfume. He felt himself losing the battle to stay neutral.

"I understand. Don't worry about it. I always have too much to say when it comes to horses."

Liz stepped closer to the truck. "Are you going to stay for Karma's class?"

Kurt's horse sense kicked in. *I should get out of this while I'm ahead.* His emotions took over.

"I guess I could, if you want me there."

She laid her hand lightly on his leg, sending a jolt of excitement through his body.

"I do."

Patting her hand, he tried to ignore the feelings stirring through him. He shifted in his seat, then reached for the key in the ignition.

"Okey-dokey. I'll be there. Right now, I'm going to run out for a bite to eat. Want me to bring you something?"

"Something light. I'm awfully nervous."

Liz watched the truck drive away. *Something's different. It's like there's an invisible barrier between us. He's there on the other side, so close, but I can't reach him.*

As she walked back to the barn, she thought about how the

hard muscles of his leg had felt beneath the coarse fabric of his jeans. Her stomach quivered. *I can't believe I did that.* She smiled to herself. The evidence of his feelings had been inescapable. *It wouldn't take much to make my fantasies about him come true.* The smile faded. She'd need to know more about him–and his past– before succumbing to any flights of fancy. Squaring her shoulders, she tucked away all thoughts of Kurt, and started psyching herself for the next class.

Karma moved restlessly around his stall, as though he sensed his big moment, only hours away.

Liz also felt unsettled. "C'mon, you. A little exercise will be good for both of us."

Thirty minutes later, she returned from the warm-up paddock and found a brown paper bag sitting on the tack trunk. Inside were a turkey sandwich and an Aliqua business card with "Good luck!" scrawled on the back.

The stallion championship class contained four entries: Karma and the first place winners for each of the other stallion divisions. Karma would compete against two-, three-, and four-year-old horses. Liz knew he had very little chance of beating out the older colts because, as a youngster, his body still had an "unfinished" lankiness to it that would eventually smooth out with maturity. The fact that he was even a contender in the class was amazing, considering the large field of horses he'd beaten to get there. Remembering Kurt's comments, Liz scrutinized the handlers. All men.

Her hands felt clammy, and Karma picked up on her case of nerves. *As if he needs any more nervous energy.* She glanced at the grandstand to look for Kurt and, again, disappointment welled up inside her. *Where in the world does he go during the classes?* She swallowed her thoughts and concentrated on keeping her colt under control as he danced around, threatening to walk on his hind legs at any moment.

Liz watched the two exhibitors ahead of her, critically comparing the horses to her own. The two-year-old chestnut was nice, but not spectacular. Liz's real competition was Bill Benton's entry, the winner of the three-year-old division. Liz turned her attention back to Karma, talking softly and trying to transmit calm confidence to him.

As soon as they stepped in front of the judge, the colt started his springy I'm-outta-here step, flagging his tail, and tossing his head. Liz tugged sharply on the lead line to get his attention. The judge tipped his hat, then walked the circle around Karma, inspecting every detail of the horse's body. Liz held her breath. At that moment, the colt transformed into a mahogany statue, stretching his long neck out even farther, and freezing into a classic Arabian pose.

At the judge's direction, Liz ran alongside Karma's breathtaking trot. He seemed to float above the ground for just a second between each stride. As Liz reversed and headed back toward the judge, the colt broke, gave a little buck, and tossed his head. *Dammit*! She yanked the lead, bringing him back to the trot. Her heart sank. *There goes the championship*. Stakes classes provided no latitude for even one mistake.

Struggling to keep her disappointment from showing, she trotted the colt over to the line and stood him up. Her throat tightened, and she cursed herself for not paying close enough attention to him, letting him break like that. The loudspeaker announced that the decisions were in, and the row of horses and handlers relaxed. She walked Karma around in a circle, partly to keep him relaxed, but mostly to take her mind off the glaring mistake.

Having conceded defeat in her mind, it took a moment to register what she heard over the loudspeaker. In dream-like slow motion, she moved forward to accept the gleaming silver bowl for Reserve Champion.

Kurt leaned against the rail at the far end of the ring. Two opposing forces pulled him as he watched Liz move up to accept the trophy. On the one hand, he worried about her continued success with Karma, and how it might affect his *own* plans. On the other hand, he was deeply moved by the freshness and enthusiasm she brought to showing her horses. He shook his head sadly. *If she stays with this rat race, she'll end up just like the rest of the women in the business—hard and cynical, ready and willing to do whatever they can to win.*

Liz's nature was so easy-going; it felt good just being around her. He didn't want to see that change for the sake of a blue ribbon.

Passing through the out-gate in a daze, Liz realized she hadn't paid attention to the winner of the class. She turned back in time to see Bill Benton accept the champion trophy for the beautiful gray three-year-old. Kurt's comments about big-name trainers taunted her as she walked toward the exit.

Kurt came forward, and pecked her on the cheek.

"Congratulations, Hon, you did real good. The judge really liked your horse, but I thought you'd lost it when he bucked."

She rolled her eyes. "Me, too."

A minute later, Benton joined them. The gray stallion snaked his neck, reaching out to touch noses with Karma. They sniffed each other's breath for a minute, then the older horse squealed and stamped.

Benton laughed, giving Liz a pointed look. "He's telling Junior who's the boss."

The two men talked for a minute, then Bill said goodbye and threw a mock salute as he turned to go.

"Good to see you getting back on your feet, man."

He nodded to Liz, then headed toward the barns.

"What did he mean, 'get back on your feet'?"

Kurt didn't look at her. "I need to talk to you about that."

A second later, his face softened and he gave her his funny, crooked smile.

"Let's get your horse put away, and I'll take you out for a celebration dinner."

The excitement of the afternoon sang through her body as Liz stood under the hot sting of the shower. *All* her wins thrilled her, but words couldn't describe how she felt about Karma's Reserve. The little guy would go places–no question.

Her focus turned to the evening ahead, and her pulse skipped. Wiping away the fog from the mirror, she saw the flush of success coloring her cheeks and the sparkle of anticipation in her eyes.

Immediately, she remembered Kurt's caution on the morning after the fire. Fear of another rejection dampened her frame of mind, and confusion took over. *If he doesn't want a relationship, why is he here?* She sighed and slipped into a sweater. *Maybe he's changed his mind, but until I know his intentions, I'm going to be very careful.*

Twenty-Two

Kurt's soft whistle of appreciation greeted Liz as she stepped outside. He lounged against the truck, openly admiring her. Warmth moved over the skin beneath her sweater and worked its way up her neck. *I love the way he makes me feel–desirable, attractive. Nervous!*

"You look gorgeous."

The compliment sent her heartbeat into a wild tumble, and she shyly lifted her cheek for his kiss. *Who would've ever thought he could be so charming?* Settled into her seat, she watched him walk around to the driver's side. His hair still glistened from the shower, and she'd caught the scent of a fresh splash of aftershave. Her senses opened the floodgates of her thoughts.

As they drove the winding road out of town, she felt his gaze touching her from time to time. She looked out the window, enjoying the excitement of the unknown. Would she finally have a glimpse into the secrets of the stranger beside her? He didn't have much to say, other than comments about the lake region. When they passed the restaurant where they'd eaten the previous night, Liz threw him a puzzled look.

He smiled. "There's a neat place on the Nevada side, a town called Zephyrs Cove. I thought we'd go there for your victory celebration."

To her pleasant surprise, Kurt's "take-charge" attitude didn't bother her, especially in view of the last six months, when she hadn't been in charge of much of anything.

When they arrived at the restaurant, the maitre d' took them directly to a secluded table in the corner, a table adorned with a large bouquet of roses tied with a blue ribbon.

The man turned and bowed. "Your champagne will be here momentarily, sir."

Liz was stunned. "You did all this? Kurt, that's so sweet!"

She opened the small card attached to the roses, then smiled up at him. "Thank you."

Impulsively, she stood on her tiptoes and gave him a soft kiss on the cheek. The spicy scent of aftershave sent a ripple through her pulse.

Floor-to-ceiling picture windows made up the entire back wall of the restaurant. The view of the lake was breathtaking at that hour, the sun still dawdling at the rim of the mountains, casting its last golden rays across the water. As she soaked in the beauty of the scene, Liz's emotions threatened to overwhelm her. She'd taken her first big step toward building Legacy, and she was with a man who made her feel wonderful.

The champagne arrived and, when their glasses were filled, Kurt raised his.

"To the future of Legacy Arabians, and your continued success."

Her eyes burned with emotion as she sipped the fuzzy nectar. The conversation turned to the day's classes, and she welcomed Kurt's critique of each one. *He has so much to offer. If we...* Liz didn't allow the thought to finish. She still needed to learn more about this enigmatic man before she dared think about opening her heart.

Kurt saw the change in Liz's attitude toward him. Her initial wariness had been replaced by almost childlike trust, an honor he knew he didn't deserve. If he could just set her aside until he'd accomplished what he needed to do, then perhaps he could think about including her in his future. *Right. Like she's going to want anything to do with me when this is all over.* He looked at her radiant face, fresh with the victories of the day, relaxed by the bubbly wine. His conscience kicked him in the head. He at least owed her an explanation of who he was.

After dinner, Liz held Kurt's hand as he led her down some steps at the side of the restaurant, then along a short path. She felt giddy, as much from his touch as from the effects of the champagne. He guided her through a thicket, then around a curve and into a charming lakeside park with lush green grass, flowering shrubs, and stone benches.

Liz inhaled sharply. "How did you know about this place?"

He looked out over the lake. "I've been here before."

An uneasy feeling crept over her. "You sure know a lot about this part of the country for being new to the area."

"Yeah. Well, that's the horse business. I've traveled a lot."

They wandered down the slope to the water's edge. A pair of ducks paddled up, clearly accustomed to being fed. Liz stood close to Kurt, the silence between them not at all comfortable, her earlier dreamy mood vanquished.

Finally, he turned and took her hand, his dark eyes searching her face for a moment.

"Let's sit down. I have something to tell you."

She settled slowly onto a stone bench, its hard surface still warm from the late afternoon sun. As she gazed numbly across the lake, the pit of her stomach filled with ice. Steeling herself for whatever was coming, she composed her face into an expressionless mask and looked directly into Kurt's eyes.

He met her gaze, then shifted his own to a point on the ground before speaking.

"The night of the fire? When I told you I didn't have room for someone in my life? That's still true, but I want you to know why."

Her chest tightened. Like it or not, she was about to learn the secret she'd so desperately wanted to know.

"I'm involved with someone from my past. I–"

Liz leapt to her feet, fury raging through her. "You mean you're *married?*"

He closed his eyes, shaking his head vigorously.

"No, not anymore...I was, years ago..." He focused on the ground. "My wife died in childbirth. My baby son was stillborn."

Liz's breath caught in her chest, a surge of pain and remorse flashing through and crushing her own selfish thoughts. She saw the desperate pain in Kurt's eyes. The beautiful brown eyes that held such excitement for her—now dull and vacant, flooded with sad memories.

Her voice cracked. "Oh, Kurt, I'm so sorry."

She sat down, and covered his hand with hers, trying to think of something to say, something that would soften the jagged edges of his pain. He sat quietly for a moment, then began to speak, his voice thin.

"I was at a horse show...I was *always* at a horse show. I wasn't even there for her at the end to tell her how much I loved her before she died."

His voice broke, and he stared out over the lake. The sun had completely disappeared, and the shadows of the mountains were spreading across the water like an oil slick. The colors, which had been so vibrant just minutes before, had taken on dull, muted tones, as though Kurt's pain had been transferred to every living thing nearby.

Liz's throat tightened and her eyes burned with tears as she silently waited for him to continue.

He rose from the bench and continued his story, slowly pacing back and forth in front of her.

"That was ten years ago. I quit my job, got in my truck, and drove all over creation, trying to find a place where the memories wouldn't follow me. There wasn't any such place...I avoided horse shows like the plague."

He swallowed hard. "About a year after she...they died, I happened to stop in Taos, New Mexico, just passing through on my way to nowhere. I saw a sign about an Arabian horse show at the fairgrounds, and the old spark ignited. I drove over there, just to have a look."

He stopped pacing and sat down again, picking up Liz's hand and caressing it absent-mindedly while he talked.

"I wandered around the barns, just absorbing the odors and listening to the sounds. Horses were in my blood, and I couldn't avoid it any longer. I wanted to be back at work. I *needed* to be back at work.

"I heard hollering and a lot of noise in another part of the barn.

I ran toward the commotion, coming around a corner just in time to meet a big horse, loose and headed directly at me. His eyes were wild and he looked scared half to death. I stepped in front of him and snapped my fingers, told him to 'whoa.' He slowed down, then reared. I snapped my fingers again, and he just stood there, shaking and breathing hard. I walked up and grabbed his halter, and started talking to him."

Liz held her breath, her eyes locked on Kurt's memory-ravaged face as he told the story.

He shook his head sadly. "That's how I got the job in New Mexico. That stupid, snap-the-fingers trick."

"I don't think it's stupid, at all. It sounds like you saved that horse from hurting itself."

"Yeah. But it also convinced the horse's owner that I had supernatural powers, something to help her win in the show ring. She was a very rich widow who owned a large Arabian breeding farm. Della Courtland offered me more money than I'd ever seen, and let me know, in no uncertain terms, that my life would get better if I played her game."

He glanced at Liz, then plunged on. "She had excellent horses, and that made my job easy. I trained, and showed, and brought home the ribbons and trophies. I buried myself in work. I didn't allow myself to think about anything except being with the horses. For Della, the win was the *only* thing. She didn't care how I did it, as long as I got there."

The light faded quickly once the sun went down, and a sliver of moon became visible just above the mountains on the far side of the lake. The air had cooled sharply, and Liz shivered involuntarily.

Kurt instantly became attentive. "Are you cold? We can go back up to the bar, if you like. It's quiet there."

She nodded, feeling more than a little chilly, perhaps not only from the temperature, but also from the story unfolding before her.

The small, cozy bar was dimly lit with old-time hurricane lamps that had been converted to run on electricity. Kurt steered Liz to a table in the corner where they'd have some privacy. He ordered cognac, and they clinked their glasses together without speaking. The golden liquor burned its way down Liz's throat, startling her with its simultaneous sweetness and fire.

Kurt set his glass down thoughtfully, apparently trying to pick up the thread of his story.

"I'd been at the farm for about five years. I was...uh, keeping the owner company..." He glanced at Liz's face. "...but I got lonely. Most women in the horse business are tough and cynical...they *have* to be to survive in such a highly competitive environment. Anyway, I met a young woman in town who had no connection with horses. She sold real estate, and was completely self-sufficient. She was charming and sexy, and we had a great time together. I needed female companionship, and she wasn't looking for a husband, so we were a good match."

A stab of jealousy surprised Liz. She didn't like to think of Kurt with anyone else. She also hadn't missed Kurt's veiled references to his intimate relationship with the rich widow. *Is that the scandal Colleen's talking about? That's not such a big deal, not these days, anyway.*

The cognac completely relaxed her. Kurt looked so vulnerable, pouring out his tragic story. She wanted to go to him, cradle his head against her breast, and tell him everything would be all right. She could *make* it all right, if he'd just let her.

Kurt shifted in his chair and continued. "Della didn't ever go to any of the small shows, but she always attended the big, important events and 'put on the dog'. That year, her horses were winning every class at the regional show in Scottsdale. She was happy 'cause it gave her the chance to flaunt her farm—and *me*—to all the other owners. It bothered the hell outta me that she always acted so possessive when we were around other people in the industry. She made my status clear, without actually spelling it out."

He hung his head. "I felt like a damned gigolo." Another long pause. "Anyway, on stakes night, Della and I were at the barn. I was prepping the horses. She was putting on a show for her friends. My lady-friend, Dottie, had decided to surprise me, and in she walked, all dressed up and looking fabulous. She'd never met anyone from the farm, and she walked right past Della as if she weren't there. She had no clue that her arrival would cause a problem. She sidled up to me, slipped her arms around my waist, and kissed me.

"Long story short: manure hit the fan, boss-lady threw a fit, Dottie realized my relationship with Della, and walked out of my life forever. My name was M.U.D."

Liz tilted her head. "What does all this have to do with me and you?"

He looked away. "There's more."

A waiter appeared and set down two more cognacs. After he walked away, Kurt continued, looking down at the table.

"After the fireworks at that show, Della made me jump through hoops like a trained seal." A grim smile crossed his face. "The old saying, 'Hell hath no fury like a woman scorned,' is true. She was an absolute witch from that time on. I couldn't do anything right, and she made it clear, in no uncertain terms, that I was no longer welcome in her...uh, as her companion.

"I tried my damnedest to keep her happy...I didn't want to lose my job. I threw myself into my work, preparing to take seven horses to the national show in Albuquerque. I felt confident about six of them, but not so sure about a gelding she'd purchased earlier that year. He'd proven to be a good performance horse and he worked nicely in harness, but he had an unpredictable streak that occasionally surprised me. I told her I didn't think we should take a chance on him, but you can guess what she said."

Liz looked down at her empty glass, amazed that she'd finished it. She felt warm and sleepy. She gazed across the table at Kurt. *I'd love to just curl up in your arms and drift away.* A peculiar expression crossed his face. *Uh-oh, I must have missed something.*

He stood up. "You'll have to excuse me a minute. I need to see a man about a horse."

Kurt had watched Liz's face soften with the effects of the brandy, the fine angles of her cheek sculpted by the soft lights in the room, a dreamy look on her face. His earlier resolve began to fade, as he pictured her lying beneath him, her silky black hair spread over his pillow. The beautiful image softened the pain in his heart, a pain that had haunted him for much too long.

Twenty-Three

Liz watched him move across the room, her need growing deep inside, her thighs tingling with desire. Never before had a man affected her this way, and she delighted in the new sensation of her sexual excitement. She wanted to make love with Kurt–soon.

When he returned to the table, her heart thumped and she looked away, afraid he would see her raw desire.

He remained standing. "Are you ready to go? I think they're going to lock us in if we don't leave."

They walked through the cool mountain night air, Liz staying close to him, intentionally brushing his arm with hers and delighting in the tingle of contact. He helped her into the truck, then slid behind the wheel.

"I need to finish my story, Liz. This is the important part. Is it okay if we just sit here?"

His direct look sent chills of pleasure through her, the coziness of the truck cab enhancing her mood. She scooted closer to him on the seat. She'd agree to anything at this point, as long as he was near. His soft voice floated between them.

"On the day I was supposed to show that damned gelding in the pleasure driving class, the drug vets did a random check. Standard procedure, no big deal.

"Two days later, the report came back positive for a foreign substance in his blood. I couldn't figure out what had happened. He acted normal, and *I* sure hadn't given him anything. I was sure it was a mistake, but once you've been informed of the results, there are a number of stages to the process.

"I couldn't find Della anywhere. I thought she was still sleeping off the party from the night before, so I went to the show office and tried to talk to the manager myself. He wouldn't discuss it with me–said I had to talk to the show vet, which I did. The guy told me the results showed a steroid in the horse's blood and urine." He shook his head. "I couldn't believe it, had no idea what was going on. Being charged with illegal drug use is not something to be taken lightly. As the trainer, I was the responsible party. I called Della's hotel, and they told me she'd checked out."

His jaw tightened, his face filled with fury at the recollection. "The bitch had gone home without even telling me. There wasn't much I could do about it. I had two more classes, and seven horses to pack up and haul all the way back to Taos."

Liz felt his pain as he composed his thoughts.

"When I returned home, two surprises waited for me. A note from Della taped to my apartment door, telling me I was fired." Sarcasm colored his words. "Big surprise."

He sighed. "The second non-surprise was a certified letter from the U.S. Equestrian drug division, a notice of charge and pending hearing."

Liz gasped. "Oh, my God, how awful! What a horrid woman. Why didn't she support you, help you sort out the drug thing?"

The minute the question left her lips, Liz knew the answer. Kurt's boss had been so angry at being two-timed, she'd wanted him out of her sight.

Kurt remained silent. Finally, he reached down and turned the key in the ignition. The engine grumbled to life, and he looked over at Liz with a matter-of-fact expression.

"So that's how I came to be in California. I hoped I'd be able to prove my innocence at the hearing, then work again after whatever penalty was lifted. I spent almost eighteen months clerking in a supermarket in San Francisco, not far from where I grew up. On my days off, I'd look up the horse farms in the area and learn all I could about them. I went to every horse show that came along, trying to get familiar with the people and the horses. When my reinstatement letter came, I started calling the farms that might be good prospects. Folks were polite, but no one would hire me."

He put the truck in gear, and they slowly coasted out of the deserted parking lot and onto the highway. Liz's mellow, sensual glow had faded, replaced by the pain of Kurt's story. She remained quiet as the truck purred along the road back toward South Tahoe.

Kurt's voice interrupted her sad thoughts.

"I *had* to tell you all this so you'd understand why I can't risk a relationship. Eve has given me a chance to get back into the ring with good horses. I have to concentrate solely on getting my life back. Without my career, I'm nothing."

Liz listened to the words, her chest lurching at the comment about relationships. A connection with the right woman could make a difference in Kurt's struggle. *Why doesn't he see the positive side of being with me?* A moment later, a horrifying thought slipped in. *What, exactly, is his relationship with Eve? Is he sleeping with her?*

The truck idled into the parking lot in front of the motel. When Kurt turned to her, pain etched his face, transforming his eyes into deep pools of sorrow.

"Liz, I want you desperately. I think you know that. But I can't ever let my personal feelings interfere with my career again. I've already paid the price. Horses are my life. They *have* to be. There's no room for anything else."

His voice softened. "I know you are attracted to me. I can feel it, and I'm to blame for leading you on when I knew how it would have to be. I should never have asked you to dance that night, but I couldn't help myself."

Embarrassed by his frank assessment of her feelings, and bolstered by her wine-induced courage, Liz became defensive.

"Kurt, I'm truly sorry for all your past pain and tragedy, but I think you have too high an opinion of your own appeal."

Face flaming with mortification and hurt pride, she pushed the door open and jumped to the ground. She'd reached the door to her room and was fumbling with the key when Kurt caught up with her.

"Liz, please don't be angry. You can't possibly understand how important my career is to me."

She whirled around and glowered fiercely at the man who'd just kicked her in the heart.

"Really? Why can't I understand? Do you think I'm any less committed to *my* dreams than you are? And what about all the obstacles you've thrown in my face every time I've told you what I want for Legacy? What have you been trying to accomplish?"

The look on his face told Liz she'd struck a chord. His shoulders sagged and he stepped back. She took advantage of her momentary edge.

"Kurt, I've had pain in my life, too. I grew up without a mother. My father became an invalid in his prime, requiring round-the-clock care that tied *my* professional goals into a knot. I've taken a huge career step that's not working out, and I've sacrificed my personal life in an effort to build something that will give me pleasure and sustain me through the coming years. The only thing I'm missing is a loving companion to share it with me. I thought it might be you, but I guess I misread your interest."

She went into her room and closed the door without a backward glance.

The painful conversation echoed in Liz's ears. She'd been on the verge of letting herself go with Kurt, and she'd as good as admitted it to him. Embarrassment, then irritation washed over her. She'd done it *again*. Floundered into his trap and made a fool of herself. *Arrogant men. Why do they always think someone's out to catch them?* She stopped in front of the mirror and smiled ruefully at her miserable reflection. *Probably because someone usually is.*

She flopped down onto the bed, fully clothed, and wide-awake. The after-effects of the emotional evening sang through her body. She pictured Kurt sitting on the bench by the lake, and the memory of his pain masked her own. Tears slid from beneath her lashes and trickled silently onto the bedspread.

Kurt stuffed a shirt into the duffel bag. The evening had been a disaster, and he simply couldn't face Liz again the next day. He rolled a sweater tightly, focusing on the motions in an effort to keep from remembering Liz's cold and sorrowful expression. A soft knock vibrated the door and, a second later, he gazed at her sad face. Her eyes glistened with the remnants of tears.

Her voice shook. "I'm sorry I was so hateful. I don't know what gets into me sometimes. Lately, I seem to be making a habit of apologizing to you."

"No, Liz. I'm the one who's sorry. I've hurt you, and I feel like a heel."

She looked so miserable he couldn't allow her to stand there a minute longer. He took her hand and drew her through the door, closing it behind him. They stood in silence, holding hands and looking at one another, each wondering how to bridge the yawning chasm between them.

In the uneasy moment, Kurt saw her gaze move to the open bag.

Surprise edged her words. "You're leaving?"

He shifted his attention to a point above her head, struggling to remain strong. Her scent filled the room, making him painfully aware that she stood within one step of his embrace. *Don't go there, man. You'll only dig yourself in deeper.*

"I really need to get back. Eve's going to have my head for being away so long, and I have horses to get ready for Stockton."

She dropped his hands and looked up at him, her eyes hooded with emotion.

"I'll leave you to your packing."

A wave of desire crashed through his good intentions, and his arms snaked around her slender body.

"Liz, please," he whispered, stroking her hair. "Don't go."

Pushing aside her fear, she melted into his arms and nestled her cheek against his chest. A musky male scent clung to his denim shirt. His breath burned against her ear as he murmured through her hair, sending shivers across her neck. His hands moved possessively down to her waist, pulling her body up against him. Thrilling shockwaves raced through her, and she slipped away into her fantasies.

❦

Twenty-Four

Four hours later, the truck headlights poked like miner's lamps through the pre-dawn darkness, illuminating the road directly ahead. Kurt stared into the shaft of light. *A damned tunnel. Long and narrow, with no light at the end–just like my life.*

As he headed home, his mood was heavy. His desire for Liz had overpowered his good intentions, and now reality tormented him. He'd taken advantage of her obvious feelings for him–a gift he didn't deserve. Not only had he exploited her trust, he'd encouraged her with the promise of more time together. He sighed. He'd meant it at the time. God knows, it had been too long since he'd felt that way. He wanted to turn the truck around and go back. Back to the woman who made him feel as though everything would be all right.

A second later, he pushed away the tender thoughts. As difficult as it would be, he had to disentangle himself from her. He couldn't promise her something he wasn't sure he could ever deliver.

His memories sifted through time to his lost wife. Like Liz, she'd been fresh and honest and trusting. He'd loved his young bride more than she'd ever known, but his own selfishness and blind ambition had taken precedence over the only bright spot in his life.

He stared into the darkness and vowed that he'd never put himself in that vulnerable position again.

When Liz arrived at the stalls the next morning, shrill, indignant whinnies filled the air.

"Sorry, Boys and Girls. I overslept." She laughed wickedly. "Actually, I had a sleep-over."

Bill Benton appeared as she filled the last feed bucket.

She grinned. "Hello, Bill. The mare still isn't for sale."

He threw her a crooked grin. "Actually, I've been thinking about buying your colt–the one you beat me with."

Liz's thoughts flew. If Bill Benton wanted to buy two of her horses, they must be pretty darn good. Good enough to keep. Good enough to make a name for Legacy Arabians.

"Sorry, I'm not selling anything right now."

He shrugged. "Let me know when you're ready."

He affected a limp salute. "By the way, you did pretty good at this show. For a woman!"

During the long drive home, Liz's thoughts were like a whirlwind. *Perhaps Kurt's right about my chances at Nationals. I probably shouldn't be so hung up on building Legacy's name in the show ring. Top bloodlines can build a reputation, too. With great horses, and the right person beside me to help the farm grow, there's no telling what could happen.* She giggled out loud. *Maybe, maybe, maybe! I'm so infatuated I can't see my hand in front of my face!*

Eve's cool greeting confirmed Kurt's prediction that she'd be angry.

"Well, hel-*lo*! Nice of you to drop in." She moved closer, frowning. "You said you'd only be away for one day. Would you care to explain?"

He shrugged. "There were lots of good horses at the show, and some big-name farms. It's important that I know who the competition is. And Billy Benton's horses kicked some butt!"

Her tone sounded menacing. "And was Miss Veterinarian there, too?"

Kurt became wary. "Yes. As a matter of fact, she's one of the people we'll need to beat. Her colt took reserve, and both her mares took firsts in their classes, *plus* a championship for the filly. Barnett has quality stock–we can't forget that."

He turned away and reached for a halter and lunge-line. He hoped Eve couldn't read whatever might show in his expression when he talked about Liz. He knew one thing for sure: he'd need to put her out of his mind, or he'd be out of a job, and right back where he started.

Liz checked the supply case in the truck, her stomach jumping with anticipation of seeing Kurt again. *I'll need to keep a strictly professional attitude while I'm working on Eve's horses. I don't think she'd appreciate knowing that her trainer's involved with her new vet.* Latching the heavy metal cabinet doors, she glanced up at the pasture. Fair Lady and her new shadow, Marcy, nibbled their way along the edge of the fence. Liz watched her beloved horses, and a feeling of well being settled into her mind.

Kurt's truck wasn't in sight when Liz arrived at Aliqua. She sighed with disappointment, but her brain told her it was probably just as well.

Eve met her at the barn door.

"Good Morning. How was Tahoe? I hear you had a successful show."

Kurt must have told her.

Liz grinned. "I did, indeed."

She followed Eve into the barn, listening to her chatter.

"Kurt is off doing whatever trainers do on their days off. We'll have to get along by ourselves today."

Eve patted the shoulder of a very pregnant mare standing in crossties.

"She's seven months along. Needs her second rhino shot, and I'd like you to do an ultrasound. She seems awfully large for this early in her pregnancy." Eve raised an eyebrow and smiled hopefully. "Maybe she's carrying twins."

"You'd better hope not. Twins are bad news."

Eve cocked her head, obviously puzzled. "What do you mean?"

Liz filled a syringe and snapped the air bubbles out of it. "Twins very seldom survive. If the mare doesn't abort, you can usually count on one of the foals being stillborn, or dying right after birth.

Once in a while, the remaining twin will survive, but it's rare."

Eve didn't respond, clearly sobered by the harsh facts.

Liz went about her work quickly and efficiently, taking the mare's vital signs, checking the udder, and listening to the sounds within the mare's swollen belly.

"Everything's fine. I hear only one heartbeat, but we'll see what the ultrasound shows."

Twenty minutes later, Liz straightened up and switched off the machine.

"You can relax. One foal, but a big one. You'll need to be on hand for this delivery in case she gets into trouble."

Eve's face had been pinched with concern, but now relaxed into a relieved smile.

"We will. She's one of my best Polish mares. The sire is also pure Polish, so this foal is an important one." She thought for a moment, then grinned. "Big, huh? *Good.* These days, everyone is looking for the larger Arabians."

Liz kept her expression neutral. *Does this woman ever think about her horses as anything other than dollar signs?*

Eve gestured toward the end of the barn. "Listen, I'd like you to take a look at another horse before you leave."

She led the way to a stall in the corner, and Liz gulped as she recognized the filly she'd rescued from the hayrack.

Eve sounded disgusted. "She injured herself at a show a couple months ago, and I think the show vet botched the stitching. She's developing proud flesh across the coronary band. Really screws me for showing her at halter."

It was clear that Eve didn't know anything about Liz's involvement with the filly's injury, and Liz didn't intend to change that fact. She knelt down beside the horse, and gently lifted the delicate foot out of the bedding for a closer look. Sure enough, the wound had healed, but ugly pink scar tissue had ruffled up into a ridge across the front of the foot. *I wish I'd had the chance to follow up on this injury.*

She stood up, shaking her head. "It's still pretty fresh. Could be repaired." She looked directly at Eve. "How valuable is the horse? Is she worth spending money on cosmetics?"

Eve tossed her head. "She's very well-bred, but not as good as some of the others. I can sell her to someone who wants performance or a pleasure horse. She could be a good broodmare someday. Scars don't matter in any of that."

Twenty minutes later, Liz steered the truck toward home. Eve's ignorance really surprised her. *She's been a breeder for a long time. How could she be so clueless about twins?* Eve's apparent lack of knowledge bothered Liz. But worse than that, the woman simply had no personal feelings for her horses. They were, as Kurt had put it, commodities, assets, goods for sale.

Liz shook her head. Her own horses were her link with life, treasured friends and companions, always there for her no matter what garbage the rest of her life handed her.

Colleen's voice bubbled through the phone. "How'd your show go? Tell me everything."

"Reserve Champion Stallion sound okay?"

Colleen squealed like a teenager at a rock concert, and Liz told her the story, complete with Karma's bucking bronco act in front of the judge.

Colleen was equally impressed with Liz's other wins.

"You are cookin'! Are you taking all of them to the regional?"

Liz hadn't thought about the regional show for a couple of days, but she spoke without hesitation.

"I haven't decided yet. I'm definitely taking Karma and Ashiiqah, but I'm still on the fence about Amy."

The conversation eventually moved to other topics.

"While you were at the show, I sold two of Marilyn's mares."

"That's great, I'll bet she was thrilled."

Colleen's tone became serious. "She hasn't been answering the phone, and I guess she doesn't have a message machine."

"Uh-oh, I hope she's okay. I'll run over and see her in the morning."

"Good, let me know. Oh, and the same buyer wants to see the ones you're keeping. His name is Frank Jones."

After saying goodbye, Liz sat for a few minutes, again mulling over her indecision about the regional show. There'd never been any question in her mind about taking all three of the horses she'd worked so hard to qualify. Why did she question her decision now? Bill Benton had ruffled her feathers, made her feel stupid, but that shouldn't alter her plans. *Maybe I should discuss it with Kurt.* The thought jarred her. *One night with him and you can't make up your own mind? I think not!*

Twenty-Five

The next morning, Liz pulled up the driveway to Marilyn's house. The windows were dark, the porch light on. An uneasy thought came with the memory of Marilyn's dazed state on the night of the fire. *What if she's unconscious in there?* Knocking loudly, Liz tried the door and found it locked. She scribbled a note and stuck it in the screen. As she climbed back into her truck, she looked over at the black lump that had once been a working barn. Her throat tightened with pain at the flashback to that terrible night– and all the changes in her own life that had come of it.

At home, the answering machine message-light blinked insistently. Annie Brown, the woman from the exhibitor party, wanted pregnancy checks on seven mares. Liz smiled with anticipation. Continue getting calls like that, and she'd be able to turn her life around, if she put her mind to it. She returned the call and scheduled the farm visit for the end of the week. Infused with confidence, she picked up the phone again and called another of the farms on Colleen's list. Fifteen minutes later, she'd scheduled a farm call with a ranch in Placerville. She closed her appointment book with a satisfied snap. *Finally. All the pieces are starting to fall into place.*

Marilyn telephoned that afternoon, her voice bright and clear.

"Been visiting my sister in Stockton. Never could go anywhere overnight when I had the horses here. Haven't seen Sis in about a year. What's up?"

She sounded pleased by the news of the sale.

"I'll get on over to Colleen's right away and sign the registration transfer papers."

A short silence hummed through the line, and when she spoke again, her tone was timid.

"Uh, Liz? Listen, I know I haven't thanked you enough for what you did for me. I just want you to know, if you need help with anything–anything at all–I'm available. Just call."

"Thank you, Marilyn. I might just do that one of these times."

Over the next few days, Liz worked to get caught up at home and in the barn. Amy and Ashiiqah were crazy to get out into the pasture, so Liz gave them some time off.

"Only for a day or two, Ladies. We have serious work ahead of us."

Karma wasn't allowed the same treat–too risky. The colt was full of himself, and Liz figured, with *her* luck, he'd get rambunctious and hurt himself. He'd have to stay in the barn until after the regional show, maybe longer, if she took him to Nationals.

While she cleaned stalls, her bad boy whinnied and pawed the floor, trying his best to convince her to let him out.

She shook her finger at him. "You have to learn that women rule in this barn. You're outnumbered."

Karma rolled his eyes and snorted, and Liz laughed out loud. *Where have I seen that body language before?*

Fair Lady had made herself completely at home, and Liz looked forward to spending some time with her. Muscala, on the other hand, remained aloof. There'd been no more rude episodes in the stall, but Liz noted that the mare kept to herself in the pasture. Miss Marcy had gained weight on the high quality grain and alfalfa hay at Legacy, and hints of her former good body were beginning to emerge. Liz groomed her daily, and the old lady loved the attention. *She really is a good mare. I'll have to look at her pedigree again–she might be an asset to my program.*

As planned, Liz spent a quiet afternoon analyzing her show schedule for the regional. She eventually gravitated back to her original plan to show all three horses, but it bothered her that she'd experienced the short period of indecision. She'd spent her life making things happen, and didn't like the concept of circumstances running *her*.

Kurt hadn't called, and Liz was old-fashioned enough to resist the urge to call *him*, now that they'd been intimate, believing that *he* should be the one to make the first contact after their night together. Besides, what would she say to him? How did one open the conversation under a new relationship? By the fourth day with no call, a cold lump formed in her stomach. Had she been a fool?

She vacillated, worrying about having been a one-night stand, then thinking up reasons for his silence. *He's probably knee-deep in catch-up at the barn, since he was in Tahoe all weekend...He's showing at Stockton this coming week. I know he gets really serious before a show...Maybe he...Stop! You're driving yourself nuts— he'll call when he's ready.*

She leaned her head on the handle of the manure rake, and took a deep breath, willing away the fear that was gathering in her chest.

Liz was impressed with the professional way in which Annie Brown's farm was run. Mr. Brown managed all the barn work and maintenance on the forty-acre spread, while Annie concentrated on her breeding program. The woman's attention to pedigree showed clearly in the mares Liz examined.

"You have terrific horses, Annie."

The tall horsewoman beamed with pleasure, her pink skin accentuating the freckles that danced across her cheeks.

"I've spent twelve years getting the right crosses on my Polish mares. I'm hoping this foal crop will be the one I've been working my butt off for."

Liz peeled off her elbow-length exam gloves, and reached for a syringe.

"I understand completely. Fine-tuning an Arabian herd isn't something that happens overnight."

A few minutes later, Annie wrote a check and beamed as she handed it over. "Such a deal. And I didn't have to wait forever to get this done. I'm sure glad you're around now."

"Thanks, Annie. So am I. Right now, I'm headed over to Beechwood Morgans. You know them?"

Annie's face lit up. "Oh, yeah, they're great people. I told them to call you."

"Thanks. Be sure you tell everyone *else* you know, too!"

As her truck moved out onto the highway, Liz smiled. *If I can keep this up, I should be in good financial shape by the time I'm ready to go to the national show.*

She chuckled. "Talk about optimism."

Late that afternoon, Liz stopped by the clinic. She hadn't talked to Doc Sams since he'd given her the okay to sift through the client files. He was just climbing out of his truck when she pulled in.

"Hi, Doc. Home for the day?"

The old man nodded and smiled grimly. "Seems like I'm never here anymore. I don't know why we got so busy all of a sudden."

Liz's skin prickled with annoyance, but she kept her tone civil. "Well, I'm available anytime. All anyone has to do is call me."

He didn't reply, but retrieved his jacket and bag from the cab. Liz brought him up to date on the work she'd been doing.

"That's good, Elizabeth. I think you'll eventually make out okay here. Just be patient."

Liz suddenly noticed how weary the elderly vet looked, and heard the deep wheeze that accompanied each breath. She felt shame for her own selfish worries and took hold of his arm.

"Doc, I'd really like to take some of the work load off your shoulders. That's why I moved out here."

"Yes, I'm going to have to slow down pretty soon. The old ticker isn't cooperating."

The words jarred her. It no longer mattered *why* the locals had avoided her, the only important thing was helping Doc Sams, so he could retire in peace, before he simply dropped dead of overwork.

"Why don't you let me take half your calls for awhile? It'll give you some relief, and I'll have a chance to meet some of the folks you've been caring for all these years. That way, when you decide to retire, it'll be a smooth transition."

He didn't say a word, just looked at her for a minute, then

beckoned her to follow him into the house. An hour later, Liz's appointment book was filled for the next month.

Twenty-Six

After such an eventful week, Saturday and Sunday seemed too quiet. Liz started working her show horses again, and also made some inquiries about stallions to breed to Fair Lady in the spring. The high stud fees for the really popular sires stunned her. She'd have to make a lot of farm calls to pay for one breeding.

Fair Lady had settled in nicely and, true to herd behavior, had politely taken over the job of Boss Mare. Liz watched the regal white lady move about the pasture, her royal status evident as the others obediently followed her from a patch of grass to the watering trough, then back to a new grazing spot.

Liz's attention moved to Muscala–the only herd member who didn't play the game. When the group moved into her grazing area, she pinned her ears and moved to another spot. Liz began to worry about the young mare's attitude. This would be her first foal, and there was always the possibility that the new mother might inflict that nasty temper on her newborn. When foaling time arrived, Liz would need to keep a close watch on Muscala.

As Colleen had promised, Frank Jones called for an appointment to see Marilyn's horses. On Sunday, his truck and empty horse trailer rattled to a stop in front of the barn. Liz watched through the window, an uneasy feeling stealing over her. *Why would he bring a trailer? To buy horses on the spot?* A burly man crawled out of the truck and looked around for a minute, then pulled a cane from behind the seat, and started slowly toward the barn.

Liz caught up with him as he reached the entrance.

"Mr. Jones? I'm Liz Barnett."

He stopped and squinted at her through thick glasses, giving her a chance to look him over a little more closely. His clothes were dirty, his hair looked as though it hadn't been washed or combed in weeks, and he stank. Liz felt a sick quiver writhe through her stomach. *A buyer for the slaughterhouse?*

She swallowed hard. "You have a farm around here?"

He grinned, exposing rotten teeth. "Yeah, I got a place over by Camino. I got Arabs and Quarter Horses, coupla Morgans. I like 'em all."

Liz couldn't decide if he was telling the truth, so she kept a neutral expression while she made up her mind. They walked slowly up the hill, Jones relying heavily on the cane. He stopped abruptly when the pasture came into full view.

"Whoa! I want *that* one."

Liz followed his gesture. He was pointing at Fair Lady. *Sure you do.*

"Sorry, she's not one of the sale horses."

He grunted, then looked at the rest of the horses, who had ceased grazing and now watched their visitors with interest.

He pointed his cane at Miss Marcy. "How about that other white mare?"

Liz was stunned by the emotion that drove her deceptive reply. "Not for sale either. She belongs to me."

Liz pointed out the horses that *were* for sale, but Jones seemed to have lost interest. As they walked back to his truck, Liz pondered her negative reaction to him. Her first instinct about him had probably been wrong. *He's nothing but a horse collector, probably a dealer, looking for a steal.*

His gravely voice broke into her thoughts. "Well, I sure wasted my time here. You ain't sellin' any of the good stuff."

She scowled. "Mr. Jones, I only have four horses for sale–those that belong to Mrs. Cook. I never said any of my own stock were for sale."

"Well, I'll think about it. Maybe that one with the scar on its shoulder. I'll call ya."

The old truck and trailer creaked down the drive, and her

thoughts reeled. *I don't want to sell you that one either.*

Liz spent the next several days in her truck, bumping along dusty back-roads. Her self-confidence faltered a little each time she met with stony silence or outright rudeness, but she went about her work efficiently, smiling bravely to camouflage her true feelings.

The appointments she'd taken over from Doc were all routine, mostly cattle ranches. As she rattled down yet another dirt lane in the middle of nowhere, she felt the fatigue of the past week as a full-time country vet. *For this I spent eight years becoming an equine specialist?* The pompous thought jolted her harder than the potholes in the lane. *C'mon, don't be a snob. If you want to practice out here, you'll have to take all comers.*

By the weekend, she'd made farm calls to five cattle ranches, a chicken farmer, and a boarding stable. She'd performed an emergency cesarean section out in a pasture where a champion dairy cow's twins had tried to arrive simultaneously. Liz's efforts had saved the calves and the mother, and the old farmer had almost wept with relief. Liz had driven away from the farm with a three-hundred-dollar check in her pocket, and the old man's assurance that she would be his vet from then on.

In addition to her busy schedule, Liz worked her show horses every morning and night, leaving her little time to think about Kurt, or the widening silence between them. However, when she fell into bed at night, she wrestled with painful memories of Tahoe that robbed her of sleep. He still hadn't called, and sadness colored all the positive changes that had occurred in her life. Her practice was slowly coming together, and she felt confident that her horses would do well at the regional show, but it wasn't enough. Her adult life had been filled to overflowing with the needs of others, and she'd willingly taken on those responsibilities, never thinking about her own future. Never allowing herself to dream about a special someone. Now that she'd opened her heart a crack, taken a chance on Kurt, he seemed to have slipped through her fingers.

Twenty-Seven

D oc Sams took his first vacation in years, and Liz was on call twenty-four/seven. On Saturday morning, she received a call from a sheep rancher in Camino.

"This is Jebediah Jameson. Doc Sams there?"

"No, he's on vacation, Mr. Jameson. This is Dr. Barnett."

Hesitation stretched through the line, and Liz felt sure he'd hang up.

"Uh, well, my best sheep dog is sick. I need a vet out here."

Liz willed herself to ignore his tone. "What seems to be wrong with him?"

"Lady, if I knew *that*, I wouldna called!"

Liz fought a nasty retort. "I'll be there in forty minutes."

"I sure hope you know what yer doin'. Dog's worth a lot of money."

The line went dead, and Liz clenched her jaw.

"Dammit! Will this job ever get easier?"

A dusty forty minutes later, a sinewy woman with tired eyes greeted Liz as she stepped down from the truck.

"Hullo. You Doc Barnett? Dog's up there." She pointed toward a low-roofed building.

Liz entered the dim interior of what looked like an old equipment shed. The only inhabitant was a black and white Border Collie curled up on a feed sack in the corner. His tail thumped once.

"What seems to be the problem?"

"Won't eat. Hasn't for two days. Jeb's real worried about him. Spunk's our lead sheepdog."

Liz offered her hand to the dog's nose, and received a tentative lick in return.

"Hey, Spunk. What's going on? Let me have a look, okay?"

Her singsong voice seemed to reassure the dog that she wouldn't hurt him, and he lay quietly while her skilled hands gently probed his belly. A minute later, she stood up.

"I suspect he ate something that didn't agree with him. You have any toads around here?"

The farmer's wife raised her eyebrows. "Toads? Yeah, tons of 'em!"

"That'll do it. There's something in their skin that makes them unattractive to natural predators, and it causes one heck of a stomachache for any animal that eats one."

She looked down at the dog, who rolled his blue eyes as though he understood she'd just exposed his folly.

"I'll give him something to clean him out, and he should be fine."

While she opened a tube of laxative paste, curiosity got the better of her. "Where's the Mister?"

The woman chuckled. "He's off up the hill, mutterin' to hisself. Don't have much confidence in young vets, much less women." She grinned and shrugged. "Men. What are ya gonna do?"

A shrill cry broke into the companionable moment.

"Mom! Mom!"

They looked up as a chubby girl burst through the door.

"Mom! Doc! Buck's hurt! He's up in the pasture and he's caught in some barbed-wire!"

Liz grabbed her wire cutters and followed the girl up the hill.

A buckskin horse was on its knees, a piece of barbed wire wrapped around its front legs. Another coil had hooked onto the halter buckle and snaked around his neck, holding him firmly in its wicked clutches. Blood trickled from dozens of small cuts.

Liz squatted beside the horse, trying to assess the damage, then turned to the girl.

"Hold his head while I cut the wire away."

The girl grasped the cheek straps on the horse's halter. Liz worked quickly and carefully, and the horse remained quiet. Once she'd freed his neck, she started on the legs. The rogue wire had wrapped itself around one leg twice, and three times around the other. Twenty minutes later, Buck was free, and Liz urged him onto his feet. The little girl wrapped her arms around the horse's neck and sobbed.

Back at the barn, Liz cleaned all the cuts and gave Buck a tetanus booster.

"He should spend the rest of the day in his stall. He's pretty worn out from his adventure."

She turned to Mrs. Jameson. "Do you use much barbed wire on the place?"

"Nope. We don't use any. I dunno where that came from."

"It looked pretty old, probably thrown into the brush when the board fences were put up. You should check Buck's pastures to see if there's more. Horses and barbed-wire don't mix."

The little girl returned, her tear-stained face glowing with gratitude. "Thank you for rescuing Buck."

Liz smiled. "You're most welcome. I'm glad it wasn't serious." Her tone sobered. "You really shouldn't leave Buck's halter on when he's turned out...I think you can see why."

"But, sometimes he's hard to catch."

Liz hesitated, trying to decide what response would make the most sense to the farm girl.

"I know, but it would be much better if you trained him to come to you willingly. If he gets caught on something again, you might not find him in time to save his life."

The child's pink face paled, her round eyes brimmed with tears, and her lip quivered as she slowly nodded her head.

Liz caught a movement out of the corner of her eye and laughed, pointing toward the front of the barn. Spunk stood in the doorway, his feathered tail waving slowly from side to side.

Mrs. Jameson chuckled. "Well, look at you! Feel better?"

The dog hung his head and rolled his eyes, then came up to them. His cold, wet nose found Liz's hand, and her day was complete.

On Sunday morning, Liz stared at the neon green display on the bedside clock. Seven. *Okay. I'm not spending any more time moping around.* Swallowing her pride, she picked up the phone and dialed. A husky voice answered on the second ring.

"Aliqua Arabians. Kurt DeVallio."

Liz's chest tightened. She'd grown to love the sound of his voice, and missed hearing it. She snuggled down under the quilt, cradling the phone against the pillow.

"I haven't talked to you in awhile. How did Stockton go?"

"We did all right. Nothing spectacular. Picked up a couple of blues and a lot of reds." He chuckled. "Eve's favorite color is blue, so she isn't too happy with me right now. What's new with you?"

Dismay flooded her thoughts. *Why are we discussing this?*

"Liz? You all right? Kinda quiet on your end."

She felt a warm rush of anger. *He's acting like I'm just a casual acquaintance.*

"I'm all right. Just surprised I haven't heard from you since...since Tahoe."

His tone was even, held no trace of emotion. "I've been pretty busy. You know how it is this time of the year."

Liz was at a loss. Perhaps Eve was standing nearby, making it hard for him to talk freely.

"Listen, Liz, I hate to cut you off, but I've got to get back to work here. Boss lady is riding me pretty hard. I'll catch you later, okay?"

She mumbled goodbye and put the phone down, immobilized by the wave of emotions crashing over her. She'd let her guard down, followed her deepest feelings, trusted Kurt. A huge mistake. The tears started softly at first, rolling down her face onto the pillow, followed a minute later by body-wracking sobs. When the storm finally subsided, she burrowed under the quilt, and succumbed to blessed oblivion.

Kurt replaced the phone on the hook, and leaned his forehead against the wall. He felt sick. *Dear God, please let me be strong. I just can't hurt her any more.* The emptiness inside him had a familiar feel to it, flooding him with sadness. He pushed away from the wall.

Casting aside his melancholy, he started talking to a leggy black colt who nervously paced circles in a stall.

"Easy, Bones, easy."

Kurt stood by the door, waiting for the animal to quiet, then stepped inside. The colt stood still while Kurt buckled the halter and hooked up a lead rope. Stroking the beautiful horse's neck, Kurt's mind focused on his work, suppressing his pain. He was a master at his craft, and before him stood a rough specimen to polish for the future.

Moments later, Kurt was in his element as he lunged the black beauty at the end of the line. The rambunctious colt should qualify easily for the regional, but Kurt couldn't allow himself to become over-confident. Plenty could happen before then. He assessed the horse's excellent conformation, whistling softly at how perfectly the colt was put together. He would be a magnificent stallion when he matured. *It's no wonder Bill Benton wants him.*

He remembered how the trainer had nosed around Liz's horses. Benton would go for the top animal, and Kurt couldn't forget that. He'd better plan on a serious contest. The two colts were perfect, an exciting match. Though he'd originally tried to subtly undermine Liz's confidence about showing, his efforts had only seemed to encourage her. The cards were on the table.

Ebony was an early February foal. The registry ruled that a horse's birth date was January First, regardless of when the actual birth took place, so, even though the colt was entered in the yearling stallion class, he would technically be closer to two years old– a distinct advantage that Kurt hoped would make a difference.

Sensing Kurt's wandering attention, the colt started skipping and hopping at the end of the line. Kurt clucked and snapped the whip. The horse stepped back into a long-legged trot, and Kurt's thoughts returned to his own plans.

If Benton purchased Ebony, Kurt could walk away from Eve Aliqua and strike out on his own. The dreams of a lifetime just might come true, if nothing interfered.

The clock said nine-thirty when Liz awoke from a deep, numbing sleep. She sat on the side of the bed and stared at the numbers, knowing the horses waited to be fed. In the bathroom, her blotchy face and swollen eyes stared back at her from the mirror and, confronted with her misery, she started to cry again, silent tears of grief. *Why am I surprised? Colleen warned me a long time ago.*

Minutes later, impatient whinnies greeted her and beautiful heads appeared over stall doors, anxious for breakfast. Liz recognized her true wealth–a barn filled with some of the finest Arabs in the country. Her first season wins at Sacramento and Tahoe were proof. In this barn lay her dreams, the dreams she'd pursued on her own for so long. Legacy Arabians and her profession were her future, not Kurt DeVallio. *I made a stupid mistake, but it's not the end of the world.*

Her eyes burned, but whether from love lost, or simply fierce pride, she didn't know.

Twenty-Eight

F air Lady pranced along beside Liz as they walked over to a small paddock behind the barn. The mare kept straining her head to look at the field where her pasture mates waited. She firmly nudged Liz's arm with her soft muzzle.

"It's okay, girl. I want to see just how difficult you are to ride."

Each day for the past week, Liz had watched Fair Lady's fascinating gait as she made her rounds of the pasture. Liz had pictured herself riding the beautiful animal along the many trails that surrounded the farm. Eve had mentioned that Fair Lady didn't like to be ridden, but Liz wanted to try anyway. She'd make her first attempt bareback, just as she'd ridden as a youngster.

She positioned the mare next to the fence, and climbed up to straddle Fair Lady's narrow back. The sensation of sitting on a horse after so many years felt wonderful. The mare flicked an ear back, listening to Liz rustle as she got comfortable. Taking a deep breath, Liz gathered the reins and touched her heels lightly against the mare's sides. Fair Lady glided forward into a smooth, rhythmic walk. Liz barely moved the reins as the horse responded to Liz's subtle leg commands.

"Good girl!" *Eve obviously doesn't know what she's talking about.*

The mare walked around the paddock once, then Liz nudged her into a trot, and gasped with pleasure. The gait felt as wonderful as it looked from a distance. Even without a saddle, Liz was able to post to the amazing, floating gait. *I'll pay for this tomorrow.* In minutes, her thigh muscles tightened painfully, and she signaled the mare to return to the walk. Fair Lady moved to the center of the paddock and halted.

"Hey, I didn't ask you to stop! You telling me you're finished with the ride?"

Suddenly, the mare lowered her haunches and sat down. Caught off guard, Liz slid off the horse and landed flat on her back in the dust, smacking her head on the hard packed dirt. The pain of the impact produced whirling stars for a moment, followed by a dull headache that spread from the back of her head to behind her eyes.

She squinted up at the mare, who was now back on her feet and standing quietly.

"Well, I guess you let me know you don't want to be a saddle horse, huh?"

The magnificent, fine-boned head turned and contemplated Liz's sprawl with huge, dark eyes. Liz groaned and climbed to her feet, brushing the dust off her jeans, her head throbbing with each movement. Slowly, she led the mare up to the pasture where the other horses anxiously waited at the fence. She opened the gate and turned the mare loose, giving her a smack on the rump.

"Okay, you win. I won't bother you any more."

Fair Lady trotted toward the other horses, snaking her neck and tossing her head as though to say, *"That ought to hold her!"*

The phone rang while Liz was dozing on the couch. She jumped to her feet, staggering with the impact of the wrecking ball rolling around in her skull. She closed her eyes tightly and, while she waited for the pain to subside, the answering machine picked up. Colleen's anxious voice buzzed through the speaker. *"Liz, when ya come in could ya call me right away? We have a foal that's limpin' real bad."*

A pretty little chestnut filly stood forlornly in a corner of the stall, its mother nervously watching Liz.

Colleen's voice was tense. "She's been favoring her left front since yesterday morning, but we can't find anything wrong with her. I thought it might be a stone bruise, but her hoof looks normal."

Liz eyed the anxious mare, then stepped inside the door and walked slowly toward her, crooning softly. She stroked the mare's neck and felt the muscles relax a little, as the wary mother decided that Liz wouldn't hurt her, or her baby.

Still, Liz used caution as she approached the foal. The maternal instincts of a mare were incredibly strong, and if eight hundred pounds of horseflesh didn't want you touching her baby, you'd better have a plan.

The foal stood quietly, watching with huge eyes as Liz approached. Placing a hand on the filly's shoulder, Liz applied light pressure, urging the foal to walk. The tiny horse stepped forward, distinctly limping.

Liz gently grasped the slim foreleg, then moved her hand slowly toward the foot, searching for a clue.

"The leg bones are solid."

She picked up the tiny foot, and examined the soft flesh above the hoof. Nothing obvious. Moving her hand up the foreleg, her fingers located some swelling. The filly grunted and jerked her leg away. Above the knee joint, Liz found the cause of the filly's discomfort.

"She has epiphysitis."

"Epiphy-what?"

"The growth plate above the knee joint is swollen. It happens in fast-growing young horses, especially if they're overfed." She glanced up at Colleen. "The mare also passes on a lot of nutrition in her milk, so the kid gets a double dose."

Colleen looked dismayed. "Is it dangerous? Can you fix it?"

Liz nodded as she dug through her kit. "You caught it early. The condition is only debilitating if it has time to seriously affect the bone growth."

She slipped on a pair of latex gloves, then returned to the stall and began massaging something into the filly's leg.

"What's that you're putting on her?

"DMSO. It'll give us a jump-start on reducing the swelling."

Liz rose and peeled off the gloves. "I want you to reduce her grain by about thirty-percent. There's a supplement called MSM—add it to her feed. It contains sulfur. It'll work on the inflammation from within." She left the stall. "Keep her inside, apply moist heat three times a day, and rub some of this ointment on the affected area every other day. Be sure you wear gloves...DMSO can be dangerous stuff."

A minute later, Liz leaned on the stall door, watching the filly bury her face under her mother's belly to take a little comfort after the ordeal. At times like this, Liz knew her calling to veterinary medicine had been the right one. Nothing came close to describing her feelings of accomplishment when she cared for a sick horse, or healed a damaged one, or delivered a new one. Granted, there were times when nothing could be done to save an animal, but it was part of the job–the bad with the good. Thinking about her spat with Eve, her resolution grew. She'd never allow *anything* to jeopardize those beliefs.

Kurt looked over the list of entries, concern creeping into his concentration. *Only three weeks until the regional.* Of the eight horses he'd gotten qualified, only five of them were actually going to San Francisco. One mare had colicked the previous week, and was recovering from surgery. The other two–a yearling filly and a three-year-old mare–hadn't made the cut at Stockton, both horses being just two points shy of the regional requirement.

If I hadn't been so busy running off to Tahoe to see Liz... He tossed the pencil onto the desk. He knew the reason his horses weren't ready, and it didn't have anything to do with Liz. If he were *really* dedicated, he'd load up the two unqualified horses and head for the nearest rated show, no matter how far away it might be. Even a third place ribbon would provide enough points to make the difference.

He recalled a time in his life when he wouldn't have given it a second thought. A time when nothing else mattered but being the best. A dark sadness crept over him, seeping into his self-confidence. *Am I just a has-been? One of those worn out horse trainers who spend their lives on the fringe, hoping for a comeback? Hoping for that big break?* His mental state was deteriorating quickly, abetted by the stress of his personal dilemma.

Though he'd thrown himself into his work for long, exhausting hours during the day, dreams of Liz had haunted his idle evening hours and his sleep. He couldn't keep the image of her tantalizing body and sweetly sensual face out of his mind. When the dreams came, he ached inside as though he'd again lost everything. Many nights had been spent staring into the darkness and wishing he knew what the future held in store.

He roused himself from the maudlin thoughts, and smiled. Ebony would be his ticket out of there, and the others didn't matter. He closed the show folder. He had only one job to do for the next three weeks.

Eve's sharp voice intruded. "I'm counting on this championship, Kurt." Her expression reinforced the words. "Don't let *anything* get in your way."

Recognizing the veiled command, he bristled and rose from the desk. "Eve, you *know* I can't promise you a national trophy. I'll try my damnedest, but there aren't any guarantees. This is one thing you can't control."

She gave him a cold, studied look.

"You think not?"

Two weeks had passed since the morning Liz had called Kurt. She'd pushed away the silence, and had concentrated on keeping her show horses humming. Even so, his face still drifted into her line of vision when she least expected it. At those times, her heart contracted painfully, and a deep loneliness threatened to paralyze her.

As she looked over her show checklist, the memory of their night together pushed into her thoughts, and hot tears rolled down her face, dripping onto the papers. She hadn't cried since the first week without him, but the pain had wedged itself firmly inside and she surrendered to the tears.

The phone rang, and she grabbed a tissue, wiping her nose as she reached for the receiver.

Kurt's soft voice came over the line, making her heart thump. She tried to keep her tone even, afraid he might sense her state of mind, or hear her pounding heart.

His tone was cautious. "How are you doin'? Everything goin'

good?"

She sensed his uneasiness with the conversation.

"I'm fine. Things are going well. And you?"

She rolled her eyes at how ludicrous it seemed, to be talking to each other like perfect strangers. Strangers who'd been lovers.

"Pretty good. Three of my regional prospects got scratched, so I'm down to five. Boss isn't happy, but there's nothing I can do about it. You still takin' that colt of yours?"

She flushed with anger. It was the wrong question–the call was a fishing expedition. He just wanted to know what the competition would be.

"Of *course* I'm still taking him. I intend to beat every horse in the ring."

He chuckled. "Well, good for you. I wish you the best of luck. I'll see you there...Maybe we can get together for a bite to eat."

She took a deep breath. "No, I don't think so, Kurt. You've made your position pretty clear."

"Liz–"

She put the phone down, her heart heavy with pain. *Used. A means to an end. Why couldn't I see it?* She smiled sadly. She hadn't seen it because her emotions had camouflaged every obvious sign there might have been. *How could winning a damned class be more important than a love affair?* Her head echoed with Kurt's warnings about the killer instincts that permeated the important shows. *We're so different. We have nothing in common, but sexual attraction. It's probably just as well that it's over. I need a soul-mate more than a bed-mate.*

She had to put him out of her mind, and move on with her life. *Fine. Now what do I tell my heart?*

Twenty-Nine

On Tuesday morning, Liz packed the truck and loaded the horses. San Francisco was only ninety miles away, but she wanted to get an early enough start that she wouldn't get tangled up in the rush hour. Pulling a horse trailer through heavy freeway traffic unnerved her.

As she settled into the rhythm of the road, her thoughts returned to the telephone conversation with Kurt. A knot formed in the pit of her stomach at the idea of showing against him. He knew everything about her horses, and she knew nothing about his. But, so what? Would information about his entries help her win? Make her lose? What really bothered her was his charade. Could his arrival at Tahoe have been a fishing expedition, too? Had their lovemaking been part of his plan to put her at a disadvantage? Her throat tightened at the painful possibility.

Deep in thought, she missed the Oakland exit and found herself sailing down the interstate toward San Jose. Disconcerted by the cars and trucks flying past her at eighty-miles-an-hour, she scanned the road ahead for another exit. The next ramp took her over a bridge spanning a finger of the bay, then into the town of Alameda, a charming village situated on an island. She needed to find a place to stop and get straightened out. She cruised slowly through the small, charming town, marveling at the lovely homes and lush gardens. A park entrance appeared and she pulled into a large parking lot overlooking San Francisco Bay. After parking the rig under some shade trees, she checked on the horses, who were looking out the windows and eagerly sniffing the wind, excited at the new smell of salt air. A quick look at the map, and she turned the truck back toward the freeway, putting Kurt out of her mind for the remainder of the drive.

As she entered the front gates of the show grounds, Liz's heartbeat skipped a little. She drove straight toward the looming building with huge letters spelling "Cow Palace" above the entrance, then cruised slowly through the exhibitor parking lot, looking for "D" Barn. A ripple of excitement ran through her at being in such a famous place. The renowned fairgrounds had been San Francisco's premier livestock show facility since the early forties. When she was small, her father had regaled her with stories of Arabian shows he'd attended there. The arena still hosted livestock shows and the Grand National Rodeo, and in recent years, had been host to several sports teams, concerts, and circuses.

She drove around behind the building, then up and down the lanes between barns. Being so new to the showing game, she'd barely made the postmark deadline for registration. As a result, she'd been assigned to stalls in one of the farthest barns from the main arena.

She finally spotted "D" barn, and parked the truck by the back entrance. Inside, the structure had been transformed from utilitarian livestock barns into elegant showcases. Rich colors and luxurious fabrics had been used to construct drapes that covered the rough wood exteriors of the stalls. An arch with a valance of matching fabric spanned the aisle between the two end stalls, giving the effect of the grand entrance to a private estate. Deep burgundy stall drapes were monogrammed in metallic gold lettering large enough to read from a distance.

To achieve these effects, farm staff worked long hours, sometimes late into the night, hanging drapes, spreading bright, fragrant wood chips or sawdust, arranging potted plants and shrubs, and installing fountains or garden statuary at the public entrance to the stalls. Invitingly-arranged wrought-iron garden furniture encouraged foot-weary barn browsers to stop and rest.

Liz moved along the outside aisle and came to a table covered with albums filled with professional photos of magnificent horses. Trophies and ribbons proudly advertised past championships to the interested visitor or prospective buyer. Business cards, farm brochures, bowls of candy, or an invitation to watch a farm video completed the enticing web with which stable owners hoped to snare a buyer.

Beyond the archway, more of the same fabric had been used to frame each stall, and small wood or brass signs identified each horse. In the aisle, director chairs, a radio, and a coffeemaker provided a private area for handlers, grooms, and owners to rest between classes.

The extent of the decorating efforts proved that showing horses was serious business. Liz looked at the lavish embellishments and felt a prickle of irritation, remembering Kurt's comments. She shook off the memory of that conversation and moved toward the end of the aisle. The fancy trimmings made her feel like a greenhorn. She had only a simple farm sign for her own stall area. *Maybe next year.*

She sighed deeply and started dumping bedding into the stalls. After checking each one for safety and filling all the water buckets, she returned to the truck to unload her precious cargo.

Kurt had just shoved the last tack trunk into the pickup when Eve appeared. He kept his expression neutral as she approached.

Her manner seemed open, as though there'd never been any friction between them. "Ready to leave?"

"Yup. Just need to load 'em and go.

He checked the cargo one last time, then started toward the barn, Eve's voice drifting behind him.

"Be sure to put up the stall drapes."

"Right-O."

He fumed. *Just what I need to worry about when I get there— decorating!*

In his previous job, there'd always been a groom or two to help at the shows, and *they* were the ones who stayed up all night designing the atmosphere. However, since Kurt was taking only five horses, Eve hadn't been willing to send along any of the barn staff. *If I have time, I'll put up the stuff. If not, well, too bad. She won't be there, so she'll never know.*

The truck moved slowly down the driveway, Kurt checking the mirrors and his view through the back window into the trailer. Satisfied that the horses were settled and calm, he headed for San Francisco.

As he drove through the late summer countryside painted with brown and gold and rust, a peaceful feeling came over him. No matter what might happen with his job, he felt good about having stood up to Eve about Ebony's championship chances. *I'll do my best–it's the only way I'll ever get out from under her thumb.*

He knew the time had come to move on. Dealing with his pushy boss had been just the prod he'd needed. A long chain of events had brought him to his current circumstances, and it would take at least the same amount of time to make things right.

Thirty

The following morning, Liz stretched, trying to work the kinks out of stiff muscles. *Man, I never thought hay could be so darned hard.*

Karma was full of himself as Liz slipped the halter over his ears. He shook his head and bobbed around, making it almost impossible for her to hook the buckles.

She smacked him sharply on the shoulder. "Quit! You're being a brat."

The feisty little horse stood still long enough to be haltered, then started hopping around again. Liz closed her eyes. *Oh, brother, I hope I can work these kinks out before tomorrow morning.* She led him out of the stall and down the aisle, followed by indignant whinnies from the mares, their message clear: *"Wait! You forgot our breakfast!"*

On her way to the exercise arena, Liz saw several people she'd met at other shows earlier in the summer, and it pleased her that she was beginning to feel a part of the show community. She abruptly remembered Kurt would be there too, and her heart pitched. Distracted by her thoughts, she was unprepared when Karma leapt into the air. The lead rope flew out of her hands, and he was loose. The colt only needed a few seconds to realize he was no longer attached to his handler, and he gleefully pranced across the gravel road toward a patch of green grass on the other side.

Liz knew better than to shout, or run after him. He loved to play "catch-me"–she'd already had that experience several times at home. Other people in the area quickly recognized the situation, and several men started after the colt. Liz watched him, her heart hammering. The lead rope dangled dangerously near his front feet. *Oh Karma, please don't run!* The colt was enjoying the game too much to run. He pranced and danced, staying just out of everyone's reach, tossing his head and snorting, his tail held high.

On Karma's far side, Bill Benton stepped out from behind a shed. The colt focused on the two men approaching him from the front. Benton was only two feet away when Karma realized he'd been ambushed. The trainer's hand whipped out and grabbed the halter, capturing the renegade colt.

Liz jogged over. "Whew! *Thank* you! He's the master of elusiveness when he gets away."

Benton handed her the lead rope, then cocked his head. "If you beat me with this horse again, I'll have no choice but to make you an offer you *can't* refuse."

Liz smiled, but said nothing. *What part of "no" don't you understand?*

Benton smoothed his hair back, and smiled engagingly.

"Listen, come on up to the sky-box this afternoon. We're having a little pre-show party. I'll introduce you around." He turned to leave, then stopped. "And good luck tomorrow. We'll have some real competition out there. Ol' Kurt's bringin' that Egyptian colt. It's gonna be *real* interesting."

Liz watched him saunter off. *As usual, I'm out of the loop. What Egyptian horse?*

After his brief escape to freedom, Karma played the obedient student. Liz lunged him a little longer than usual to be sure his movements were good, and that he responded quickly to her commands. He went through his paces as though there'd never been any question about his performance.

At four o'clock, she checked the class schedule one last time, then glanced around at the spotless aisle and nodded, satisfied that everything was in order. Show halters were polished and ready. The horses had been exercised, and now quietly nibbled their hay. *I'm as ready as I'll ever be.* After combing her hair and swiping her mouth with lipstick, she headed across the road to see how the other half lived.

At the box office, she flashed her Exhibitor Pass and asked for directions to the skyboxes, located on the upper level. Security guards patrolled conspicuously up and down the corridors filled with bejeweled women and well-dressed men whose raucous laughter ricocheted off the tile walls. Liz knocked on Fire Stone's door and a tall, handsome man with sharp blue eyes opened it immediately.

"Come on in. I'm Sean."

Liz shook his hand, aware of his light grip. "I'm looking for Bill."

Sean's slim fingers fluttered in the direction of the corner. "He's over there, with one of the customers. Can I get you something to drink?"

"No thanks, I'm fine."

He patted her arm. "If you need anything, just holler."

He walked across the room and coyly sidled up to another attractive young man, who was deep in conversation with an older woman. Liz studied the trio for a moment. Unworldly as she was, Liz recognized the scent of ambition.

The woman was dumpy with over-bleached hair, over-blue eyeshadow, and a red gash for a mouth. Her fingers glittered with diamonds and her sagging, wrinkled neck was wreathed in gold jewelry. She laughed coquettishly at her young companions' comments. The two men hovered over her as though she were a gorgeous twenty-something girl. Liz turned away, a bad taste forming in her mouth.

The large room was tastefully furnished with comfortable sofas and easy chairs awash with soft southwestern colors. Thick, lush carpet the color of French vanilla ice-cream covered the floor. Art Deco chrome and glass coffee tables held baskets of flowers, bowls of fruit, and trays of hors d'oeuvres. Soft lights cast faint-edged shadows on the pale cream walls, and airbrushed the edginess from the aging faces in the room. The front wall was floor to ceiling sliding glass panels, opening onto a private sitting area with a commanding view of the arena. The skybox was nothing like she'd expected. *It must cost a fortune to rent something like this for a week.*

"Hi, Liz. Glad you could make it."

Bill Benton smiled and took her hand. "Come on over and meet Celia."

Celia Franklin, rich heiress and owner of Fire Stone Farms, was nothing like the woman Liz had studied earlier. Celia's clothes were elegant, her jewelry minimal, but expensive, and her face and body well preserved. Liz felt completely out of place.

Celia's voice oozed curiosity. "Billy tells me you have outstanding horses. How long have you been in the business?"

Liz blanched. "This is my first year."

Celia's eyebrows lifted ever so slightly. "Oh. Are you enjoying it?"

Liz struggled to slow her racing pulse. "So far. I'm working to promote my farm name and bloodlines."

Condescension magnified the woman's response. "Rea-lly."

Okay. Two can play this game. Liz looked Celia squarely in the eye.

"Yes, my father is Ben Barnett. I have the cream of his Double B herd as my foundation."

A smile of recognition changed Celia's face to a friendlier mask.

"Oh, I remember Ben! What a wonderful trainer!" She tilted head and looked sympathetic. "I was so sorry to hear of his death."

Liz couldn't believe how far south the conversation had gone, and desperately wanted to leave. Bill stepped in to save her.

"Let me introduce you to some of our other clients."

Celia took his cue and offered her hand.

"It was lovely to meet you, Liz. Come see us at the farm sometime."

In the space of the next half-hour, Liz met over a dozen people who were deeply involved in the Arabian industry, including Jane Van Wilten, the garish woman who'd been hanging on Sean earlier. The extent of the wealth and power in that room made Liz painfully aware that she viewed only the tip of the iceberg. *What am I doing here? This isn't my world.*

"So, are you going to sell me that colt, or not?"

Bill was grinning mischievously over the rim of his wine glass. She laughed. "You never give up, do you?"

"My dear, in the horse business, 'give up' is a dirty word." He glanced over at his boss holding court in the corner with Sean and his shadow. "Celia expects me to show the finest horses in the country, and win all the ribbons." He winked. "I do my best to keep her happy."

Liz nodded thoughtfully, briefly thinking of Kurt's past. Being at the top of the heap had its disadvantages: there was no place to go, but down. She couldn't begin to imagine the stress that went with such a life.

Bill called out across the room. "Sean, I'm taking Dr. Barnett down to the stalls. Keep an eye out for Broderick, tell him I'll be back in a while." He grinned. "Come on, I'll show you the horses."

The main show barn housed most of the larger farms, breeders who'd been showing at the facility for years, and had firmly acquired the right to particular blocks of stalls. The stall trappings were more luxurious, more expensive, more anything than Liz had seen in "D" barn. Fire Stone held a block of twenty stalls directly in front of the main entrance to the arena–a plum position.

Benton's manner was relaxed as he guided her along the aisle, stopping at each stall to introduce her to the occupant. Liz was overwhelmed–the horses were so perfect they were almost unreal. Benton's pompous tone emphasized his words as he pointed at the bay mare that had placed second to Ashiiquah.

"Jane Van Wilten paid eighty-thousand for this mare as a yearling. The horse is worth twice that now." He shook his head. "She was not pleased about losing to your horse."

Liz stared at him, trying to comprehend the mind-boggling prices he'd just thrown out.

He continued. "That gray mare over there brought a hundred-thousand, and the colt you beat just sold for sixty.

He leaned against a stall door. "Arabians are big business, Liz. You should get with the program." He narrowed his eyes, a sly grin playing with the corners of his mouth. "If you won't sell, how about letting me show your horses for you? I can make them worth a fortune, if you'll let me."

She finally found her voice. "Thanks, Bill, but I'm not in it for the money."

He blinked. "What the hell else *is* there?"

Thirty-One

Kurt expertly maneuvering the large rig through heavy traffic, and thinking about the colt in the trailer. Ebony had been in great form the day before, moving through his paces effortlessly, and attentive to each command, taking only seconds to assume a proper halter stance.

Kurt glanced in the rearview mirror and smiled. "Bones, I think you're gonna be my ticket back to the real world."

Two hours later, he pulled through the front gate of the Cow Palace and started hunting for his barn, peeved because his stall assignment was in one of the farthest buildings from the arena. Eve insisted on handling the entries, *always* managed to be late mailing them, and Kurt paid the price with a rotten stall location. Straight ahead, he spotted a barn with a huge white "D", and started searching for a place big enough to park the truck and trailer. The hour was late, and the exhibitor parking lot was jammed.

The Legacy Arabians truck sat close to the cinderblock building, and his pulse skipped. *Man, I'll bet she's in the same barn. I can just see us stalled near each other.* The thought triggered another, more intimate vision and he closed his eyes tightly. Since she'd hung up on him, he'd wrestled with his emotions, wanting her even more, but still fearing the complications it would create.

Cool it. You have absolutely nothing to offer her. The way things stand right now, she can't be part of your life. He leaned his head back against the seat. *Why am I even thinking like this?*

Liz's face floated behind his closed eyes–looking up at him

from her barn work, looking up at him in anger, looking up at him from the pillow beside him. He was haunted by the woman he didn't want to want.

Burying the images, he jumped out of the truck and entered the dimly lit barn. He walked the empty aisles, looking for the stalls that would be his.

A handsome bay face peered through iron bars.

"Hey, Karma, how ya doin'?"

The horse nickered and bobbed his head. Kurt reached through and scratched the colt's chin, then looked around. Liz had brought all three horses she'd qualified in Tahoe. An empty director chair sat by the tack stall, an open magazine on the seat, a thermos sitting on the floor beside it. *Hmm, she must still be here.* His heartbeat faltered for a second. *Be strong.* He turned back to the colt who begged for more attention.

"See you in the ring, little man."

The barn buzzed with activity when Liz woke at five-thirty the next morning. Opening day of a show generated lots of nervous excitement, and she loved the crackling atmosphere. She checked the class schedule to see that the starting time of Karma's class hadn't mysteriously changed during the night, then turned on the hose, and started filling water buckets.

Grabbing the latch on Karma's door, she peered through the bars. "Hey, you still sleeping, you lazy butt?"

The colt stood in the corner, head down, eyes closed. He didn't respond to her voice, and panic rose in her chest. Apathy at feeding time meant trouble. Deeply frightened, she dropped the hose and snatched open the stall door. Karma roused slightly at the sound, raising his head and looking at her with glazed eyes. With a leaden heart, Liz knew she was seeing the end of her dreams.

She moved quickly to the colt's side and ran her hands over his smooth neck. He didn't feel hot, but a fine layer of sweat glistened on his coat. *Colic.* She'd seen the symptoms so many times, but had never had the bad luck in her own barn. Fear wrapped a cold, clammy blanket around her. A horse with colic could recover quickly–or require surgery. Or die. She squatted down and placed her ear against the colt's flank, listening closely. His gut sounds were normal, strong and gurgling, not the ominous silence of a blocked or twisted intestine. She racked her brain for another diagnosis.

Show regulations required that any ill animal had to be examined by the show veterinarian. As the owner, she couldn't give him anything. He nickered softly and took a step toward her. His knees buckled and he went down. Struggling to his feet, he swayed a little, but stayed upright, trying to focus dull eyes. Liz thought her heart would break.

The lights were on in the show office.

"Is the vet in? I have a sick horse!" she gasped, breathless from her sprint.

The clerk behind the counter nodded and gestured toward an open door. "I think he just came in."

A short, balding man stood at a table, loading syringes into a large, black bag. Liz rapped her knuckles on the doorjamb as she entered.

The vet's voice had a crisp edge. "Good Morning. What can I do for you?"

"I have a sick colt this morning–of all mornings."

"What's the problem?"

"He's sweaty, dull-eyed–"

"Did you change his feed? Sounds like colic."

"No, it's not colic. I–"

"And how do you *know* it's not colic?"

His patronizing tone sparked Liz's frustration and fear. "Because I'm a licensed veterinarian, and I guess I'd know colic when I see it!"

"Oh, sorry." He smiled sheepishly. "Let me grab my bag."

He peered inside the medical kit, then snapped it shut. Liz stepped out into the main office and fidgeted while she waited for him. *What could have caused Karma's problem? I didn't change his feed...maybe the different water...he might have eaten some of the wood shavings.* The vet finally joined her, and they walked in silence toward the barn, Liz struggling to quell a sense of impending disaster.

Karma still stood in the corner with his head down. The vet left his bag in the aisle, and went in to examine the colt. Seconds later, he turned and leveled a solemn look at Liz.

"This colt entered in a class this morning?"

"Yes, the first one."

"You'd better scratch him."

He turned back to the colt and pulled back the eyelids, peering closely into the pupils.

Liz's anxiety tied her stomach into a hard knot.

"What's the matter? Is he going to be all right?"

The vet came out of the stall, throwing her a disgusted look.

"I don't know who you think you're fooling. What did you give him?"

She stared at the person who'd just destroyed her morning. The pitch of her voice rose higher than she'd intended.

"What are you talking about?"

"I mean, what did you give him? Something to calm him down a little before his class?"

Liz drew herself up to her full height and scowled.

"I'm a veterinarian. Do you think I'd *accidentally* overdose my own horse to the point that he couldn't even stand up, let alone show in a class? Does that make any sense to you?"

She became aware that people up and down the aisle had stopped their work, gathering in groups to watch. A minute later, the vet brushed past her, carrying a syringe filled with bright red blood. He stowed it in his bag, then turned and spoke in an even tone.

"I'll send these samples up to Sacramento today, but we won't have results back for at least twenty-four hours."

Liz heard, but barely digested his words. Her horse had been drugged right under her nose.

"Will he be okay?"

The man shook his head and his tone softened. "Whatever tranquilizer he got will probably wear off on its own, but you know how unpredictable some of these drugs can be." He threw her a knowing look. "And you'd better hope the U.S. Equestrian vet doesn't show up for a random drug check."

He turned and walked away, leaving Liz standing in the aisle with an audience that had witnessed the entire exchange.

Farther down the row, heads bobbed together, and snatches of speculative conversation drifted into Liz's anxiety.

A woman called out, "Everything okay? Need any help?"

Liz shook her head and retreated into Karma's stall. Shock ricocheted through her body and she started to tremble. She leaned against the wall, then slid down into the soft shavings, barely able to breathe, her stomach churning. Closing her eyes, she leaned her head against the rough wood, trying to think straight. *My poor little boy. How could this happen? Who wants him out of the class?*

She got to her feet and stepped up next to the colt, smoothing her skilled hands over his young body, feeling him tremble beneath her touch. Kurt's warning echoed in her head. *"There are folks who would do bad things to keep a good horse from winning."* The loudspeaker crackled through the barn. *"Liz Barnett. Please come to the show office. Liz Barnett to the show office."*

Karma sighed deeply and cocked his hip, leaning heavily against the wall. Gone was the feisty glint in his eye, and the prancing arrogance. His ears drooped, his lower lip hung open, and his tail dangled like an old mop.

Leaving the stall, Liz stared with unseeing eyes at the cement beneath her feet, her thoughts tumbling over one another, searching for an answer. Shamefully, she remembered how she'd lashed out at Kurt's implication of skullduggery at important shows. And she'd slept through the attack. Her eyes burned. *I might as well have turned him out with a pack of wolves.*

The aisle was deserted, the curious onlookers having apparently returned to whatever they'd been doing earlier. She suddenly felt as though she'd suffocate, and moved toward the door, wanting to fill her lungs with fresh air, feel the sun, make the nightmare disappear. Outside, the real world settled around her, and she leaned against the building, still trying to comprehend the situation. Too many emotions rolled through her body, flooding her with a feeling of helplessness. How had life gotten so screwed up?

The loudspeaker barked in the background, and another idea

came to mind. *Bill Benton.* His reference to the old lady's displeasure at her horse taking second place now took on a more ominous meaning. *He's just ambitious enough to try to win by any means.* Reinforcing her thoughts were Benton's comment about getting beaten by Karma again, plus his eagerness to have the colt under *any* circumstances. She latched onto him as the culprit. *He was so smug yesterday, even referring to Kurt's horse as being serious competition. Oh God! What if his horses have been attacked, too?* A chill raced across her shoulders as she headed for the show office, despair washing over her like rain.

Thirty-Two

Liz's hand moved slowly through her signature. The clerk handed over copies of the scratch form, then turned back to his business, seemingly unconcerned by her horrible predicament. Her thoughts moved back to the night intruder. When had all this happened? *That* was the mystery. She scowled, willing away the dull headache that was forming at the base of her skull. If she was going to protect her horses from whoever was out to ruin her, she'd have to stay awake.

The PA system crackled a welcome message across the show grounds. Pain tightened its grip on her throat. The entire year had been thrown away by the actions of one selfish person. Someone desperate. Someone with no conscience. Liz trudged along, looking at the dusty ground, lost in thought, no longer under any deadline.

"Whoa!"

Strong arms caught her as she collided with a solid body.

Kurt grinned. "Hello out there?" His eyes widened with concern. "Hon! What's the matter?"

Liz's distress disappeared briefly at the sight of his face and the warm brown eyes that had haunted her for weeks.

"Kurt! Is your colt all right?"

Confusion sharpened his features. "What? What colt? What are you talking about?"

He gently guided her over to the side of the building.

"Tell me what's going on."

He remained expressionless while Liz related the horror story.

162 Toni Leland

She looked earnestly into his eyes. "I think someone was afraid I'd win the stallion class."

He didn't speak, but placed his hands on his hips and turned away. The puzzling reaction sent her thoughts reeling in a new, chilling direction. *Could it have been him? Could he want his reputation back so badly that he'd sacrifice mine?...No, I won't believe that.* Her heart ached with the terrible accusation she'd made in her mind, then logic took over. *But why else would he have backed away from me so completely in the past few weeks?* The pain of suspicion again knifed through her thoughts.

Kurt turned back to her, on the verge of speaking, and Liz attempted to mask her expression, not wanting him to see what had flashed through her thoughts. She wasn't quick enough. He took one look at her face, then silently turned and walked away.

Liz moved slowly down the aisle toward her stalls. A woman stepped out of a stall in the adjacent area.

"Is your horse all right? I couldn't help overhearing the vet."

Liz nodded numbly, not wanting to talk about it.

The woman offered her hand. "I'm Shelly Ireland. I own Kelly Green Farms in San Jose."

Liz shook the work-hardened hand. "Liz Barnett. I live in Garden Valley. Legacy Arabians." She sighed. "He's all right, I guess. It was a tranquilizer of some kind." She stared at the ground. "I can't imagine how this happened. He seemed fine when I left last night, then I found him all goofy this morning."

Shelly's tone was sympathetic. "I hope he'll be okay. Maybe you'll get lucky and find out who did it."

Liz said nothing, the recent conversation with Kurt still painfully sharp in her head.

A short, bow-legged old man came around the corner and walked up to Shelly.

"They'll deliver another four bags of shavings about two o'clock," he said, glancing curiously at Liz.

"This is Patrick. He's my barn manager, looks after everything at shows, and is basically indispensable."

Patrick colored at his boss's compliment. "Pleased ta meetcha.

Ain't you the gal whose horse was drugged?"

She winced and nodded. "I'm really at a loss. When I left here last night around nine, he was eating his hay."

Patrick thought for a minute. "Well, le'ssee. I was here 'til about eleven. I did see some guy standing down there by your stalls, but I didn't think much about it. Thought he was with you."

"Do you remember what he looked like?"

She held her breath, waiting for a description of the intruder.

"Mmm. Tall. Uh, kinda dark, like he mighta been a foreigner or somethin'. Moustache...he had a moustache. That's about all I remember. Like I say, I thought he was supposed t' be there."

Liz's stomach rolled. Numb with pain, she nodded and mumbled her thanks, then turned and walked on to her stalls. Karma seemed to have regained some of his composure. His eyes had lost their dull glaze, and he'd moved to his water bucket. His muzzle glistened with the remnants of a drink.

"I'm so sorry, Baby. I'm going to get to the bottom of this if it takes me all year."

Kurt leaned against a post, watching Liz talk to some people in the aisle. Even from a distance, he saw her despair and his heart tightened with anger. He should never have told her about his past. He glanced at his watch and leapt forward. Ebony's class was in fifteen minutes.

Racing back to the stalls, he pulled the colt out into the aisle, and slipped on the fine, gold-chain show halter. He'd already groomed and blanketed the colt earlier, which would give him a little advantage, but it would be tight. Without bothering to change his shirt, he grabbed his jacket off the hanger and slipped it on, dusted off his pants, and grabbed his hat. He pulled the blanket from Ebony's back, and started toward the door at a dead run as the loudspeaker blared the last gate-call.

Kurt looked at the blue ribbon in his hand, and glanced at the bouncy black colt walking beside him. Thinking about everything that had happened in the last hour, he remembered his father's words, so many years ago, long before the trouble in New Mexico. *"You'll reap what you sow."* Kurt had sown some foolish seeds, and he had no one to blame but himself for the bumper crop. His ambition had screwed him up again, only this time, his heart was involved.

He toweled the sweat from Ebony's neck, and analyzed the line-up of possibilities for the fiasco. Maybe Benton wanted to protect his interest in Bones. *Nah, he wouldn't risk his career on something like this. He'd just buy Karma instead of Ebony.* Remembering Eve's cold confidence about winning the class, he felt the prickle of suspicion crawl across his shoulders. Protecting *her* interest in the championship made more sense. He shook his head, a sick feeling crawling through his gut, as another painful reality intruded. *Liz has every reason to think I might have been involved, since she knows about New Mexico.*

He put the colt away and leaned on the stall door, lost in a barrage of thoughts as he examined each one again.

Through the barn door, Liz caught a familiar movement. Across the gravel road, Kurt led a gorgeous black colt, a youngster almost twice the size of Karma. *That must be the Egyptian horse Bill mentioned.*

She focused on Kurt's uncharacteristic body language. A slow and shuffling step replaced his usually confident, almost swaggering stride. His shoulders drooped, de-emphasizing his height. The self-assured manner had disappeared, his bearing now one of defeat–despite the blue ribbon in his hand.

Seeing him so discouraged, Liz knew she'd judged him unfairly, jumped to conclusions without proof. The floodgates of an emotional dam opened, filling her with determination to learn the truth. She desperately wanted to believe that he had nothing to do with the drugging, and her thoughts returned to her original choice for bad guy–Bill Benton.

Amy ambled up to the bars to beg for treats, and Ashiiqah dozed quietly in the corner of her stall. Liz clenched her jaw. *Whoever is out to get me isn't going to mess up any more of my horses.*

Thirty-Three

At the fairgrounds security office, Liz approached a buxom black woman wearing a gray uniform. A wide belt sat on her ample hips, hung with gun holster, radio, billy club, and keys. Liz tried not to stare. *How does she keep that thing up? It must weigh twenty pounds.*

"Someone came into my stalls last night, and dosed my horse with a tranquilizer."

The security officer picked up a pad of paper. "Any idea who'd want to mess up your horse?"

Liz felt uneasy, not ready to name names. "No, but it's possible another exhibitor might have wanted my horse out of the halter class."

The implication of her own words jumped out at her. *Someone* thought Karma was so good he couldn't be beaten. A chill of the unknown followed the brief flush of pride.

"So, exactly what is it you want us to do, Miss...?"

"Barnett. Liz Barnett. I want you to call the police. This is a criminal act. I'm also worried about my other horses. What should I do if someone tries to tamper with them?"

The woman thought for a moment. "We have a security guard who patrols the barns from eleven at night until five in the morning. But he has four barns to cover, so he only gets to any one location about three times a night. Do you have a cell phone?"

Liz nodded, and the woman handed her a card.

"If anyone comes around your stalls, acting suspicious, call this number. The patrolman will get right over to you. Maybe you'll get lucky and catch whoever did it. I'll give the sheriff's office a call right now."

Liz thanked her and left, mulling over the new batch of information. If the patrolman made it to a certain location three times in six hours, then there were several two-hour periods when the horses were unprotected. Plenty of time for someone to slip into a stall and do whatever ugly deed they'd planned. She shuddered at the vision of someone sneaking through the night and plunging a needle into Karma.

She pushed the dark thoughts from her mind, and headed toward the barn to prepare for Ashiiqah's class. As she approached her stalls, she saw two men standing in the aisle. She strode toward them, anxiety gnawing at her gut.

"May I help you?"

"Doctor Barnett, I'm James Gibbson, the show manager. This is Dr. Franklin from U.S. Equestrian Equine Drugs and Medication Program."

Liz thought she'd throw up. The nightmare was about to get worse.

The fresh-faced young vet smiled. "How ya doin'? He gestured toward Ashiiqah's stall. "Would you bring that mare out, please?"

While Dr. Franklin drew blood, Gibbson said, "The results of these tests will be available before the championship classes on Saturday. If there's a problem, we'll let you know."

A few minutes later, Liz watched the two men walk away. Her legs began to wobble and she dropped onto the tack trunk, her thoughts flying. *Man, random really means* _random_. *He could just as easily have asked for Karma.*

Kurt moved through the next two classes like a robot. He'd lost the exhilaration of being in the ring, the excitement he'd always loved when showing horses. It wasn't the same when you were there because you'd been commanded–no, bribed–to win. Twice, he'd left the ring with a second place ribbon. Not much to crow about, but the points counted enough to qualify the horses for the Nationals. Ebony's classes were the only ones that mattered to Kurt.

His thoughts returned to the current state of chaos. If his suspicions were correct, Eve had committed an act that could ruin her. He hadn't yet decided whether he'd throw his job away and follow his heart, but he was coming close.

With a few hours before his next class, he might try to approach Liz again. He'd checked her stalls earlier, but the area had been deserted, except for an old guy sitting on a chair outside the tack stall, the same man who'd been talking to Liz earlier. *She's probably afraid something will happen to her other two horses.*

He felt terrible, knowing the only target at Legacy Arabians had already been hit.

Later in the afternoon, Liz struggled to stay focused on her class, feeling completely undone by the disastrous morning. She glanced at Ashiiquah as they entered the ring. As usual, the lovely mare pranced in an animated and regal attitude, attended to Liz's commands, and created a fabulous picture. Liz led her horse to their place in the line, and let her mind wander for a moment as she looked around the ring at the other exhibitors. Could the culprit be there in the ring with her? An icy finger ran down her spine. She scrutinized every exhibitor in the line-up. Two women and three men she'd never seen before, plus Sean, Kurt, and Bill Benton.

Kurt was the next handler to go before the judge. Watching him, her heart faltered in a familiar, sweetly painful way. He directed all his attention to his mare, keeping the animal alert and positioned properly. A second later, he moved forward and followed the judge's instructions, posing the chestnut beauty to show off her faultless conformation. He trotted the mare out, staying close to her shoulder, the two of them in perfect cadence. Kurt's expert movements and smooth transitions from one command to the next impressed her. *I could learn so much just from watching him.*

A slight commotion off to the right caught her attention, and she turned in time to see Bill Benton struggling with a rearing mare. The animal's eyes rolled with fear and her nostrils flared. Liz's chest tightened. She hadn't cared much for Bill Benton the first time she'd met him, and things hadn't changed much. He had an arrogance about him, a core of selfishness, and he'd revealed his true nature the night she'd visited the skybox. She watched with disgust as he yanked hard on the mare's lead, bringing her back to all fours. Throwing a quick glance over his shoulder at the judge, Benton smacked his crop sharply on the mare's tender underbelly. The animal leapt sideways, then stood still, quivering.

Liz turned away, unable to stomach the cruelty. *And he wants to handle my horses. Like hell!* The display fostered another thought. *I suspect he would be capable of doing something to a horse to keep it from winning. Well, Mr. Benton, if it was you, you've certainly succeeded. And I intend to find out!*

She glanced at the man next to her and gave him a sorrowful look.

He shook his head and spoke in a low voice. "He's such a jerk, always yanking and snatching his horses. I don't know why Celia keeps him on."

The comment caused Liz to think again about Kurt's assessment of the Arabian industry, and what made it tick. Her own situation seemed to confirm that he was right. The blood test on Ashiiqah would come back negative, she was certain of that. Clearly, Karma had been the only target, which meant *someone* was out to win the championship, no matter what it took.

She looked over at Kurt again, watching him pose his horse and pay strict attention to the class. She smiled, amused by her thoughts. *Here we are, competing against each other, and I'm not even nervous.* Her smile faded. She needed to talk to him. He might have some ideas that would help her sort out the mess.

"Step up, please."

Liz woke up with a jolt. The judge was looking directly at her with an expectant expression. *Oh, Lord, how long has he been waiting for me to come forward?*

She went through her routine, but the voice in her head told her she'd probably blown the class by not paying attention. The judge scribbled on his clipboard, then motioned for her to trot the horse away. Ashiiqah floated above the ground, appearing to move in slow motion. Liz concentrated on her horse, putting all other thoughts out of her head.

As they returned to the line-up to wait for the results, she caught Kurt's eye. He nodded and smiled, sending hope through her heart. Five more exhibitors performed before the judge turned in his decisions. Liz felt like a spectator. She hadn't connected with the class, her mind lost on other things. *It will probably cost me, and even if I win something, I could lose it again. Why am I even bothering?* Feelings of defeat weighed heavily on her shoulders. She glanced at Kurt again, but he concentrated on keeping his mare looking good. *He'll stand out in everyone's mind when they think about this class. I guess that's one of the differences between a professional and an amateur.*

The loudspeaker crackled, and while the announcer's voice droned on, Liz's mouth grew dry. *I'll probably get the gate.* She smirked when Benton took a fourth. Nervous excitement grew in the pit of her stomach, a queasy, unpleasant feeling. Kurt's name hadn't been called yet, either.

"In second place, number three-eighty-five, Aliqua Anika, owned by Eve Aliqua, and shown by Kurt DeVallio!"

Kurt trotted the mare over to accept the red ribbon, his face showing neither pleasure nor disappointment. As he left the ring, she heard the announcement. *"...owned and shown by Elizabeth Barnett!"*

Her stomach pitched. *I can't believe it! We won a class against big name trainers!* As she circled the arena with her mare, the little voice in her head scolded her: *Ashiiqah won the class, not you.*

Kurt waited for her at the out-gate, a tentative smile brightening his distinctive features.

"Well done, Liz!"

Her eyes burned with the wide range of emotions raging through her.

She lowered her voice. "I really didn't deserve that win. I couldn't concentrate for more than two seconds at a time."

He chuckled and patted her shoulder. "Your mare is a natural. She knows what she's supposed to do, and obviously loves doing it."

Liz looked up at him, suddenly feeling brave. "Could I talk to you? I need–"

"Yes, that's why I waited for you. I need to talk to you, too."

He slipped his arm around her shoulders and gave her a quick hug. In comfortable silence, they walked their horses toward the barn.

At the door, Kurt turned toward his own stalls, calling over his shoulder, "I'll be there in a few minutes."

Thirty-Four

L iz put Ashiiqah in the crossties, then turned to Patrick. "Everything okay?"

She moved over to Karma's stall and looked inside. The colt seemed to have recovered from his ordeal. His eyes were bright, and he whinnied a long greeting.

Patrick stepped up beside her. "He snapped out of it pretty good. Whatever he got wasn't very strong."

"Doctor Barnett?"

Liz turned to face a stocky man in a brown uniform. He tipped his wide-brimmed hat.

"I'm Officer Stanton from the San Mateo Countywide Security Unit. Fairgrounds called, said there was an attack on your horse."

Liz nodded and gestured toward Karma. "Yes, he was drugged sometime during the night."

"Is the horse valuable?"

"He's valuable to *me*."

A brief flicker of scorn crossed the officer's face at her sentimental response.

"I understand. Why would someone drug him?"

"The only thing I can think of is that someone was afraid I'd win the stallion class this morning."

"Ahh. Eliminating the competition, huh?"

Stanton scribbled something in his notebook, then looked up. "Any idea who might want to sabotage you?"

She took a deep breath. "Well, this is an important show. Anyone who wants to get to the nationals would be interested in a win."

"Do you know who was in the class?"

Liz shifted uneasily. Did she dare make accusations without proof?

"The exhibitor list for that class is posted in the show office."

Patrick's voice interrupted. "Hey! There's the guy that was hangin' around the stalls last night!"

Kurt stepped up to the group, a confused and wary expression darkening his face.

Liz's heart thumped against her ribcage. *Oh, God Patrick!* She hastened to defuse the situation.

"This is my friend, Kurt DeVallio."

Patrick turned back to his own area, clearly disappointed that he hadn't caught the villain.

Officer Stanton addressed Kurt. "You were here last night? What time?"

Kurt's face revealed nothing. "Late, past eleven. I came through on my way to my own stalls. No one was around."

Liz frowned. *Where was I when he came by?* How long would it take someone to slip into the stall, give the injection, and slip away? Liz held her breath to slow her racing heart. Five to seven minutes would be plenty of time.

Officer Stanton threw another question at Kurt.

"Was the horse okay when you saw him?"

Kurt's face had turned to stone. "He was fine. I scratched his chin and left."

"How do you spell your name, Mr. DeVallio?"

A minute later, the deputy put away his notebook, and shook his head. "These crimes are hard to track down, but I'll check around, see if anyone saw anything, talk to the other exhibitors in that class."

Liz watched Stanton walk toward the doors. Taking a deep breath, she looked at Kurt squarely, hoping her voice wouldn't betray her feelings, her hope that his visit the night before had been to see *her.*

"What *were* you doing here last night?"

He didn't smile. "I was looking for my stall assignments, and just happened down this aisle. The colt came to the door and wanted some attention. That's all. I saw a magazine and thermos by the chair, figured you were over at the restroom."

Before she could respond, his eyes narrowed. "You think *I* did it, don't you?"

The question was too direct, and Liz faltered. "Well, no..."

He took two steps away and looked up at the barn roof, the rigid set of his shoulders proof that he fought to control his anger.

When he turned back, his soft voice had turned to steel. "Well, of *course* you do! After all, I have a past reputation for drugging my horses. I guess I can't assume we're close enough that you *don't* suspect me."

His face clouded with emotion and anger. Liz's heart was beating too fast, and she couldn't think. Things were headed in the wrong direction. He might have helped her, and she'd just insulted him.

"No, Kurt. That's not the way—"

Her roller-coaster thoughts were impossible to explain, and pain tightened her throat.

Kurt's usually pleasant face had assumed an ominous look, his fine features carved into hard edges. His sensuous mouth had drawn into a straight, thin line, shadowed by his moustache. However, the worst change reflected in his eyes. The deep brown pools—always warm, inviting, flirtatious—had lost their sparkle, and now looked like pieces of obsidian lying in murky waters.

He stepped up close, his voice low and menacing.

"Liz, let me tell you something. No matter what my past record *says* I did, I have never in my life abused a horse, or given drugs, or done anything artificial or illegal to win a class. When I win, it's because I'm the *best*—and because I have the best horse. I did *not* drug Karma. I wouldn't need to do that to beat you."

He turned on his heel to leave, then spun back. "But you know what else? The saddest thing about this whole mess is that I believe your colt could have beaten mine, hands down, but I'd prepared myself for a good fight. I really looked forward to facing you in the ring. But I guess you can't see who I *really* am. Only what people *think* I am."

He turned and strode away, his long legs covering the ground rapidly.

She started after him. She had to salvage the situation, try to explain. She stopped. What could she say to him? Her obvious discomfort had already made him think she'd considered him a suspect. Didn't matter, she had to try.

He disappeared around the end row of stalls, and she had to run to catch up to him.

"Kurt, wait!"

He didn't stop. She closed the distance between them, and grabbed his arm. He stopped short and glared down at her, sending her pulse into a frenzied, erratic rhythm. Not one hint of interest or caring colored his expression. She faltered, suddenly afraid to say anything. She let go of his arm and stepped back.

"Kurt, please let me explain."

"Liz, there's nothing to explain. Your opinion is pretty clear."

"But–"

"Not now, Liz. Maybe later, but not now."

He turned and disappeared into his tack stall.

Her shoulders sagged, and she walked dejectedly back to her stalls. A soft nicker greeted her. Ashiiqah stood patiently in the crossties, waiting to be put into her stall.

⚘

Thirty-Five

Adrenaline pumped through Kurt's system, fueling his pain and anger. He dropped onto a bale of hay in the tack stall and put his head in his hands. *So much for the support of a good woman. She didn't even hesitate to think I did it.* The small, dark enclosure felt close and suffocating. He peeked through the drape to make sure she'd gone, then left the barn, striding out into the bright sunlight. He headed toward a rodeo arena located on the far side of the exercise pen.

From the top row of the bleachers, he viewed the expansive grounds of the Cow Palace. On the horizon, the ever-present thin fog hung over San Francisco Bay. The fresh air and solitude of the empty arena calmed him a little, and his pulse slowed. He sucked in a deep breath to clear his head. He needed to repair the damage of the day.

I can't blame her for suspecting me. I <u>did</u> tell her all the gory details about New Mexico. Except the important part, the rumor that Della had paid someone to drug the horse. A sharp jab of derision ran through him. *And I was too torn up to defend myself.* He exhaled to lighten the weight in his chest, remembering the despair that had consumed him after that debacle. All his hard work, his determination to quell the grief, sidestep the mourning process, had distracted him from the ruthlessness of his employer. When everything fell apart, all he'd wanted was to die. He looked up into the pale blue expanse of sky above the arena, remembering the hollow feeling of helplessness.

A large hawk caught his eye, as it circled, floating effortlessly on the air currents, scanning the ground below for prey. Kurt watched the bird for a few moments, letting the distraction soothe him. He dropped his gaze to the dusty ground below the bleachers and his anger passed, leaving him empty and exhausted.

Months ago, he'd accepted the fact that too much time had elapsed for him to do anything about correcting the New Mexico fiasco. However, today's events were déjà vu. Now, he had to rectify both situations–his *and* Liz's.

Sitting on a bale of hay in the quiet, dimly lit tack stall, Liz took some time to think. All she wanted to do was pack up her horses and go home. *I've had enough fun for one day.* Her practical nature told her she might as well salvage the efforts of the past week, take Ashiiqah back into the ring for the championship class that night, but she couldn't muster much enthusiasm for the idea. Depression settled into her bones. *What's the point? There's no way I'll ever find out who destroyed a full year's work and my reputation.*

Amy's class was scheduled for the next day, and Benton's taunt eased into her thoughts. What, exactly, *is* the purpose of showing a broodmare? Amy's foals were exquisite. Her outstanding pedigree spoke for itself–Karma was a perfect example. The atmosphere of the Fire Stone party, and Benton's casual references to the exorbitant prices people paid for Arabians, contributed to Liz's feelings of isolation.

I don't need to show Amy to sell her foals. She suddenly felt foolish, and shook her head. *So far, I've resisted selling any of my horses, or even Marilyn's, for that matter.* The simplicity of the situation surprised her. *I'm on the wrong track for the wrong reason. Maybe I just wanted to show off a little, feel like I belong somewhere.* The events of the past six hours had painfully clarified her naiveté, and made her sharply aware that she was embroiled in a world she didn't like.

"I'm here to scratch an entry."

The entry clerk looked up from his computer, sighed, and rose to his feet. He pulled a two-inch-thick sheaf of computer printouts from beneath the counter. "Name?"

"Elizabeth Barnett. BB Amy's Pride."

He removed the entries, and attached a scratch form to fill out and sign. When she'd finished, the man replaced the ledger, and turned back to his desk without looking at her. Liz's cheeks warmed, his attitude making her feel a little like a criminal.

However, on the way back to the barn, her step acquired a little bounce. *This is the right thing to do. I can concentrate on building my practice, and just enjoy my horses.* Her springy step faltered. She'd still have to find a way to turn this mess around. It was the sort of taint that would give her a bad name as a horse-woman *and* as a vet, and the black cloud certainly wouldn't help her convince the locals of her competence to care for their animals.

Kurt was the only person she knew who might have helped her figure out what to do, and she'd ruined her chances there. Her light mood sank at the realization she'd have to wait until Kurt felt ready to talk to her.

She took Karma out of his stall, and started grooming him, trying to take her mind off her problems.

"I'm so sorry, Baby. You missed your chance at stardom, and it's all my fault."

She pulled the shavings from his tangled tail, her mind turning over ways in which she might have prevented the attack. *How can you fight an enemy, if you don't know you have one?* Kurt had warned her, and she hadn't taken him seriously. As she worked, she recalled every detail of the previous twenty-four hours, trying to find some small clue in the mystery. Karma had been fine at nine-thirty. Patrick had seen Kurt at the stall around eleven. Karma had been heavily drugged when Liz had found him at five-thirty. *Heavily drugged. Damn! That's it!*

She racked her brain for a minute, finally dredging up her pharmacology course from vet school. Most tranquilizers absorbed rapidly, with peak blood levels at the one- to two-hour mark. The injection couldn't have been given at eleven, because the drug would have almost worn off by the time she'd awakened. That meant the dose was probably given sometime after three a.m. She almost wept as she mentally completely exonerated Kurt from any wrongdoing.

Karma shifted restlessly in the crossties and pawed the ground, annoyed with Liz's distraction. Cooped up since late the day before, he had a lot of excess energy singing through his young body. Liz tossed the currycomb into the tack stall, and took the colt out to the exercise pen.

As she lunged him, her spirits lifted.

Later, while Liz visited with Shelly, the loudspeaker crackled overhead. *"Kurt DeVallio, you have a phone call at the show office. Kurt DeVallio."*

Shelly chuckled. "Mmm, Mr. Gorgeous. He certainly is the mystery trainer."

Liz gave her a puzzled look, and the woman shrugged.

"No one knows much about him. He's obviously a great trainer–always in the ribbons–but there he is, working for some nobody out in the middle of nowhere. With his talent, he should be working for one of the top barns, making tons of money."

Liz recalled Kurt's sad story, knowing the reason he was working for "some nobody."

Shelly giggled. "Oh, jeez, I just remembered...you beat him in the two-year-old class. How did *that* feel?"

"Pretty darn good, but I only won because my horse stayed tuned in. *I* was a wreck! All I could think about was this morning's fiasco, wondering if the villain stood there in the ring with me."

"Yeah, that must have been tough. What are you going to do?"

Liz's smile faded. "I'm not sure there's anything I *can* do. The sheriff is looking into it, but he didn't sound optimistic that they'd turn up anything. In order to clear my name, I'd have to know who did it. That's a pretty long shot, don't you think?"

Shelly nodded in solemn agreement.

Kurt relaxed in the truck, mulling over Eve's telephone call. Interestingly enough, she'd already heard that Ebony had won the colt class that morning, smugly informing him that she'd cleared a spot in the display case for the championship trophy. Her bold tone had raised his hackles. He hadn't yet figured out how he would trap her into an admission of responsibility for the drugging, but he'd eventually think of something.

He stared through the dusty windshield, feeling something akin to despair. *I need to find Liz and apologize for this morning. I can't blame her for suspecting me. After all, I am a complete stranger, regardless of our night together.*

That memory stirred up the desire lurking deep inside him and, for a moment, he wanted to throw away his old dreams and make new ones, with Liz as a part of his life. Shaking his head at the silly, sentimental notion, he headed back to his stalls to prepare Ebony for the championship class that evening.

Thirty-Six

Late that afternoon, Officer Stanton returned to Liz's area with the report on his investigation. He'd questioned the other exhibitors in the colt class, but no one had seen anything.

Liz pushed a little. "What about Bill Benton?"

The deputy gave her a curious look. "Do you think *he's* the one?"

She gulped. "Well, he's been trying to buy my colt, or get him in training. Seems like–"

"He's clear, Dr. Barnett. He has an alibi for the entire night."

She cocked her head. "What is it?"

Stanton smiled. "I'm not at liberty to reveal his whereabouts, but the alibi checked out."

She was confused. What could the big secret be? *Oh! He's probably sleeping with Celia. How could I be so dense?*

Stanton closed the notebook and shook his head. "Sorry. Wish I had better news. I'm not sure what else to suggest. I'll file the report, and if anything else comes to light, I'll let you know."

That evening, exhilarated by a strong class and bursting with pride, Liz walked Ashiiqah back to the barn. *Legacy Ashiiqah: Regional Reserve Champion Mare.* Liz looked at the large tri-colored rosette and gleaming silver trophy in her hand, feeling a shiver of pleasure at her victory. Every first place winner from all the filly/mare divisions had been in the class. A field of ten. The best of the best. The champion had been Kurt's entry, a four-year-old gray, straight Egyptian horse. *If I have to take second place to Kurt DeVallio, that's fine by me, but Ashiiqah and I held our own out there.*

She did a quick replay of the class. Kurt had looked absolutely gorgeous in his tuxedo, wearing the formal attire with the ease and confidence of a professional. Her own sequined jacket and black satin trousers made her feel very glamorous, very much a part of the high society of the ring.

She slipped out of the elegant garment and looked around her stall area. It was finally over. She'd leave the disappointment and pain of this place, and go home where she belonged. Thoughts of being back on her lovely farm filled her with excitement. *I'll pack tonight, get some rest, and leave early.*

She began collecting all the items strewn around the tack stall, tossing them into the open trunk. Seeing her sleeping bag, she shivered. The thought of being all-alone in the deserted barn with an unsavory character roaming the night was more than a little unsettling. She checked the battery on the cell phone, then placed it on the sleeping bag beside the card with the emergency number.

"Patrick! You busy?"

Ebony had sailed through the championship class, his performance breathtaking and perfect, but the win felt hollow for Kurt. Too much had been sacrificed for the sake of a title and a price tag.

As he walked toward the barn, Bill Benton fell into step beside him, his movie-star teeth gleaming through a pompous grin.

"Well, Kurt, I see you pulled it off. Pretty clever."

Kurt stopped abruptly and glowered.

"What *exactly* does *that* mean?"

Benton's eyes glittered with malice, his expression mocking.

"Come on! You know what I mean. Pretty clever to sedate Liz's colt to keep him from making the class this morning."

Kurt lunged forward, nearly knocking the man off his feet.

"Benton, that's a damned lie, and if I find out you're spreading it around, I'll break your scrawny neck!"

The trainer backed out of Kurt's reach, and threw out one last barb.

"You take good care of *my* horse, ya hear?"

Kurt watched him saunter off, astonished that the trainer had been so bold in his accusations. *Of course! It's a perfect cover for whoever did it, since my past record is already tainted.*

He stowed Ebony's trophy in the tack trunk, and angrily flung the exhibitor card into the corner. He was now *damned* sure that Eve Aliqua and Bill Benton were conspirators.

He took a deep breath and started down the aisle. He'd rehearsed over and over what he would say to Liz, but nevertheless, his stomach tightened at the prospect of apologizing. He'd done a helluva lot of it since meeting her. When he walked into her stall area, his heart fell. The old man was there, which meant that Liz wasn't.

Patrick looked up, a frown spreading across his weathered face, his tone possessive.

"What'er *you* doin' here?"

Kurt's smile faded and he glowered at the belligerent old man.

"I came to see Dr. Barnett."

Patrick turned his attention back to his magazine.

"She's over watchin' classes."

The pleasure driving class had just started, and a large crowd of spectators filled the arena. Kurt scanned the seats on both sides of the ring, but didn't see Liz. *She's probably not very interested in performance classes.* After looking around once more, he headed back to his stalls, his thoughts turning to another woman.

Eve seemed pretty damned sure of herself about the outcome of this show. Thinking about Benton's veiled accusation, anger rushed in, but common sense told Kurt that his original notion was valid: Bill Benton would not jeopardize his career for Eve Aliqua, no matter how much he wanted Ebony. Kurt came to terms with the suspicion that his boss really *was* the culprit. *Now, how to prove it?*

Liz emerged from the restrooms in time to see Kurt leave the arena. Her pulse jumped. *Was he looking for me?* She started after him, then hesitated, unsure she wanted to face him. *Maybe he was in the arena for some other reason.* He'd very likely still be angry.

If she apologized, would he even accept it? Probably not. She'd badly bruised his ego by doubting his honesty, and that would be hard to repair with a man as strong as Kurt.

The Native Costume class had just entered the ring, and Liz stared, fascinated by the elaborate and expensive costumes of horses and riders. The native trappings of the Middle East magnificently enhanced the classic beauty of the Arabian horse. The riders in the ring below had obviously researched the customs and raiment from many of those countries, coming up with exotic outfits that sparkled under the lights and flowed on the air currents generated by the cantering horses. Liz watched the entire class, the gorgeous display transporting her to distant lands, her problems forgotten.

By the time she headed back to the barn, it was late. Kurt hadn't returned, reaffirming her suspicion that he'd been in the arena by coincidence. She said goodnight to Patrick, and retired to the tack stall, exhausted and unable to think of anything but ending the day. The barn lights dimmed and the noise level dropped to a distant hum. She squirmed, trying to get comfortable on the hard bales of hay. Checking the phone once more to be sure it was working, she exhaled and gazed up at the dim angles of the barn rafters. The tension eased out of her muscles, and she drifted into a hazy, half-conscious state.

In an instant, she came fully alert, her pulse racing. *Footsteps?* Raising herself up on an elbow, she listened hard, trying to filter out the sound of her own heart crashing against her ribs. A shadow fell across the doorway.

"Liz?"

Kurt stepped into the stall, and she fell back against the hay, closing her eyes, fighting a sickening wave of fright.

She struggled to sit up. "You frightened me nearly out of my wits!"

He sat down next to her on the bale, his face even with hers. His features were soft and Liz searched them for a hint of his feelings. He reached over and stroked her hair, concern shadowing his face. His shirt cuff brushed her cheek and she inhaled deeply, the scent bringing back the memory of their night together. A familiar longing came over her, and she leaned her head into his hand, savoring the warmth of his touch. His voice caressed her mind.

"Listen, you go to sleep. I'll stay up with the horses."

She felt deeply moved by his efforts to make amends. *Now's my chance to tell him how wrong I was.* She raised her eyes, but Kurt was looking at the ground.

"Liz, I have something to tell you. You'll probably hate me forever, but I owe it to you."

The warm feelings disappeared, and a chill blew through her chest. She watched his face closely as he struggled to begin.

"When I told you about my past, I neglected one important detail."

As he looked at her, a rosy glow crept over his cheeks.

"A few months after my suspension, I heard a rumor that my boss had hired someone to drug that horse. She'd been so jealous of my girlfriend that she'd set out to destroy me. And she succeeded. I had suppressed my grief, tried so hard to push the past aside. When everything came crashing down, I no longer cared about anything. Everything I'd touched had crumbled, without exception. I never tried to get my record cleared. I just let Della get away with it. I was paralyzed."

Liz spoke softly. "Why are you telling me this? I already *know* you weren't responsible for what happened this morning."

He took a deep breath. "Because I think I know who drugged your colt."

Her voice cracked. "Who!"

His hands came up defensively. "Hold on, I might not be able to prove it, but I'm almost positive Eve had something to do with it."

Liz said nothing, her insides turning to lead. *Why would Eve do something like that?* In the next instant, an answer slammed into her brain. She rose and stalked over to the stall door, trying to suppress the urge to scream insults at him. She took a deep breath and turned back to face him.

"So, you've been sleeping with Eve to keep your job. Just like New Mexico. Is that what you're saying? That when you made love to me, it was just recreation?"

He rose to his feet, visibly shaken. "No! Liz, please sit down and hear me out. You're on the wrong track."

She crossed her arms over her chest. "I can hear you just fine from here."

He took a deep breath. "First of all, I *haven't* been sleeping with Eve. I learned my lesson good on *that* one."

A small twinge of relief sneaked through Liz's anger.

Kurt continued. "Bill Benton offered Eve a huge amount of money for Ebony, on one condition–that the colt win the regional title so Bill could take him to the nationals."

Liz narrowed her eyes. *Bill Benton, again.*

Kurt walked to the side of the stall and absent-mindedly fingered a lead rope hanging there.

"Eve offered me a double commission on the sale. A lot of money, Liz...my big break."

The emotions scrambling through her brain made her dizzy, but she felt mostly despair, followed by anger.

"So, all your attention over the past couple of months has only been about business. You were spying on me?"

He shook his head. "In the beginning, yes, but I–"

She didn't let him finish. "You gave Eve the ammunition she needed to remove Karma from the class. To ruin me."

She felt used and naïve. Both Kurt and Eve had taken advantage of her.

Kurt stood quietly until she'd finished her tirade, then came to stand directly in front of her. He searched her face with his sad, dark eyes.

"Liz, I never dreamed she'd go to such lengths. I'd planned to try to win the class fair and square. Our horses were perfectly matched, it would have been thrilling." He looked down at the floor. "I've made a real mess of my life, and as a result, you've caught some of the backlash."

He looked up again, directly into her eyes. "But I promise you, I'm going to get to the bottom of this, and clear your name."

She didn't even try to keep the contempt from her voice. "Just get out!"

Thirty-Seven

"My treasures do not chink or glitter,
They gleam in the sun and neigh in the night."
                                        –Old Arab Proverb

Liz stood in the center of her cozy kitchen, soaking up the rich warmth of the oak barn-board paneling that glowed with the late afternoon sun streaming through the window. The comfort of being back home wrapped around her like the security of a cocoon. The events of the past few days had drained and saddened her. She felt as though she never wanted to venture out again.

Through the window, her beloved red barn was a bright spot against the brittle, late-summer colors. Legacy was her treasure, and she had the control to make it as large or small as she desired.

I'll never again let shallow ambition bring harm to my beautiful horses.

In her mind, Liz had left the business of showing Arabians. During the drive home from San Francisco, she'd thought long and hard about that decision. At first, she'd questioned herself about cowardice, about being a quitter. However, the longer she thought about it, the more convinced she became that it would be possible to breed and sell fine quality horses without putting them through the rigors of the show ring. She didn't need to prove anything to anyone. More importantly, she did *not* want to be one of the desperate players in the risky winning game.

The sun dropped behind the mountains, casting soft shadows

over the land as she walked toward the barn. Heads popped over stall doors, eager for supper, and Liz beamed at her stable of beauties.

"You'll all live like royalty. I promise."

Later that day, the woman who'd cared for the horses during Liz's absence stopped by to pick up her check. Her uneasy manner told Liz something was wrong.

"Hi, Mandy. You don't look very happy."

"I'm tellin' you, that gray mare is a piece of work. First, she pinned her ears at me when I went into the stall to feed her. That made me kinda nervous. Then, the next day, out in the pasture, she wouldn't come, and wouldn't let me catch her to bring her in."

Mandy hesitated, prefacing her words with an apologetic look. "I left her outside all night. It was getting dark, and I had to leave. I'm really sorry–I know you never leave your pregnant mares out at night."

Liz inhaled slowly, telling herself to remain calm. Mandy had been around horses all her life, and Liz had assumed she could handle most situations. This one must have been particularly difficult.

"How'd you get her back into the barn?"

"The next day when I turned everyone out, she'd gotten over her snit, and wanted to come in. She spent all day inside."

Fearing she'd say something she might regret, Liz decided not to discuss the issue further. After Mandy left, Liz went to the barn and watched Muscala for a while.

"I wish I knew what your problem is."

Eve showed up in the tack room bright and early, her manner brisk and confident. "Where is it?"

She looked around the room, spotted the trophy sitting on the file cabinet, and quickly moved over to pick it up.

Kurt watched her out of the corner of his eye, seeing greed work its seductive magic on his boss. She turned, her face glowing with self-satisfaction.

"You did a great job, Kurt–thank you. Billy says the colt was fabulous in the class." She laughed. "This was one time he didn't mind losing."

Kurt nodded, but said nothing. *Interesting. She's already talked to Benton.*

Eve parked herself on a stool in the corner and watched him work for a few minutes. He sensed she had something to say, but he kept his head down, polishing the cold, steel bit in his hands. The silence grew thick and, finally, she spoke.

"Billy's going to pick up Ebony tomorrow morning. He wants plenty of time to work with him before the nationals."

Kurt's gut tightened. *The game plan has changed.* He narrowed his eyes and looked directly at her.

"He's already signed the contract?"

She shifted her gaze to the floor. "Not yet, but I've agreed to let him keep the horse at Fire Stone while I'm drawing it up."

Kurt exploded. "Eve, that's ridiculous! *Nobody* lets a valuable horse go to a buyer without a signature. *And* insurance!"

She gave him a disdainful look. "Well, that really isn't any of *your* business, is it?"

Kurt knew immediately where the rest of the conversation would go. He rose from the bench and stepped toward her, his chest tight with anger.

"When do I get my commission?"

She looked away and cleared her throat. "I won't be able to pay you until I have most of the money. It'll be six months, at the most, but probably sooner."

She tried a sincere smile, but her features were rigid with deceit.

"That wasn't the deal, Eve."

She straightened up, her face cold with power. "And what *deal* are you talking about? I don't recall signing any agreement."

Fury raged through his head, unleashing a barrage of thoughts. He wanted to tell her to go to hell, but a voice in the recesses of his brain reminded him that he needed to sort out the mystery of Karma's drugging. He quelled his anger.

"I did what you wanted, Eve. I saw to it that Ebony won the regional championship."

She snorted and rose from the stool. "Well, *that* couldn't have been too hard, since Liz–" Her eyes widened almost imperceptibly, and she clamped her mouth shut.

He caught the slip-up, and his stomach jerked. "What about Liz?"

Eve recovered quickly. "Oh, nothing. I just heard she had to scratch her colt from the class. It was sick or something?"

Kurt moved to the doorway and wedged himself there. "Now, where did you hear *that*?"

She frowned, feigning scorn. "Well, Billy, of course! And it disturbs me a great deal that *you* didn't tell me about it. I mean, after all, you were right there in the same barn with her."

He heard the words and his stomach dropped. She knew too much, too soon. It was becoming clear that Bill Benton and Eve Aliqua had arranged the whole incident to look as though Kurt had been involved. Kurt, who'd had a juicy carrot dangled in front of him. Kurt, who'd been seen at Liz's stalls late at night. Kurt, with the questionable past.

Now, not only had Liz's reputation been destroyed, but Kurt also had no way of getting his sales commission from Eve, until– and if–she decided to give it to him. The current state of affairs made the mess in New Mexico look like a hiccup.

Thirty-Eight

Colleen was horrified by Liz's description of the ordeal with Karma and the show officials.

"How awful! Who would want to destroy your reputation?"

A vivid image of Eve Aliqua flashed through Liz's head.

"I can't imagine...I contacted security and filed a report. The sheriff questioned a few people, but didn't find anything."

"What did the lab report say?"

"Diazepam, like Valium. It certainly isn't a common drug for calming show horses. A more logical choice would have been Reserpine. God, Colleen, what's really upsetting is that, whoever dosed Karma, knew exactly what he or she were doing, injecting just enough to keep him out of the class."

Colleen's voice was subdued. "What about all your hard work, and the Nationals?"

Liz swallowed hard. "I'm through showing horses. I really believe I can raise and sell quality Arabians without jumping through horse show hoops. It's nice to have the ribbons to show off, but my horses will prevail by their bloodlines."

The line remained silent. Colleen probably thought Liz had lost her senses.

"Good for you, Liz. I've *always* believed that, but try telling it to some of these rich owners."

After the conversation, Liz disappeared into a mire of personal thoughts that temporarily crowded out her professional concerns.

How could I fall in love with someone so unsuitable? She sucked in her breath sharply at the admission, and the pain of her true emotions. Then she reminded herself that Kurt had warned her. She'd chosen to play a dangerous game, and she had the wounds to prove it. An instant replay of their last conversation at the show flickered through her head, and Kurt's stricken face appeared in her mind's eye. At the time, she'd been so devastated, angry, and unbearably embarrassed by her naïveté, that she'd never wanted to see him again. Now, second thoughts were creeping in.

Who am I to judge him? His past life has shaped his present situation. He's a strong, independent man shackled by circumstance, a man who's fighting for survival.

Though the thoughts churned through her brain, she couldn't help feeling that she *did* have a right to care about his actions, if they affected *her*. And they certainly had.

Liz went about her comfortable, predictable morning routine, filling each feed bucket. She'd always loved starting her day with the horses. Lugging the last pail toward Muscala's stall, Liz remembered Mandy's problem with the cranky mare. Muscala must have thought she could take advantage of a new person, just like a little kid tests a new babysitter. At the stall door, she stopped and scrutinized the animal. Muscala's swollen belly promised a large foal. A ripple moved beneath the mare's flank as the fetus shifted position. The mare's ears flattened and she snapped a hind leg up to kick at the movement. Liz shook her head. *I don't like the direction this pregnancy is taking.*

She entered the stall and dumped the grain into a bucket in the corner. Without warning, Muscala lunged, teeth bared, eyes wild. Her heavy body slammed Liz into the wall, huge teeth grinding through Liz's light work shirt. Pain seared through her shoulder, and she struggled to regain her balance. A well-aimed, powerful kick caught her in the thigh, and she tumbled into the shavings. Muscala grunted and stamped her feet. Liz instinctively rolled over onto her stomach and covered her head with her arms, bracing herself for another blow. As suddenly as they'd begun, the horse's movements stopped, and stillness settled over the stall.

Liz lay for long, agonizing minutes, waiting for whatever might be next. *How am I going to get out of here?* She slowly lifted one arm and turned her head so she could see the mare. Muscala stood in the corner, munching grain as though nothing had happened. Moving very slowly, Liz sat up, watching the animal every second for signs of another attack. Muscala seemed unconcerned. Liz gingerly rose to her feet, and pain exploded in her shoulder. She gritted her teeth and backed toward the stall door, never letting her eyes leave the mare. As she fumbled with the latch, the horse suddenly wheeled and dived straight at her, ears pinned, flared nostrils gaping above bared teeth. Liz leapt out the door, slamming it just seconds before Muscala hit it. The mare's heavy head hit Liz's cheek, knocking her off balance. She crashed to the cement floor, her injured shoulder taking the brunt of the fall. Pain came in a wave, threatening to take her into oblivion.

Large amounts of adrenaline pumped through her system, and her thundering heart struggled to handle it. *Oh, my God, I don't believe this just happened!* Delayed tears of fright ran down her temples, trickling into her hair. She lay still for a few minutes, staring at the ceiling, then slowly sat up. The only sound she could hear was her own ragged breath.

The walk back to the house was long and painful. She gingerly peeled off her shirt, and inspected her damaged shoulder in the bathroom mirror. Blood oozed from several open wounds, and several shades of blue and purple already colored the entire area. Nausea threatened, and she closed her eyes. *I should have someone look at this.* On closer inspection a second later, she saw a jagged, bleeding scrape on her face, and a large bruise darkening her cheek and jaw. *I can't believe she did so much damage.*

She moved slowly into the study, and picked up her cell phone. She was beginning to feel woozy as she dialed Colleen's home number. Her friend's perky voice on the answering machine prompted her to leave a message. Liz hung up and dialed the barn number. The phone rang several times, while she struggled to clear her head. A man answered and, through the fog pushing into her brain, Liz heard that Colleen had just left for Sacramento.

Resting her head on her arms, she tried to decide if she'd be able to drive herself to the local hospital. She felt shaky and disoriented. The phone in her hand was making a peculiar noise. She lifted it to her ear, and the sound of Kurt's voice confused her even further.

"Aliqua Arabians. Hello?"

"Uh, Kurt?"

"Liz? Hey! What's wrong?" His voice rang with concern.

"I've had a little accident..." A wave of dizziness closed in, and her voice trailed off.

"Liz, are you at home? Liz! Talk to me!"

"Yes. I'm sorry to bother–"

"I'll be right there!"

The line went dead and she stared numbly at the dark display. A minute later, she eased back onto the couch, and succumbed to the heavy darkness that pressed her into the cushions.

Thirty-Nine

Kurt's fear burned into his brain as the truck sped toward Liz's farm. The winding road between Placerville and Garden Valley seemed to go on forever. One thought hammered itself against his skull. *"Please, let her be okay."* A tractor and overloaded hay wagon pulled onto the highway about a hundred yards ahead, and Kurt swore under his breath. His usually careful, somewhat sedate driving habits disappeared, and he punched the accelerator to fly past the creeping vehicle. In the rearview mirror, he saw the farmer shake his fist.

The truck skidded to a stop in Liz's driveway. He pushed through the screen-door into the kitchen, calling her name, and was met with silence. As he slowly started down the hall, apprehension overwhelmed him. Entering a large, comfortable living room, he stopped for a moment, listening in the hushed atmosphere. A small, muffled sound came from a doorway off to his left, and he bolted toward it. The small, crumpled body on the couch brought his heartbeat to a dead stop. In two strides, he knelt beside her. The sight of her bruised and swollen face sent a wave of despair through him.

"My God, Honey! What happened?"

Barely moving her lips, she managed to croak, "horse."

The emergency room at the community hospital in Placerville wasn't busy at that hour of the morning. An orderly wheeled Liz directly into an examining room, and Kurt waited nervously in the lobby.

Two hours later, Liz reappeared in a wheelchair. The nurse addressed Kurt.

"It's a nasty bite, but it should heal up all right. The doctor gave her a tetanus shot, just to be on the safe side."

Kurt's surprised expression made Liz giggle, then flinch.

"I'll tell you on the way home," she mumbled through stiff lips.

Looking up at the man who'd come to her rescue, her heart swelled with love. His expression was tight with genuine concern for her, and with that, all the past questions and problems faded into insignificance. They could be answered or solved later. Nothing mattered now, except that he was there with her.

As Kurt maneuvered the truck along the highway between Placerville and Garden Valley, he glanced over at Liz and grinned.

"Okay, you gonna tell me what happened?"

Liz unfolded her story slowly and painfully, and with each disclosure, the lines on Kurt's face deepened. When she'd finished, he remained silent for a few minutes.

He finally spoke, his tone angry.

"I knew that mare would be trouble when you first bought her. I tried to talk to Eve about it, but you know how she is–always has to have things her own way."

Liz remembered the heated conversation she'd overheard between them. Even back then, Kurt had been thinking of her best interests. The revelation made her happy, but also ashamed that, through the past few weeks, she'd let her emotions and bruised pride overshadow her good judgment.

Kurt parked the truck close to the house, then opened Liz's door to help her out. As he gently steadied her, the memory of their first embrace wiggled its way into his brain, and sadness flooded his heart. Lost chances. Would he ever be able to start over with her?

Her legs were wobbly, but with his arm around her waist, she managed to walk into the house. He helped her into the study, and she sank onto the couch, releasing a long sigh. She leaned her head back against the cushions and looked up at him.

"Thank you for coming to get me."

Pain and exhaustion shadowed her eyes, and his heart rolled with sadness.

"Thank you for calling me."

After she drifted off to sleep, Kurt wandered up to the barn. Heads appeared over stall doors, and anxious nickers echoed through the rafters.

"Okay, you guys, she's fine."

He looked at Muscala, the only horse in the barn who hadn't responded to his presence. The mare stood haughtily against the stall wall, ignoring his stare. *Eve should never have purchased that mare, let alone sold her to someone else.*

Shaking his head at the disastrous hand of fate, he grabbed halters and started taking the other horses out to the pasture for the day. Muscala would stay in her stall until he decided what to do about her. As he led the horses out, two at a time, he had a chance to look around at the lovely hillside and tidy paddocks. The farm was pleasant and peaceful. He understood why Liz loved it so much.

He'd never had a place of his own. His entire life had been spent working for someone else, showing someone else's horses, and doing someone else's bidding. His strong drive to "be the best" had kept him from considering the idea of being his own master. Until New Mexico. He'd been shaken by the sordid reality of his unhealthy relationship with Della and, from that, a plan had grown to strike out on his own, nurtured by dreams of a second chance at life. However, Della's jealous fury had effectively ended those dreams.

Chagrin worked its way into his thoughts. *And here I am again, at the mercy of another unscrupulous woman.*

His shoulders slumped. He had a long road to travel before he could ever consider being independent–or sharing his life with anyone again.

Liz awoke from a troubled sleep, gasping at the deep pain in her shoulder. It took a few seconds to remember the chain of events, and her trip to the hospital. Struggling to sit upright, she gritted her teeth against the sharp pain. The doctor had given her some pain pills, but she had no idea where they were. *I wonder if Kurt is still here.*

As if summoned by her thoughts, he appeared in the doorway.

"Can I get you anything?"

"Yes, please. Drugs." She smiled painfully. "I think they're in my handbag, wherever that is."

He disappeared, and returned a few seconds later, swinging the bag.

"This color really doesn't go with my outfit."

She laughed, then grimaced. "Oh, please! Don't!"

He handed her a glass of water, then sat down next to her while she took the pain pill. A minute later, he gently slipped his arm around her and pulled her to him. She nestled into the soft warmth of his shirt, feeling the comfort of his nearness and savoring the security of his arms. *It's almost as though we've never had any problems at all.*

In the peaceful snuggle, she felt Kurt's voice rumble through his chest.

"I'm going to see if I can fix the problem with that mare."

She raised her head and looked at him, her addled brain trying to figure out where the statement might be headed.

"Do you think you can work with her, make her less crazy?"

He shook his head. "No, that's not what I mean. She's a dangerous horse. Eve had no business selling her to you–or to *anyone*, for that matter. Eve knew the mare had a nasty disposition. That's why she wanted to get rid of her."

"What are you going to do?"

"I'll insist she take back the horse and void that part of your contract."

Liz thought for a minute. "She won't go for it. You know...'buyer beware' and horse sales. I should have been more careful, but I was so enchanted with Fair Lady that I didn't really pay close attention to Muscala."

"That doesn't matter. Eve knowingly sold you an unstable horse, and didn't give you any indication there might be problems." He looked directly into her eyes. "You're very lucky to have gotten out of that stall without being kicked in the head."

She shivered, remembering her panic as she'd tried to fend off Muscala's vicious attack.

Kurt's voice became brisk. "Let me fix you something to eat, then I have to go back to the farm for a couple of hours. I'll be back this afternoon to bring the horses in and feed."

Confusion blurred her thoughts. "You mean I put the horses out before I went to the hospital?"

He chuckled. "No, I did it earlier this morning while you were sleeping."

"Whew! For a minute there, I thought I *had* been kicked in the head."

Minutes later, she listened to kitchen sounds echoing from down the hall, and her thoughts hummed. *Why does this feel so right, after everything that's gone so wrong?*

Forty

Kurt pulled up in front of the barn just as Eve came out of the house. Even from a distance, he saw her scowling features, and braced himself for the storm.

She caught up with him at the barn door. "Where in the hell have you been?"

"I had an emergency this morning."

He walked through the dark entrance, Eve close behind him.

"What kind of emergency?"

He stopped short. *I've had just about enough of this pushy witch!* He turned and glowered at her.

"I've been at the hospital with Liz Barnett."

She blinked. "Liz Barnett? What happened?"

"That crazy mare you unloaded on her came unglued this morning, and hurt her badly."

Eve's eyes widened. "*Muscala?*"

He snorted, his words oozing with sarcasm. "Yeah, that's the one."

She didn't reply, and Kurt continued.

"I'm going over there to pick up the mare and bring her back here. I'd advise you to release Liz from the contract, unless you want a lawsuit."

Eve bristled. "And just who do you think *you* are–Perry Mason? I don't have to do any such thing. Someone buys a horse, they take their chances."

She turned away, the conversation over as far as *she* was concerned.

Kurt's voice rose a little. "I'd suggest you reconsider, Eve. There's a lot at stake here."

She turned back and narrowed her eyes. "Meaning what?"

"Meaning, if you don't, I'll see that the story gets around about all your shoddy business practices. *And* I'll help Liz in any way I can if she decides to sue you. In fact, I'll *encourage* her to press charges."

Eve's face shadowed with anger and she stared at him for a full minute before she answered.

Her voice snapped with tension. "Fine. Go get the damned horse!"

Kurt watched her retreating figure. When he put all the pieces together–selling a dangerous horse, making under-the-table deals, reneging on a sales commission–Eve came up smelling pretty bad. What would keep her from making sure her horse won–by any means? *There has to be some way I can find out if she's behind the drugging.* He sidelined his thoughts for the moment, and followed her into the house.

An hour later, he drove through the foothills, the empty trailer bouncing along behind the truck. *I could almost drive this road with my eyes closed.* He glanced down at the paper lying on the seat next to him. He'd stood by while Eve had typed up a contract release and signed it. She'd been cool toward him, but had apparently gauged her liability and decided it would be best to cooperate. On reflection, Kurt's instinct told him that her sudden cooperation was a good indication that she feared he'd start nosing around–which was exactly what he intended to do.

Liz was sitting at the kitchen table when he stepped through the door. She looked so pitiful that he wanted to gather her up and cradle her in his arms like a small child. Instead, he leaned over and kissed the top of her head, then sat down across from her.

"You look a little perkier."

"I *feel* like I've been run over by a tank."

"You have–that's a very large horse."

He stopped smiling and leaned forward, taking her hand into his. "I brought the trailer to pick her up. Eve has released you from the contract. I have the papers in the truck."

Liz's face tightened with her emotions. For all his evasiveness, and all the problems they'd had between them, he knew she'd seen through his macho charade. For one fleeting instant, he wanted to throw caution aside and tell her how much he loved her. Then, the frightening impulse disappeared, and he looked away from the woman who had him hog-tied.

Liz's voice caressed him. "You're amazing. Thank you."

He rose and looked down at her. "It's the least I could do, considering all the trouble I've caused you."

He headed toward the door to finish the business at hand.

An hour later, he returned to the house.

"Horses are in and fed. I followed your schedule on the feed room door. Is there anything else I can do for you before I leave?"

"You could help me up the stairs to my bedroom. I think I'd like to sleep for a week."

As he steadied her with each step, his thoughts ran wild. A deep comfort level had developed between them, the kind that usually came only with time spent together in quiet, ordinary situations–something they'd never had. It felt wonderful being there to help her, protect her...love her. He wanted to be a part of her life.

In the bedroom, her unique scent perfumed the air, stirring his senses. The room was feminine, but understated–like the woman herself. He sat on the edge of the bed while she disappeared into the bathroom. A few minutes later, she emerged, wearing a long white nightgown that caressed her small, shapely body. His gaze hungrily took in the soft globes of her breasts and the lovely outline of her bare arms. A deep stir overwhelmed the noble thoughts of earlier in the day. He wanted nothing more than to take her in his arms and make love to her again.

She looked embarrassed at being in her nightclothes in front of him, and he dropped his eyes to give her some privacy. She sank onto the bedside, releasing a deep sigh.

He reached over and caressed her good shoulder. "You okay?"

She nodded, then turned and slipped her body under the covers. When she met his gaze again, the message there sent a wave of hope through him. A promise for the future?

She smiled shyly and took his hand. "Thank you again for being here." Her expression became seductive. "When I'm feeling better, I think we have some unfinished business."

His heart lurched, and he leaned down and kissed her forehead, wishing he knew what lay ahead.

The last light of day dwindled as Kurt headed to the barn to get Muscala. The fire burning inside him consumed his thoughts, strengthening his determination to clear his own name. There'd be no future with Liz if he didn't.

Muscala dozed in the corner, but flicked an ear toward the door at the sound of his voice.

"Time to go, mare."

He opened the stall door and entered. She raised her head and flattened her ears in one small attempt to intimidate him.

"Hey!" he barked, moving forward aggressively.

Her ears came back up, she shifted her weight, and stepped back, watching him carefully. He slipped a halter over her head and clipped on the lead rope, working in a confident manner that kept her submissive. She meekly followed him out of the barn and into the trailer. Behind them, several soft, nervous nickers drifted from various stalls. Kurt shook his head. *No love lost here.*

Forty-One

The next morning, Kurt noted Eve's contrite expression as she entered the tack room.

"I'm really sorry Liz got hurt. Is she okay now?"

"Yeah. It was a pretty nasty bite, but the rest of the damage is just bruises and scrapes."

He gave her a hard look. "She could have been killed. I don't know what you intend to do with that mare, but you need to understand that she is a serious liability."

Eve looked down at the floor. "I know. I've been scared to death of her ever since I bought her. I'd hoped *you* would be able to work with her, but then I had the chance to get rid of her, so I did." She looked up with apparent sincerity. "I really *am* sorry."

Her chameleon personality had taken years to develop. She'd been caught up in the glamour and intrigue of the Arab business and, somewhere along the line, greed had taken over and she'd lost her integrity.

He nodded. "So am I."

She relaxed and smiled, as though she knew the worst of the storm had passed.

"Why don't you come up for a cold beer after work? I'd really love to hear all about the show, and who was there–you know, everything."

Kurt recognized the attempt to smooth things over. *Might be a chance to find out a thing or two.*

He smiled. "Sounds good. I'll be there around four-thirty."

Eve turned to go, then stopped.

"By the way, I've been wondering...Why would Liz Barnett call *you* when she got hurt?"

Kurt watched his boss walk back to the house, and his skin prickled with irritation at her parting shot. He hadn't answered her– it was none of her damned business, and fortunately, she hadn't pursued the subject. Still, as the morning progressed, the incident fueled both his anger and his determination to get some answers. While he unloaded tack trunks, he reviewed the events of the San Francisco show. Eve had telephoned him every single day. And each day, she'd already known what had happened. *Someone was cluing her in. Was it Benton?*

He snapped the latches on the empty trunk and sat down on it, pursuing his train of thought. *If someone else did the actual drugging, I don't have a prayer of finding out, or proving it.* His brain started playing out a scenario. *Suppose...just suppose, Eve did it. She'd have had to know exactly where Liz's stalls were located. That would be easy, Benton could have told her, or she could have called the show office. Benton could also have given her the security patrol schedule, or she could have just watched and waited for an opportunity. She knew I'd be at my motel, so there'd be no chance of running into me.*

He frowned. There were loopholes in the fictitious scene, and Eve was too smart to involve anyone else. Such collusion would leave her vulnerable to discovery, or even blackmail. Again, Kurt's professional regard for Bill Benton subtracted the trainer from the plot equation. *If Eve did it, she did it alone.*

He rose and started for the barn door, his thoughts picking up momentum. In order to keep her secret, she'd have had to drive to Daly City and back in one night, but that wasn't an impossible task. Climbing up into the truck cab, he began maneuvering the long horse trailer into its regular parking spot. A glance at the trip odometer showed a round trip of 288 miles, a long drive by any standards. *She'd have to be pretty damned determined, making the trip in one night all by herself. Could she have paid someone else to do the dirty work at the show?* Kurt's mood darkened. *If she did, how the hell am I gonna find out?*

He put the mystery out of his mind for a while, while he cleaned out the horse trailer and closed it up. He dragged a hose across the driveway and began to rinse the dust from the gleaming blue Dodge Ram. His reflection in the smoke-tinted windows reminded him that he was, again, someone else's lackey.

Kurt was very particular about maintenance of the farm vehicles, and his after-show routine included a thorough cleaning, inside and out. Losing himself in the mindless task, his thoughts drifted to the last conversation with Liz that night in the tack stall. Her anger had been justified–he couldn't argue with that. She'd viewed him as the source of all her problems, an opinion not far from the truth.

He grabbed a rumpled show schedule from the floor of the truck and stuffed it into the trash bag, then removed his hotel receipt from the dashboard to give to Eve for reimbursement. He squinted at the receipt, and an idea began to take shape. Leaning back in the seat, he looked through the windshield at the big house. Eve reclined on the deck, enjoying her usual midmorning sunbath. He looked from her prone figure to the red Corvette parked next to the truck. *If she did drive to Daly City and back, she had to get gas somewhere along the way.*

He jumped to the ground and walked around the truck to the other side, crouching down between the two vehicles. His pulse jerked as he reached for the door handle of the Vette. He looked up again to be sure she couldn't see him and, praying that she hadn't set the alarm, snatched the door open and slipped inside.

Eve's car was always a pigsty, and he grimaced at the careless treatment of a beautiful vehicle. He poked through the rubbish on the passenger seat and, finding nothing of interest, leaned across the console and checked the floor. *Dammit, I was so sure!* Discouraged, he sat back in the soft leather seat, and checked on Eve again. He reached for the door handle, giving the interior one last cursory glance. He spotted a flash of yellow tucked deep between the driver's seat and the console. He pulled it out, and grinned triumphantly. It was a parking violation warning, written up by Cow Palace Security and dated the day of the stallion class. The time written on the ticket was 3:05 am. He stuck it into his pocket, and checked the crevice beside the seat again, digging a little deeper. When he withdrew his hand, he had the answer: a dated credit card gas receipt from a station just east of Oakland, stamped with Eve's name and the time the gas had been pumped–3:55 am.

Forty-Two

Kurt stared at his image in the mirror as he combed his damp hair. Sharp features stared back at him, dark eyes challenging. What he was about to do seemed slimy and underhanded, but his determination to get to the bottom of the drugging incident spurred his resolve.

Remnants of the shower still glistened across his shoulders and chest, and he whisked them away with a towel. Splashing aftershave over his neck, he winced at his blatant preparations to charm Eve into disaster. A few minutes later, he glanced in the mirror again, noted the hard look in his eyes, and headed out the door. The warmth of the sun had faded, a sure sign that October was on its way. Walking across the lawn toward the big house, he felt a deeper chill.

Eve wasn't in sight when he stepped onto the deck. He rapped lightly on the open door, and she peeked out of the kitchen.

"Hi, come on in. I'm defrosting some steaks." She gave him a sly smile. "Hungry?"

His stomach tightened. *Does this woman have a conscience?*

She walked toward him, her red hair loose and flowing over her shoulders, her face glowing with an almost flirtatious expression.

He smiled. "My, my! Don't *you* look nice."

His conscience chided him for how low he'd sunk.

Out on the deck, he purposely selected a seat that would give him face-to-face space with Eve. She handed him a frosty mug of beer, leaning over and providing him with a glimpse of tanned cleavage. He caught the scent of her freshly washed hair and heavy, exotic perfume. The ploy was transparent, and his determination deepened.

She settled herself into the chair next to him and raised her glass. "Here's to good times ahead."

Her eagerness was like that of a child waiting for a bedtime story. "Tell me everything about the show."

Choosing his words carefully, Kurt delivered a day-by-day description of the event, the classes, the other exhibitors, and the winners. He didn't mention Liz's attendance at the show, preferring to bide his time until Eve brought it up. He knew she would, thinking she was home free.

The sun dropped, taking the temperature with it, and Eve gestured toward the house.

"It's cold out here. Let's go inside. I'll get the steaks going."

While she fired up the grill, Kurt glanced into the dining room. Fine china, crystal glasses, flowers, and a bottle of wine were set up on the lace-covered table. She clearly thought he'd be easily manipulated. His jaw tightened with distaste. *Is _she_ ever in for a big surprise!*

Eve had almost finished her second glass of wine when Kurt pounced.

"Bill Benton tried to buy Liz's colt the day before the class."

Her glass stopped in mid-air, and a frown knitted her eyebrows. "What are you talking about? He's buying Ebony."

Kurt kept his tone soft and even. "He's not stupid, Eve. He knows a great horse when he sees one, and Liz's colt has fantastic potential."

Regaining a little of her composure, she shrugged. "Well, he certainly never mentioned it to me. He said she had a problem with her horse, that's all. Illegal drugs or something."

Kurt's face stiffened with anticipation. Her guilt showed in the way she held herself while she lied to him. He glanced down at his plate, mentally suppressing the urge to walk out. When he looked up again, Eve was pouring herself another glass of wine. Her face was flushed, and her hands trembled, causing red drops to splatter across the white lace, but she didn't seem to notice.

Her voice took on a hard edge. "So, tell me. Did she have a problem or not?"

Kurt sat back in the chair, and arranged himself into a relaxed pose. "You tell *me*."

Her self-control was slipping. In a matter of minutes, he would have enough to nail her. She set the wine bottle down hard, causing the silverware to jump.

"Kurt, why do you keep acting like you don't know anything? Billy said you were with her every time he turned around." The green eyes narrowed maliciously. "In fact, Billy seems to think *you* had something to do with knocking the colt out of the class..." She paused and smiled wickedly. "Which makes sense, since you *did* have a large commission riding on Ebony's title."

Kurt sat forward, cold resolve infusing his thoughts. His moment was near, and the excitement of moving in for the kill was almost seductive.

"I wonder if *Billy* would appreciate knowing you're the one responsible for the colt's disqualification."

Eve's exaggerated look of astonishment added a theatrical effect to her words.

"You *have* to be kidding! You *know* I was right here the whole time. You talked to me on the phone every day."

He watched her pretense for a moment.

"Yeah, I did. But once you got your obligatory phone call out of the way, you'd be unaccountable until you called me again the next day. You had all night to get the deed done."

Her expression changed rapidly, moving from indignant to downright ugly.

"How *dare* you accuse me of this! Who do y–"

Kurt rose to his full height and stared down at her.

"*You* drugged the colt, didn't you?"

She said nothing, just looked down at her glass. A minute later, she raised her eyes in defiance.

"I've struggled for years, trying to take Aliqua to the top. My horses are outstanding, but I've never had anyone to help me. Then you came along with your magical powers over them, and I thought

I could have my dreams. Ebony was going to be my chance. I counted on you, and you screwed it up."

Kurt didn't flinch. "Did you, or didn't you drug the colt?"

She lifted her chin self-righteously and squared her shoulders. "The horse wasn't hurt. He can be shown again next year."

Kurt felt the bile rise in his throat, and he took a deep breath, resisting the urge to shake the daylights out of her.

"The horse is fine. Liz is *not*. Her record has a damaging smear on it, and *you* have to fix it, whether you wielded the needle yourself, or paid someone else to do it."

She rose and looked him straight in the eye. "You have no proof that I had anything to do with it."

He gave her a cold smile. "You think not?"

Forty-Three

Liz awoke to sun streaming through the bedroom window and the smell of freshly brewed coffee drifting on the air. She smiled and closed her eyes again, knowing Kurt was downstairs taking care of things, taking care of *her*. A quiet rustle caught her attention and she looked toward the door. A handsome face peeked around the doorjamb, and her heart thumped. She felt an overwhelming urge to beckon him to her bed, and lose herself in his arms.

His soft voice prodded her back to reality. "Good Morning. How are you feeling?"

"I don't know. I haven't moved anything yet."

She took a deep breath and attempted to sit up, sending excruciating pain through her shoulder. She gasped and fell back on the pillow.

"Easy, Hon. You're going to be very sore for a while."

He moved to the side of the bed and slipped his arm under her back for support while she tried again. When she'd managed to gain an upright position, he plumped the pillows behind her back, then stroked her hair lightly, sending arrows of delight through her thoughts.

"Ready for coffee? Breakfast? Drugs?"

She noticed her face didn't hurt quite so much when she smiled.

"Coffee and drugs, please. I'll wait on the breakfast for awhile."

He disappeared through the door and she heard his quick tread on the stairs. He whistled softly under his breath, and she listened after him. How comfortable and *right* it felt to have him there. *You've come a long way, Lizzie. Now if you can just get your ego under control, you might have a chance for happiness with this guy.*

As Kurt fixed a coffee tray for the patient, his brain churned. *Should I tell her about last night with Eve?* His first inclination was to leave it alone, given his track record when it came to explaining things to Liz. They'd finally come to a point where they weren't at each other's throat every time he turned around. He did *not* want to jeopardize that.

Anyway, it'd be better to wait until I've really proven Eve's involvement. If that's even possible. He stared at the milk jug in his hand. *I have good, strong evidence, but I'm really an uninvolved bystander. Liz has to be the one to press the issue.* He slowly set the milk on the tray. *Does she have the gumption to do it?*

A few minutes later, he sat on the edge of Liz's bed and cradled a steaming mug between his hands as he brought her up to date on Muscala.

"Eve feels real bad you got hurt."

"It's my own damned fault. I should have–"

"No! Horse owners have a responsibility to inform any prospective buyer about a horse with problems. It doesn't matter what kind of problem–training, personality, foaling quirks– whatever. I don't believe even a pre-purchase exam would have given you the information about that mare's weird personality. It was fully Eve's responsibility to tell you about it."

"Temperament *is* hard to assess in a single exam...But, you know, I *had* seen her strange behavior–and worried about it. You'd think I'd have been more careful."

He stood up. "Eve takes care of Eve. Don't ever forget that." He stroked her hair softly. "I have to go. I'll be back later."

After he'd gone, Liz's thoughts turned to business. She needed to check in with Doc Sams. She felt terrible that she'd let him down, after convincing him to allow her to step in while he rested. However, he'd been very concerned and sympathetic, telling her to take it easy, that he was fine and the work would still be there when she felt better.

She gazed at her battered reflection in the mirror. The woman who stared back had many bruises, and not all of them were physical.

By mid-afternoon, she broke down and took more pain medication, eventually falling into a deep sleep filled with fractured dreams of Muscala, Kurt in armor on a charging black steed, and Fair Lady with a unicorn horn. Someone sounded a trumpet, and she jerked awake.

Kurt's voice on the phone sent shivers of happiness across her skin. "Did I wake you?"

"It's okay, you can't imagine the dream I had."

A chuckle. "Is it censored?"

Her face warmed. "No, just crazy."

"I'll be over around five. I just wanted to see how you were doing."

She put the phone into its cradle, and lay back again. *I could really get used to this.* The phone rang again, and Colleen's voice bubbled through the receiver.

"I got your message. What's up?"

Liz's tale left Colleen aghast.

"God! Do ya need me to come over an' help out?"

Liz's joy formed her smile. "No, Kurt is taking care of everything."

Colleen's tone sounded wicked. "Mmmmm, *That* must be a treat!"

Liz ignored the invitation to expand, then changed the subject.

"By the way, Colleen, what's in Sacramento?"

"A guy! I met a really neat guy, and guess what? He's *not* in the horse business–he's a *real* person!"

Liz laughed at their private joke that anyone in the horse business had to be either crazy or retarded. Colleen's happiness was deep and genuine as she described her new friend. A few minutes later, she brought up the subject of the homeless horses.

"How much longer are we going to baby-sit for Marilyn?"

Liz frowned, remembering Frank Jones's visit.

"I don't know. I pretty much squelched any more sales to that

Jones guy. There was something about him I really didn't like. And he only wanted to buy *my* horses."

She flinched a little at the white lie, but didn't know how to explain her reluctance to sell anything to the man.

"Yeah, he was kind of creepy, but his money's as good as anyone's."

"What if he's a buyer for the killers?"

Colleen was silent for a few seconds. "Well, if he is, then the horses he bought here are already dogfood."

Liz gulped at her gaff. "Oh, Colleen! I'm sorry. I guess I'm just a little paranoid."

Before hanging up, Colleen promised to come by and visit sometime in the next couple of days.

In the quiet of the study, Liz reflected on Colleen's tone. Though the opinion hadn't been voiced, it had been clear that her friend viewed Liz as being too personally involved with the horses to make good business decisions.

That evening, after a light supper of grilled cheese sandwiches and tomato soup, Kurt cleared the table and washed up the dishes, humming as he put everything away in the cupboards. Liz sat at the kitchen table, enjoying the spectacle. His shirtsleeves were rolled back, revealing muscular forearms dusted with fine black hair that sent erotic messages to her brain. He glanced over and winked, and she opened her mouth to tease him about being a good househusband, then recoiled. *Good grief, don't you ever learn?* She remembered the results of the last time she'd alluded to permanence, and her pulse jumped.

A second later, his features took on a strange expression. He grinned and tossed the dishtowel on the counter.

"And what, exactly, is going through that pretty head?"

She blushed and looked away. "Nothing. Just thinking about getting back to work tomorrow."

He slipped into a chair and took her hand. "Don't rush it, Hon."

She savored the warmth and gentleness in his soft touch, wanting the moment to last forever.

"The drug report from U.S. Equestrian came today. Ashiiqah

was clean...like I had any *doubt*." She gazed down at their clasped hands. "But my big plans for Karma sure got screwed up."

Kurt's fingers tightened around hers, his voice firm.

"Liz, you'll get through this and be able to continue. This winter, you can work on your show techniques, polish your green horses, do any number of productive things that will make you a more formidable opponent in the ring." He grinned. "You put another year on Karma, and his wins will mean a lot more as young stallion than as a cute baby."

His efforts to make her feel better didn't work. She shook her head vigorously.

"No, I'm through with the whole thing. I no longer want any part of the show circus."

He sat back and looked at her thoughtfully.

"Quitting? I find that hard to believe. I distinctly remember a conversation about not wanting to be 'just another breeder'."

"Right. That was before I was steamrolled in front of God and everybody."

"Liz, if you decide not to show your horses any more, it needs to be an informed decision, one that you make based on a great deal of thought, not an emotional knee-jerk. Breeders show their horses for a reason–to provide a record of excellence for the animals they hope will reproduce those qualities and traits that make them outstanding horses."

Liz started to protest, but he held up his hand.

"Hear me out. If the whole mess were erased tomorrow morning, would you still want to take Karma to Nationals?"

"Of course, but–"

"Case closed. Give yourself some time to work through the anger of the raw deal, then start making plans for the future."

She nodded and looked down at their entwined fingers. She felt chastened, knowing that he spoke the truth from his own painful experience.

"You're probably right. I'll give it some thought." She looked up, viewing him through narrowed eyes. "Do you know much about Bill Benton?"

"I know he's one of the best trainers in the business. Some

folks think he's a little heavy-handed with the horses, but most people don't understand what's involved with keeping these animals under control. Why do you ask?"

"I just wondered if you knew he was sleeping with his boss."

Kurt shook his head. "Liz, it goes on all the time, but it's really no different than any other industry. Ambitious people do what they must to get where they want to be."

Again, he spoke from experience, sending an uncomfortable ripple through Liz's stomach.

He released her hands and sat back. "How'd you find *that* out?"

"The sheriff talked to every exhibitor in the colt class. He said Bill had an alibi, but was cagey about telling me what it was. I just put two and two together."

Kurt looked away toward the window. "Yeah, he grilled *me* pretty good, too."

A flash of guilt surged through Liz's chest, remembering the tense scene in the aisle.

"I'm awfully sorry about Patrick. I'm sure he just thought he was being helpful."

"Yeah, big help. Listen, you never told me what drug was used on Karma."

"It was Diazepam–which I thought was a strange choice. It's usually used on aggressive stallions to keep them from savaging the mares when they breed."

As she watched, a veil of anger descended over Kurt's dark eyes.

Later that evening, Liz reviewed the conversation, and Kurt's puzzling reaction. She'd tried to pursue the subject, but he'd been evasive. *Even if he suspects Eve, I can't imagine how he could prove anything.*

She sighed and turned her thoughts to the coming week. Doc Sams had insisted that she take a couple more days to recuperate before trying to resume her farm calls, but with each day, she felt better and itched to get back to work.

The phone rang and she grabbed it, hoping to hear Kurt's husky voice. To her disappointment, Marilyn's greeting rattled through the receiver.

"Hi, Liz. I wanted to tell ya, I've decided to move to Oakland to live with my sister. I'm leavin' next week."

Liz couldn't hide her surprise. "What about your farm? And the horses?"

"Farm's for sale...an' I thought I'd just sign all the registration papers over to you. You can do whatever you want with the horses. If you sell 'em, fine. Keep the money for their upkeep. I've caused you so much trouble, it seems only right."

Liz was stunned. The woman was going to walk away from the only life she'd ever known.

Kurt scowled at the invoice for supplies he'd ordered two months ago. Two vials of Diazepam had been logged into the farm inventory, enough to carry them through breeding season, which wouldn't begin for another two months.

He moved into the tack room and unlocked the medicine cabinet. A minute later, he nodded with nasty satisfaction. Only one vial remained on the shelf. Though he couldn't prove anything by it, the extra information strengthened his resolve about what he needed to do.

Forty-Four

By the following afternoon, Liz's muscles had loosened up and she moved around comfortably. The shoulder still hurt quite a bit, but she was able to manage most ordinary tasks, like showering, dressing, and making tea. Five days away from the barn had taken its toll on her psyche, and she needed a "horse fix."

She strolled through the empty barn, delighted to see how well Kurt had cared for it. He'd picked the stalls and filled them with fresh bedding, water buckets brimmed, and the aisle floor had been swept spotlessly clean. She wandered into the feed room and stuffed some treats into her pocket, then went out into the sunshine, heading up the path to the pasture. Fair Lady lifted her nose from the sparse grass and whinnied loudly. The herd followed the beautiful mare as she trotted down to the fence, and Liz's heart ached with love. Warm, velvety muzzles carefully gobbled alfalfa cubes from her palm, then eagerly checked her pockets for more.

Miss Marcy pushed her way to the front of the group, making soft noises in her throat. She stretched her head over the fence and nuzzled Liz's cheek.

Stroking the old lady's neck, Liz murmured, "I'll never sell you. You're mine now."

Marilyn's generosity with the horses had been a big surprise, but Liz knew it would be foolish to try to keep all of them. They didn't fit in with her carefully laid plans for Legacy. She looked at the animals she'd acquired as a result of the fire. The gelding with the shoulder wound was a polite and gentle young man, and would make someone a nice saddle horse. He'd be easy to sell. The other three horses were mares of varying ages and quality, also saleable. She sighed. *Guess I better call Jones back. I can't be so picky about this.*

Fatigue caught up to her and she left the fence to settle in her favorite place on the farm–a huge boulder surrounded by lush green grass and spongy moss. She gingerly lowered herself to the ground, and watched the horses return to the serious business of grazing.

Once she started back to work, there wouldn't be much time for such leisurely luxury. The thought saddened her. She'd loved being home, caring for her horses and making plans for the future of Legacy, even though it had been as a result of her failing practice. She reviewed the two weeks just prior to the regional show, carefully analyzing each farm call she'd made, and the atmosphere attendant on each one. The ranchers' rigid resistance to her had lessened, and she'd begun to feel optimistic that her career could flourish in the beautiful foothills. Diligence and patience, that's all it would take. Though she couldn't think about it right then, she'd have to decide if her pride would let her take a shot at showing horses again. Only time would tell.

A familiar voice from down by the barn interrupted her thoughts, and she looked at her watch. *Five o'clock. Right on time.*

"I'm up here by the pasture!"

Kurt emerged from behind the trees and, a moment later, dropped into the grass beside her.

"Just couldn't stay away, could you? How are you feeling?"

"Pretty good. I think I can start doing my chores again, with the help of pain-killers."

She glanced at his profile as he watched the horses graze. She loved having him there on a regular basis. Her return to work would bring an end to the delightful arrangement. *Maybe I could pretend for a little while longer.* He turned and looked at her intently, as though he could read her thoughts.

She grinned. "What? Did I drift? It's the drugs."

He patted her hand. "I don't want you to push yourself to get back to work. I can help out as long as you need me."

Need you? I need you non-stop. His dark eyes showed a tiny flicker of emotion, but an instant later, it disappeared and he looked away.

She laid her hand on his arm. "You've been so good to help me the way you have...especially since we've had so much trouble between us."

He turned, his eyes filled with compassion, his face softened by the shadow of his thoughts.

"Liz, I haven't been very good at explaining myself, and I know I have a defensive streak, but I am *so* sorry for all the pain I've caused you, both directly and indirectly."

She leaned over and brushed her lips against his warm cheek. "Let's put it all behind us."

He gently pulled her into his arms and kissed her, long and tenderly. She kissed him back, her heart overflowing with the magic of being with him. When their lips parted, she gazed invitingly into his eyes, her face warm with the excitement of the kiss. *I don't ever want to be without you again. Do I dare tell you that?*

Gently, he released her, his voice husky with emotion. "Let's get you back down to the house, and I'll bring the horses in."

Her heart fell with disappointment at the abrupt ending to the romantic moment. She tried to catch his eye, but he avoided looking at her as he helped her up. Minutes later, they walked silently hand-in-hand down the hill.

When he returned to the house, he sat down and searched her face from across the kitchen table. His manner seemed subdued, almost sad.

"Liz, I want you to think about something."

Her heart faltered. "I'm listening."

"I want you to seriously consider suing Eve for Karma's attack."

The idea surprised her so much she couldn't reply. He reached across the table and took her hand.

"I mean it. You are the only one who can flush her out."

"But I have no proof!"

He smiled wickedly. "No, but *I* do." He reached into his pocket and withdrew a small folded square of paper. "These prove that she was at the Cow Palace in the wee hours, just long enough to give Karma an injection."

Liz stared at the gas receipt with Eve's name imprinted. The timing was perfect.

"But, these don't *prove* she did it, just that she was there."

"I know, but I think if she finds out that you're pressing criminal charges, she might be willing to make a deal. She may have no conscience, but she definitely has a brain, and I don't think she'd chance being convicted."

"You're basically talking about a bluff."

"That's right. Winner take all."

Liz sat back and closed her eyes, unable to consider all the facets of such a plan.

"I'll think about it. Right now, I need to go to bed."

She rose, and Kurt stepped up close.

"Are you sure you want to start working again? I can come back tomorrow."

She feigned confidence she didn't feel. "I'll be fine. I feel pretty good–after all, I've had five days off."

He grasped her hands, holding them firmly, his eyes dark with apology, his somber expression driving through the pit of her stomach.

"I have to go out of town for awhile. Will you call Colleen if you need help?"

Her heart thumped with apprehension, and she looked down at the strong, capable hands holding hers so gently.

"Where are you going?"

She felt awkward with the question, but couldn't help herself.

His smooth features revealed nothing. "I have to take care of some business. Now, promise me you'll call Colleen."

"I promise."

He pulled her close, holding her firmly, his chin resting lightly on top of her head. She heard his heart thudding steadily between them. Her own pulse slowed, and her uneasiness faded as she basked in the warmth of his arms and the tenderness of the embrace. Unwilling to think otherwise, she told herself that everything would be all right.

Forty-Five

Kurt tossed the last of his meager belongings into the back of the truck, then looked around at the generous pastures and elegant barn. *Too bad. Well, there's always something better on the horizon.* He spotted Eve heading toward him. *I hope she doesn't make a scene. I just want the hell outta here.*

She looked ten years older than when she'd hired him. Her features were tight, but she forced a smile.

"Kurt, I wish you'd change your mind. I know you're upset with me, but you could really make something of yourself here at Aliqua. I can pay your commission now, and I'll–"

"Eve, this is the way I want it. I can't stay here under the circumstances–I've already told you that. And you can keep the commission. I don't want any part of money involved with a shady win."

Eve colored, but plunged on. "But, it's so late in the season– what am I going to do for a trainer? Who's going to show my horses?"

Kurt snorted. *Well, it sure didn't take her long to start worrying about herself and <u>her</u> future, did it, Buddy Boy?*

"You'll find someone. There are dozens of trainers out there who'd give their right arm for the chance to show horses like yours." His jaw tightened. "Especially now that you're *on the map*, as you like to put it."

He gave her a hard look. "I hope your conscience will guide you to do the right thing."

She reached for his arm. "Kurt, I–"

He took her outstretched hand, dropped his apartment key into it, then tipped his hat.

"Well, Eve. It's been real."

With that, he climbed into his truck and drove down the hill through the giant pines, never once looking into the rearview mirror.

Liz had eaten half her breakfast when Colleen breezed through the screen door.

"How's the victim? Whoa! Nice shiner!"

Liz grinned. "I'm still awfully stiff, but at least nothing hurts too much."

"Is there anything I can do to help ya today?"

Liz finished the last of her coffee. "Actually, yes. You can help me take the horses out. I'm so slow that by the time I get them out there, it'll be time to bring them back in."

A few minutes later, Liz opened the barn doors, and anxious whinnies echoed through the air.

Colleen laughed. "Pretty spoilt, I'd say."

"Yes, they certainly are. I'll probably pay the price for pampering them so much, but I love it, and that's the way it will stay."

Colleen looked around at the horses who eagerly anticipated their morning turnout.

"Where's that mare that attacked ya?"

"That's right, I haven't told you the outcome of that mess. Eve took the mare back."

Colleen looked astonished, and Liz nodded. "Can you believe it? Kurt pulled it off somehow."

Colleen's expression changed, became serious, and she peered closely at Liz.

"That's pretty amazing, don'tcha think? I mean, horse contracts being what they are, and Eve being the way *she* is. Do ya know how he did it?"

"No, I didn't ask. Does it matter?"

Colleen stepped over and slipped her arm around Liz's waist.

"I hate to keep playing devil's advocate, but ya know nothin' about Kurt, or his relationship to Eve. Don't you have questions about him?"

Liz searched her friend's face for some clue to the thoughts behind the caution.

"Is there something you know, that I *should?*"

Colleen's expression changed to pity, and she sighed. "No, nothin' specific. I just see ya getting tangled up with a man who can't even come up with a past, let alone promise you a future."

Liz hesitated. *I should level with her, let her know everything's okay. She's only trying to be a good friend.*

"Grab a horse and I'll fill you in on the way to the pasture."

Later, Colleen lounged back in the kitchen chair, clearly mulling over the tale of the past two months of passion and despair. Finally, she leaned forward and looked at Liz seriously.

"Sounds like a day at the carnival–thrilling rides, and peril at every turn."

Liz smiled weakly, recognizing that Colleen's analogy was proof her opinions about Kurt hadn't changed.

"Colleen, he dropped everything to come here and take me to the hospital, then stayed and looked after me and the horses. Doesn't that say something?"

Colleen didn't answer right away, then shook her head.

"I'm not sure. It could, but it could also say he just had a severe case of guilty conscience for all the pain and trouble he's caused ya."

Liz became exasperated that she couldn't convince her friend of Kurt's sincerity. However, as her annoyance grew, a nagging worry also took root. *What if she's right? Maybe I'm too close to the situation to see clearly...And too much in love.*

As she sorted through the disturbing thoughts, Colleen's voice broke in, her tone sympathetic.

"Liz, I'm not sayin' he's bad. I just think ya should take things real slow. In the short time you've known him, you've been riding a roller coaster of emotions. Can ya imagine a lifetime like that? Just think about it, okay?"

She rose to leave. "Do ya want me to come by tonight and help ya bring everybody in?"

Liz felt very tired.

"Yes, please. And thanks for the pep talk–I appreciate your concern. I'll be careful."

After a short nap, Liz settled onto the couch with her medical journals to catch up on the backlog of reading. She thumbed through the pages, picking and choosing articles that might apply to a rural practice. She planned to drive over to Doc's place the next day, and set up her schedule again. Thinking about the future, a thrill of eagerness curled through the pit of her stomach. Would Kurt be any part of that future? A tiny shadow of worry crept into her brain.

Reviewing all the things that had happened since she'd met him, Liz saw the sharp contrasts in his behavior. The original macho surliness had been replaced by a pleasant, but hands-off, attitude. After his soul-baring confession in Tahoe–and their passionate night together–he'd retreated again, but had bounced back into her life at the regional show. The memory of *that* horrible experience rolled over her. Kurt's attitude had changed again, but by then, she didn't trust him, or herself. Yet, when she'd needed him, when it had been critically important, he'd been instantly at her side. *Talk about a roller coaster ride...Kurt's the one who's been all over the park.*

She sighed and closed the magazine. *I'll just have to wait and see what happens after he comes back from wherever he went.*

Forty-Six

Thinking about the possibility of a future with Kurt made Liz all the more determined to find out something about him.

Colleen picked up on the second ring, and Liz worded her request carefully.

"I'm researching some bloodlines for prospective studs. Do you have any back issues of the *Arab Horse* magazine? I thought it might be a good place to start."

"Sure, how far back do you want to go?"

Liz pretended to think for a minute. "Um, about ten or eleven years. That should give me an idea which stallions have maintained popularity, sired winning offspring, stuff like that."

Colleen promised to bring the magazines over on the weekend, and Liz hung up, feeling pleased with her ingenuity.

Feelings of satisfaction changed to anxiety as she dialed an attorney's office in Sacramento. She'd given Kurt's idea a lot of thought. It hadn't occurred to her that anything might be done outside the confines of the industry, but logically, since the attack had happened in a public place, civil law should have some jurisdiction. Even if nothing came of it, she owed it to Karma to see if she could correct the situation.

Forty minutes later, she hung up, feeling encouraged. The lawyer had been interested and sympathetic, offering to start by sending a letter to Eve. Liz made copies of her evidence, put them in an envelope, and walked out to the mailbox. As simple as it seemed, having made a decision felt good.

Liz spent the next few days traveling from ranch to ranch, taking care of all kinds of routine problems–some big, some small. For the most part, the clients she called on were polite, but distant. One afternoon, she received an emergency call to one of the cattle ranches in the area. During the drive, she tried to sort out the differences between practicing in rural California, as compared to the big barns of Kentucky–her only measuring stick. Thoroughbred operations were carefully controlled, with a dozen or so people involved with the horses, their care, and their reproduction. All aspects of the business were confined to limited areas, and nothing was left to chance. Veterinary care was easy to retain, and the larger facilities usually employed a resident veterinarian, or shared one with a farm close by.

She guieed the truck across a bumpy cattle guard, then headed down a long, dusty road. In the distance, the ranch house and sprawling barns of Rocking M Hereford Ranch looked like miniature buildings arranged on a model railroad layout. The cattle operation was a perfect example of the opposite end of Liz's comparative spectrum. Beef cattle herds were every bit as valuable as race horses, but the hundreds or thousands of acres required to keep so many animals placed the ranches a long way from civilization, turning a routine farm call into a travel adventure.

Based on her experience so far, it seemed that her clients' distrust came from a need for self-preservation, more than anything else. Doc's assessment of the locals was valid. Life in those parts was not easy, and the loss of valuable livestock due to a vet's ineptitude wouldn't be tolerated. It would just take time and patience to gain the confidence of the ranchers.

The truck rolled to a stop beside one of the large brown barns, and Liz looked down at the schedule. She'd been called to examine some newborn calves. The sound of hoof-beats caught her attention and she turned, just as a stocky sorrel Quarter Horse came to a dusty stop, three feet away. The jowly man perched in the saddle stared at her for a second, unsmiling. When he spoke, his chest wheezed, most likely from a lifetime of cigarettes.

His tone was terse. "Where's Doc?"

Oh, great, another battle.

"He's taking some time off. He hasn't been feeling well. Where are the calves you want me to examine?"

If the cowboy's expression served as any indication, he wanted to send her on her way. He grunted, then slid off the horse and walked toward the barn. Liz followed, irritation pushing against her self-restraint.

They entered the dim barn, and the rancher hollered at someone on the far side.

"Nick, git up here!"

A minute later, a skinny man in dusty jeans and a stained work shirt joined them. The three of them stood beside a small holding pen containing a couple of cows. Two tiny calves lay curled up in the trampled straw, apparently asleep.

"Nick brought 'em in a coupla hours ago. Thinks they mighta been attacked by coyotes or somethin'. Got them bloody spots all over 'em."

Liz shuddered. Calves as young as these wouldn't have survived a coyote attack. They'd tangled with something else. She stepped into the pen, carefully gauging the anxiety level of the cows. They seemed unconcerned, watching her with large eyes and chewing their cuds.

She knelt beside one of the small brown bodies. The soft baby fur was ragged and crusted with dried blood in dozens of places across the calf's chest and neck. Liz leaned closer and lightly touched one of the larger areas. The calf opened its large dark eyes and struggled to get to its feet, without success. Liz continued examining the area, feeling the heat in the skin and observing the distribution of the wounds. Moving to the other calf, she noted that the sores and distribution pattern were identical.

"Where did you find them? Were they together?"

The skinny man answered. "Off in a grove of trees, away from the rest of the herd."

Liz thought for a minute. She rose to her feet and looked at the two silent men standing outside the pen, then took a deep breath and plunged in.

"I think they got tangled up in a hornet's nest."

The big cowboy threw his head back and guffawed loudly.

"Oh, brother! That's real good!" He pinned her with his ugly beady eyes and snarled, "Is that what they're teachin' vets these days?"

His response came as no surprise, but Liz'd had enough. She stepped up to within inches of his fat paunch and glowered up at him.

"Would you like to bet money that I'm wrong?"

He blinked with surprise at the confidence behind her words. She didn't give him a chance to answer.

"I'll tell you what. I'll give these calves a shot of antihistamine, and if they don't get better, you don't have to pay me."

The two men looked at each other as though they thought she'd lost her mind. She turned and strode out to the truck, muttering to herself and shaking her head. Most animal owners never considered the simple things like bee stings, poison ivy, toxic plants...toads. *Those poor little babies don't yet have the immune system to tolerate a serious hornet attack.*

The two ranchers were leaning on the rail when she returned. Neither of them said anything as Liz entered the pen, but their smirks infuriated her.

Twenty minutes later, both calves were on their feet, bawling and hungry. Liz entered the pen again and caught one of them. She moved her fingers over the sores, satisfied that the allergic reaction had almost dissipated. She gave the rancher a triumphant look.

He nodded and removed his hat. "Ma'am, I owe you an apology."

She grinned. "And ninety-eight dollars."

On Saturday, Liz was putting out the evening hay when Colleen showed up. She followed Liz into the feed room, a mischievous grin playing across her pert features.

"Hey, can I get a job at this-here fancy facility? You know, now that you're so busy with your practice?"

Liz raised an eyebrow. "How could *you* help me? What about Fairhill?"

"The Sharps're thinkin' about reducing their herd by half, and they're not breedin' any mares next season. Effie said they'd been worried about how their retirement plans would affect *me*, since they'd only need me half-days. So, I'm yours part-time, if you'll have me."

"Will I ever!"

Lately, one of Liz's biggest concerns had been how she'd be able to care for her horses and manage a full practice at the same time. She'd have to break down and hire someone, but disliked the thought of having a stranger in her barn.

"I can't pay you much right now. I'm still scraping the bottom of my financial barrel, but things are starting to pick up. Can you live with that?"

"Sure. Listen, I have those magazines you wanted."

Five minutes later, Colleen reached into the back of her truck and hauled out two large bundles of magazines tied with baling twine.

"Thanks, Colleen. This will help a lot."

Her friend climbed up, settled behind the wheel, and peered through the window, an impish grin brightening her face.

"Be sure an' let me know if you find out anything juicy about him."

As she pored through the stack of heavy magazines, Liz felt foolish at how transparent her charade must have seemed. *At least she's quit nagging me about him.* Turning the glossy pages filled with tales of success, she became lost again in the world of showing expensive Arabian horses.

An hour later, only two issues remained unread. Her disappointment was sharp. She'd been sure there'd be some professional information about Kurt in the magazines, but so far, there'd only been a show photo of him, posed with a blue-ribbon mare at a small show in Colorado. She dropped the magazine onto the pile and sighed.

If he was so good, why wasn't anything written about him? Suddenly, she grabbed up the magazine again and peered at the date.

"Well, no wonder! This is too old, maybe even when he was just starting out."

She picked up the remaining two issues and checked the dates, matching them with Kurt's story. *Bingo! October and November of the last year he worked for Della.*

On page twelve of the October magazine, Liz found a trainer interview with Kurt DeVallio, touted as the Arabian industry's "rising star." Barely breathing, she absorbed every word in the article.

Interviewer: "Can you tell us how you've achieved such success with the Arabian breed?"

DeVallio: "Training starts with attitude. Attitude involves understanding a few things about horses and the way they think. Horses have a short attention span, from about five minutes to a maximum of twenty. Working in that window is the key–and remembering that you're dealing with the mentality of a two- or three-year-old child."

Liz could hear his husky voice saying those words.

Interviewer: "Do you start training your horses very young?"

DeVallio: "Absolutely. I never let them get started with nipping and biting, especially the colts. They learn right away that I'm the boss, and they accept that. A horse has to respect you, or you can't teach him anything."

Interviewer: "What about horses that are already trained?"

DeVallio: "Same thing. Respect. If you're having a problem, you have to go back and figure out what happened before you got the horse. What kind of training has it had, and how can you reverse the bad habits. It all goes back to a trainer's attitude. The horse knows. He feels everything you think through the lead rope."

Liz grinned, remembering his skill with Karma.

Interviewer: "Anything else important to training?"

DeVallio: "Always let your horse know when he does it right. Praise him, pet him...He'll want to repeat it. You want the horse to respond because he wants to, not because he's afraid <u>not</u> to."

The end of the article listed Kurt's long list of important wins with Arabians, including several national championships the year before, and predictions for his future as one of the nation's top horse trainers. Anticipating the end of the story, she eagerly picked up the November issue. Six hundred pages glistened with lavish photographs, show results, and congratulatory advertisements for all the champions of the national show that year. Forty minutes later, Liz dropped the book back onto the pile. Not one word about Kurt, not even a small picture. It was as though he'd ceased to exist.

Liz's busy schedule had pushed her anxiety about Kurt's silence to the farthest recesses of her brain. However, in quiet moments, and at night when she wrestled with sleep, her misgivings muscled their way into the forefront. Researching his past didn't help her frame of mind, either, only reinforcing her admiration for his skill and his deep understanding of horses.

Recalling the look on his face before he'd left her, and the quick surge of panic she'd felt, a cold fear of abandonment crept into her heart.

Forty-Seven

Kurt lounged against the polished mahogany doorjamb of the office, watching a tall woman leaf through papers in a file cabinet in the corner.

"Hello, Della."

She wheeled around, her tanned face wide with unpleasant surprise. "What are *you* doing here?"

He stepped into the familiar surroundings and offered a humorless smile.

"It's time to play truth or consequences."

She snapped the file drawer shut, then moved briskly to the desk to shuffle some papers.

"I can't imagine what you're talking about. What do you want?"

"I've been talking to some of the locals. There are a few who would like to see you go down in flames."

She said nothing, but her face tightened with tension.

Kurt continued. "I need you to clear my name with the show board, and let me pick up the pieces of my life. You're the only one who can do that, and I'm asking you politely."

He moved to the trophy case that housed only a third of the honors he'd won for the farm. The remaining trophies were lavishly displayed in the big house. His heart twanged at the thought of how close he'd come to real success as a professional trainer. He'd been within a few months of going out on his own, never again forced to answer to anyone but himself. His only crime had been wanting to have a normal life, a warm and loving relationship with Dottie.

Della's voice broke into the distant thoughts.

"You *are* kidding, of course? Your illegal activities nearly cost me my reputation."

He stepped up close, his eyes almost level with hers.

"*Your* reputation? Who do you think you're kidding?"

A curtain of apathy descended over Della's features. "I'm not kidding anyone. Now please leave my property."

He stepped back, keeping his tone level. "Okay. If you won't help me, I'll find someone who will."

He turned and left the room, walking down the aisle of the elegant, pretentious barn, through the open doors, and into the thin October sunshine.

After three weeks had passed with no word, Liz began to worry that Kurt wouldn't be coming back. She swallowed her pride and called Aliqua.

A male voice answered. "Hello, Aliqua."

"Is Kurt there?"

"Nope. Don't work here no more."

Her heart slammed against her ribs, her breath stilled.

The man spoke again. "Do ya wanna talk to the boss?"

She exhaled sharply. "No, that's all right. I–"

She quickly hung up the phone.

He'd left her.

For weeks after that call, Liz's sadness filled every waking minute. Finally, she'd accepted the reality, and plunged into her work with all her strength, keeping her innermost thoughts at bay, thinking of nothing but her work and her horses.

One afternoon, she received an envelope from the attorney's office. She'd almost forgotten her feeble attempt to compromise Eve. Liz read quickly, hoping for positive news. The lawyer had contacted Aliqua, outlined the complaint, and described the consequences of being convicted of "intentional damage of property."

"...Unfortunately, Dr. Barnett, while your evidence is strong, it is purely circumstantial. Without an eyewitness to the crime, I don't

hold much hope of bluffing Ms. Aliqua into clearing your record.
 If you wish to pursue the matter, I'd suggest contacting every-
one you can find who might have been in the barn area that night.
Someone may have seen something you can use...."

 The pain of the past few months welled up, fresh as it's beginnings, and Liz wept.

 The weather in Taos remained balmy in late fall, at least during the day. The sun warmed Kurt's back as he strolled along the
sidewalk, taking in the familiar sights. The huge, annual art and
pottery festival had kicked off that day, and the town was jammed
with tourists. He'd loved living in the rustic old town that had survived the ravages of the modern age. Hundreds of artists made their
homes in the area, inspired by the magnificent scenery and crisp,
clean light.

 Stopping in front of one of the galleries, Kurt admired a small
clay Pueblo bowl, steeped with the magnificent colors of the native
earth. *I should buy that for Liz.* He closed his eyes for a minute.
She'd been on his mind almost constantly since he'd left California. The intimacy of the few days when he'd cared for her had
awakened old memories–painful memories that he'd suppressed
for almost ten years. Gradually, those memories had been replaced
with fresh, vibrant experiences with Liz that gave new meaning to
his life. *I have to get myself straightened out. I can't drift around in
Never-Never-Land forever.*

 He glanced at his watch. Only ten minutes to get to Leona's
Café. His future depended on this meeting with Buddy Carroll, and
he didn't want to chance missing it. He'd return to the gallery later.
For the moment, he'd sideline thoughts of Liz so he could concentrate on his bold plan to expose Della's treachery.

 As he'd nosed around his old stomping grounds over the previous two days, he'd learned from some of the locals that rumors
had flown wildly after he'd left town. His instinct told him that if
he pressed hard enough and looked long enough, he'd find answers.
Sure enough, Buddy Carroll, a former assistant trainer at one of the
big Arabian farms in the next town, had telephoned Kurt, promis-
ing to reveal critical information about the scandal.

As Kurt approached the door to the café, his heart thumped. The guy might be nothing more than another sleazy, wannabe trainer trying to act important.

In the far corner of the room, a small, wiry man rose and waved. Kurt shook his hand, then slid into the booth. Buddy's unkempt hair and wrinkled shirt gave him a down-on-his-luck appearance. *Not a good sign.*

Kurt spoke first. "So, what do you have to tell me?"

As Buddy started to answer, a waitress appeared beside the table, holding up a coffee pot and smiling invitingly at Kurt.

"Can I get you anything?"

"Just coffee. Thanks."

The girl poured the coffee and moved off to another table, and Kurt returned his attention to Buddy.

"Your information?"

The man hesitated, appeared nervous, as though he'd lost his nerve. "Well, I heard you were trying to find something to bring down Della Cortland."

Kurt remained silent and Buddy continued.

"When you were working for her, my boss, Stan Wilson, was... uh..."

Buddy stopped talking. Worry creased his forehead, as though he feared his revelation might jeopardize his own personal safety.

Kurt pushed his coffee to one side and leaned forward, arms resting on the table. He tried to keep his tone level and non-threatening.

"Go on."

"Stan was courting Della–and her money." He hesitated, looked closely at Kurt, then continued. "One night, Stan came into town for something, and he saw you and that real estate girl. What was her name?" He stopped, thought for a minute, then shrugged.

"Anyway, I think Stan suspected that Della was sleeping with you, which didn't fit in with *his* plans to combine the two farms. I guess he wanted you out of the way."

Kurt leaned back in the booth, Buddy's words stampeding through his brain. *Della was sleeping with someone else the whole time? If that's the case, why would she care about my friendship with Dottie?*

Buddy's voice interrupted Kurt's mental turmoil.

"I know the rumor went around that Della drugged her horse out of jealousy, but it was really Stan who did it."

Kurt spoke for the first time during the story.

"How do you know this for sure?"

Grim fury etched Buddy's weathered face. "Because I was there, and *saw* him. It was late at night, I was headed for the can, and just happened to see him come out of your horse's stall. He went the other direction and I followed him. He tossed something into the trashcan and left the barn. I looked in the barrel and there was a syringe layin' right on top of the rubbish."

Kurt reeled at Buddy's account of the drugging incident. Anger boiled up, almost choking him, and he leaned forward again, glowering at the man sitting across the table.

"Why the hell didn't you ever come forward? Do you have any idea what my life has been like since that show?"

Buddy shook his head sadly. "You have no idea what *my* life has been like since that show."

Forty-Eight

As time passed, Liz accepted Colleen's assessment of Kurt's actions. Whether out of a sense of responsibility or remorse, or something else, he must have felt the need to come to her aid after Muscala's attack. The shoulder had healed well, but her heart still ached, an open wound.

On a crisp, fall Sunday afternoon, she relaxed in her study, leafing through the latest issue of *The Arab Horse*. The magazine was thick and heavy, filled with the recent Arabian National Show results from Albuquerque. She idly looked through the pictures, feeling totally disconnected from that world. A full-page photograph drew her attention.

Bill Benton posed beside a magnificent black horse, the ground in front of them lined with trophies. The print below the picture read, "National Grand Champion Stallion, Aliqua Ebony, owned and shown by Bill Benton." Liz's jaw tightened, thinking about the price *she'd* paid, so that Bill Benton could show a national champion. The magazine dropped into her lap and she thought about Eve's bribe. Pain and anger percolated into Liz's mind. *I guess Kurt just took the commission and split.*

Images of the handsome cowboy had haunted her for weeks, sneaking up on her when she least expected it. When she cleaned stalls, the video loop in her brain clicked on. The memory of him leaning against the door, watching her on that afternoon so long ago, replayed itself repeatedly. Alone in the quiet barn, her thoughts would inevitably return to the magical night they'd shared in Tahoe.

In self-defense, she'd finally locked her emotions away into a dark place, deep inside where they couldn't hurt her anymore.

Now, without warning, the lock popped open and her feelings bubbled to the surface, as fresh as when they'd been stashed. *Face it. You are so in love with the man, you'd forgive him everything if he asked.* She looked down at the picture, now blurred by her tears.

Colleen came down with a cold, which turned into pneumonia, and Liz made the trip to Placerville to visit her sick friend in the hospital. Pale and small against the crisp hospital sheets, Colleen attempted a smile, but it came across as a small shadow of her usual bright countenance.

"Ain't this the pits?" she croaked.

"I *thought* you might be trying to burn the candle at both ends."

Colleen struggled to sit up. "Yeah, well, you know *me*, I gotta do it all. What's new?"

Liz told her the story of the rancher and his calves. Colleen hooted with laughter, sending herself into a coughing fit.

A frowning nurse stuck her head in. "You all right?" She turned her focus to Liz. "Don't tire her out. She needs a lot of rest."

The head disappeared and Colleen made a face. "That's not my favorite nurse, believe me. Now, go on with your story. I'll try not to breathe."

Liz finished the story, then thought for a minute. "Did you see the picture of Bill Benton and his new champion?"

Colleen nodded, but remained quiet, wariness creeping into her expression.

Liz probed a little. "Did you know Kurt doesn't work at Aliqua any more?"

Colleen nodded and looked embarrassed. "Yeah, but I didn't want to be the one to tell ya, since I've done nothing but put him down since ya fell for him."

"Any idea where he might have gone?"

Colleen looked very sad. "No...I sure wish I did."

"I've really made a mess of it, Colleen. What can I do to fix this? I don't even know where to start looking for him. When he left that day, he said he had to go somewhere on business. I just figured it was for Eve. Apparently, he went somewhere else, and my damned pride kept me from calling Aliqua soon enough to find out."

Silence dominated the room for a few moments, then Liz sighed. "I guess I'll just have to live with my mistakes, unless he shows up again. If he does, you'd better believe I won't let him get away this time." She stood up. "I'll get out of here now, before ol' Nurse Brutus returns. Be back in a couple of days."

Colleen smiled. "I'd like that. In the meantime, instead of just mopin' around, why don'tcha see if ya can figure out a way to track down your man, and bring him home?"

Kurt stole a sideways look at the small man walking beside him.

"I really appreciate your help, Buddy. After all this time, I wasn't sure I'd be able to find any evidence to clear my record."

"Yeah, well, I'll *never* clear mine. Wilson blackballed me in the whole area, made my life miserable. I'd like to see him pay for his treachery. I sure don't have anything to lose."

Kurt pushed open the heavy glass door to the Taos Community Bank, and the two men stepped inside. Buddy pointed toward a small Notary Public sign perched on a desk in the corner. Fifteen minutes later, they stepped back out onto the sidewalk.

Kurt folded the sheet of paper and tucked it into his jacket. "I'm headed out first thing in the morning. Why don't you meet me for breakfast at the Leona's?"

The following morning, Kurt finished his second cup of coffee and glanced at the clock. *I guess he decided to pass on breakfast. Not that I blame him. Dragging up all the old crap couldn't have been very pleasant.*

According to Buddy, he'd approached Stan Wilson and hinted that he knew the whole story, hoping to improve his own position at the farm. Stan had given him a large raise, with the understanding that the subject would never come up again. As soon as the furor had died down, he'd been fired.

Kurt shook his head, feeling a familiar bond with the down-and-out trainer, knowing how it felt to be discarded like yesterday's hero. But poor Buddy had been out of work for over six years, subsisting on odd jobs and seasonal work. Stan Wilson had spread lies about the man, making it impossible for him to find another training job.

A shadow darkened the table, and Buddy slid into the booth.

He looked embarrassed. "Truck wouldn't start. You already eat?"

"Nope, been nursing my coffee while I waited."

Kurt deliberately refrained from mentioning their previous conversation, instead, making small talk about the town and how it hadn't changed much. Breakfast arrived, and the two men ate in companionable silence.

When the dishes had been cleared and the check paid, Kurt pulled an envelope from his pocket and laid it on the table in front of Buddy.

"It isn't much, but it might be enough to get you out of Taos and into another area where you can find work. Competent horse trainers are hard to come by. I'm sure there'll be something out there for you."

Tears welled up in Buddy's eyes, and his shoulders sagged with gratitude as he stared at the envelope.

His voice broke as he picked it up. "Thanks. I hope you can fix your life, too."

As he drove out of town, Kurt remembered the clay bowl in the gallery window. He turned the truck around and headed back toward the shopping district, mentally reviewing the events of the last two days.

He shook his head. *The power of money. I took the hit for the drugging, and all this time, I've thought it was Della. No wonder she acted so obnoxious when I showed up here.*

Twenty minutes later, he was back on the road. He glanced at the package on the floor and smiled, picturing Liz's face when he presented her with the beautiful bowl. The smile faded abruptly. Why did he think she'd even speak to him, let alone be thrilled with a gift? He'd been away for almost two months, and hadn't even called her. Not that he hadn't picked up the phone every other day, desperately wanting to hear her voice. *I deserve whatever wrath she's going to hand out.*

Buddy's notarized testimony was tucked safely into the duffel bag, along with the money from Kurt's old savings account–fifty thousand dollars. *The sales commission on Ebony would have been nice, but this'll be enough to get me started, maybe a down payment on a place of my own.*

Kurt's optimism about the future grew, his thoughts filled with exciting ideas and plans. He'd finally left all the pain of the past behind him. The loose ends were almost tied up, and he felt really good about himself for the first time in a long while.

As he headed north, he read the looming road-sign: Denver 439 miles. One more stop, then he'd be able to go home to Liz.

Forty-Nine

S ince her father's death, Liz had found Christmas holidays to be almost unbearable. Without family to share the season, she'd taken refuge in a trip to one distant place or another, trying to dispel her loneliness. This year, her thin financial cushion wouldn't allow for any extravagant winter travel.

She leafed through a brochure for Arizona, wondering if a brief getaway to the sun would help her mood. Scottsdale was supposed to be wonderful in the winter, and also one of the best places to see fine Arabians. If she visited some farms and looked at mares, she'd be able to write the trip off to farm business.

Melancholy washed over her. Stepping back into Bill Benton's glitzy world of show horses would only make things worse. She wanted no reminders of her brief trip through that dark tunnel. She stared out the window at the hills and pastures, brown and dormant, waiting for spring. A sharp stab of homesickness ran through her. At this time of year, the Kentucky landscape would be blanketed in soft white snow, the trees and fences and rooftops and hills sleeping peacefully beneath the white cloak.

Kurt entered her thoughts, as he had so often during the past month. She'd called the secretary at the Arabian registry office, but had been told in no uncertain terms that member information was confidential. Liz's long history of keeping to herself had put her at a disadvantage, leaving her without even a network of horse friends who might know where he'd gone.

She shook off the dismal thoughts. Colleen had returned home from the hospital, but remained too weak to work, so Liz wore many hats those long days. As she headed out to the barn to do her chores and bring the horses in for the night, she focused on more positive subjects.

Surprisingly, the bright spot in her life had become her practice. She was busier than she'd ever dreamed possible in such a short time, and her bank account was slowly recuperating from its near-fatal low balance. *Darn good thing. The stud fees for breeding three mares will be hefty.*

She'd finally reviewed Miss Marcy's pedigree, and had decided that the mare was worth breeding if she found the right stallion. She'd made deposits two studs, a pure Polish and a Polish-Egyptian. Come spring, Marcy, Amy, and Fair Lady would have husbands.

Liz's heart warmed at the mental image of foals frolicking in the pastures again, their contented and watchful dams grazing nearby. As she cleaned stalls, she considered the future of Legacy Arabians. Well-bred horses always brought decent prices. Nothing like Benton's inflated price tags on animals that were boosted into stardom by God-only-knew what means–but certainly prices that would fit within the market. Her ambitious dreams of being a sensation in the show ring now seemed so shallow, and she questioned her motives again. *Why did I feel I needed to prove something?* The very fact that she'd kept some of her father's horses and had continued the bloodlines was, in itself, a memorial to Ben Barnett, but she hadn't seen it until recently. She smiled with fond memories. *One famous horse trainer in the family is surely enough.*

Trekking up to the pasture to collect the horses, an idea struck her. *Maybe I felt I had to justify having such excellent horses–do something important with them, more than just love and enjoy them.* She watched the mares follow Fair Lady down the hill toward the gate. Karma meekly brought up the rear, and Liz chuckled. Men do *not* rule in a horse herd. The females make the decisions, and the males obey.

Her mirth faded. *That's exactly what I did with Kurt. I enforced the rules, and true to herd pecking order, he followed them to the letter.*

That evening, Liz lay curled up on the study couch, reading

about a new medication for colic. After ten minutes of fighting to keep her eyes open, she rolled off the cushions and tossed the medical journal onto the desk. As she flicked off the light, the phone rang.

She groaned. "Oh, please, not an emergency right now. I need to go to bed."

She composed her voice. "Dr. Barnett. Legacy Arabians."

The line echoed with long distance.

"Hey."

Her heart leapt into her throat.

"Kurt! Oh, my God!" She shivered with delight–and relief at finally hearing his voice again. "How *are* you? *Where* are you?"

She heard the smile in his voice–probably amusement at how giddy she sounded.

"I'm good. How 'bout yourself?"

"I'm fine, really busy."

She couldn't believe the mindless exchange. She had a million things she wanted to say, but fear of another rejection reared its ugly head. A heavy silence thickened between them. She swallowed hard, then opened her mouth to say something else–anything to break the quiet.

His voice sounded solemn. "I've really missed you, Liz."

Anxiety tightened her chest. She'd waited so long to hear from him, and now she couldn't even speak.

His voice continued its soft, melodic voyage. "You have every reason to hang up on me. I've treated you badly, and caused you a lot of trouble. I just wanted to hear your voice again, and tell you I'm sorry."

His voice dropped as though he were going to end the conversation.

"No, wait!" She struggled to regain control. *I'm not going to let him slip away again.* She willed herself to be calm. She *had* to keep him on the line. "I heard you quit Aliqua. Where *are* you?"

He cleared his throat. "I'm on the road again."

A crackling noise echoed in the silence between them, then he spoke.

"When I realized what Eve had done to you, my long-lost

conscience jumped up from wherever it had been hiding all those years, and I had to make a serious decision. It scared the hell out of me, thinking about giving up the job I'd had such a hard time getting, but I knew I couldn't work for dishonest folks any more."

Listening to the strength in his voice, her heart swelled with love and admiration for his courage.

His tone became more confident. "Even before the end of the regional show, I'd planned to see if I could trap her into admitting she'd drugged Karma. When I returned to the farm after that show, she started hedging about Ebony's sales commission, and that really ticked me off. Then the damned mare attacked you, and that did it. Seeing you battered and bleeding as a result of Eve's unethical dealings put me right over the edge."

Liz reflected on the days he'd spent, tenderly caring for her and her horses. His voice brought her back to the present.

"I packed up and handed over my keys. It felt *really* good."

"You knew you were going to quit when you left here?"

"Yeah, and I'm sorry about that. I just couldn't tell you, because I wasn't sure if the truth would ever come out, and I was afraid you wouldn't pursue it."

"I did, and the attorney was fairly optimistic in the beginning, but not long ago, he wrote and told me that the only way to clear my name would be to find someone who saw something that night. I simply haven't found the strength to pursue it."

She winced at how wimpy she sounded.

His tone was sympathetic. "I was afraid of that. Finding old witnesses is a tough call."

Liz wanted to move past the subject. "Where've you been for the past two months? Looking for work?"

"Yes and no. I headed for New Mexico first. I had some old business to finish."

Liz waited. Further explanation didn't seem to be imminent. The unfinished business probably had to do with his original suspension. *How can I get him to tell me where he is?*

"Liz, I know it sounds like I'm hedging, but I've done a lot of soul searching about my past...and my future. I'm in the process of getting my name cleared on the old mess in New Mexico, and it's taking longer than I expected." He sounded nervous. "I didn't want to call you until I could tell you the good news, but it looks like I'll have something in writing any day now. I hope."

"That's wonderful! *Then* what are you going to do?"

He hesitated for a moment, as though choosing his words carefully. "I don't know yet. Depends on some other things in my life."

His guarded tone made her very nervous.

A second later, he spoke again. "Are you planning to go to that Arab art show in Oakland, the week after next?"

The abrupt change of subject caught her off guard.

"I have the invitation, but hadn't made any plans yet, because Colleen just came home from the hospital. She's not supposed to go out for a couple more weeks."

"Meet me there. Please?"

She closed her eyes, imagining herself standing next to him again, feeling his strong arm around her shoulders, inhaling his wonderful scent. His voice pierced her thoughts.

"Liz, please. I want to see you again. Start over."

She pictured his face, the corners of his eyes crinkling with his beautiful smile. Leaning into the phone, she felt their lips so close, yet so far.

"Me, too."

Ten minutes later, the phone rang again. Colleen's still-weak voice held breathless excitement.

"Liz! Have ya seen the new issue of the registry bulletin?"

"No, what's going on?"

"Eve Aliqua's been permanently suspended! *And* that black colt she sold to Bill Benton was stripped of its national title! I'll bet ol' Billy's ticked!"

Liz reeled with the news. "Are there any details?"

"Nope. Nary a one."

Colleen fell into a coughing fit, and managed to squeak out a good-bye.

Liz stared at the phone. *Had Eve actually found her conscience?*

❧

Fifty

The California Arabian breeders group had quite a reputation for putting on fabulous fund-raising events. Liz hadn't attended the last two galas, and she looked forward to this one.

The auction invitation had promised works by many famous and popular equine artists, including a piece by Robert Vavra. Liz's happiness grew as she flew down the highway. Even though she couldn't afford to buy anything, the prospect of being with Kurt again made her heart sing.

I'm not going to make any more stupid mistakes with him. Wherever he's been and whatever he's been doing, it's none of my business. Now *is the only thing that matters. It's time to take a chance.* She gulped at the thought. Taking a chance could mean things might not work out the way she wanted. Then, her father's words from the past echoed in her head. *"Lizzie, if you don't ever take any chances, you'll never know the opportunities you missed."*

She passed through the outskirts of Oakland, and found the street leading to Mills College, where the auction would be held. Stone gates towered twenty feet over the drive, marking the entrance. She drove slowly down the beautiful, tree-lined road, watching for signs to the College Art Museum.

The daylight had faded into dusk by the time she pulled into a parking space in front of the elegant Spanish Colonial building that housed the museum and art center. Old-style lanterns around the stucco building cast their golden glow on the ivory-colored walls and the lush shrubbery planted below.

As Liz locked the truck, the area around her suddenly exploded into brilliance, illuminated by thousands of colored Christmas lights. She gazed at the display, feeling a sense of joy and longing that had been locked away since her father's death. *I want all this back.* Resolving that she would shop for Christmas decorations the very next day, she started toward the entrance to the building.

As she climbed the wide steps, she looked up at the immense, marble Chinese dogs grinning down at her from their guard pedestals. Inside the door, she showed her invitation to the man at the registration desk, and took an auction number. She tucked it into her purse, feeling guilty that she wouldn't be using it.

The entrance to the exhibit lay straight ahead. *I'll just wait here 'til Kurt arrives.* She'd agreed to meet him around seven, but he hadn't said where. She settled onto a marble bench in the entrance hall and watched the large crowd of guests milling around, sipping wine, talking, laughing.

Each time the doors to the museum opened, her heart stopped. Each time, it wasn't Kurt. She stepped outside twice to see if he might be waiting by the front door. At seven-twenty, her stomach felt as though she'd swallowed lead. She rose from the hard bench, and followed the signs down the stairs to the restrooms. Her pain reflected in the mirror, and she blinked furiously. *He's just caught in traffic or something.*

Taking a deep breath and trying to compose herself, she headed back upstairs. *I'll wait in the lobby for another fifteen minutes. If he doesn't show up, I'll go in and look at the exhibits. If I'm being stood up, I might as well enjoy the artwork before I head back.*

Her chin quivered at the thought.

Okay, I've had enough of this foolishness. Liz rose and walked stiffly toward the entrance to Gallery One.

"Liz! Wait!"

Bill Benton strode up to her, smiling like a long-lost friend. Startled to see him, she wasn't sure what to say.

"Hi, Bill. Fancy meeting *you* here."

"I'm Celia's lackey tonight. She donated the food, and a couple of paintings. I'm supposed to be shopping for clients." He grinned wickedly. "You ready to talk business yet?"

Liz shook her head, feeling her shoulders droop.

"No, I'm finished with that stuff. It's not my world."

He cleared his throat, his face shadowing with sympathy. "It can be a real snake pit, that's for sure." He met her eyes, traces of apology tightening his jaw. "What a mess. I sure wish you had sold me *your* colt. Ebony was a waste of a good horse and a lot of my time."

Liz felt a surprising twinge of compassion–she knew the feeling of deep disappointment.

"You can still show him next year."

"Nah. Celia's suing Eve Aliqua for fraud. The horse will most likely be sold. And frankly, after all the scandal, I'd just as soon not have anything to do with him."

"What happened? If you don't mind me asking."

His face darkened with recollection. "At Nationals, after the stakes classes were finished, we were all partying in the skybox. Eve got a snootful." He shook his head. "She's never been able to hold her liquor. Anyway, just about everyone had gone, and Celia was joking around, using the trophy for a mirror. You know, fluffing her hair and so on.

"Out of the blue, Eve says, 'You should be thanking *me*, Celia. You'd have been in deep shit if that Barnett woman's horse had been in the ring.'"

Liz's stomach lurched, and she felt the blood drain from her face. Bill nodded at her recognition of his disclosure.

"You don't know Celia, but she's never been able to stand Eve Aliqua. The stupid bitch stood right there and as good as confessed to taking your colt out of the running. In front of witnesses."

He chuckled. "Celia wasn't about to let a chance like *that* go by. She filed a complaint with ASC, and that was it." He smiled sheepishly. "What is it they say? 'You can't win 'em all'?"

Liz shook her head in wonder. *I think it's, 'what goes around, comes around.'*

Bill offered his arm. "You going in for the auction? They're getting ready to start."

"No, I'm waiting for someone, but thanks. Maybe I'll see you later."

A large number of art pieces had been donated for the event. Three rooms of the museum were hung with exquisite oils, watercolors, pen & ink drawings, and photographs–all of magnificent Arabian horses. Several pedestals held fine sculptures in bronze or marble.

Gazing at the beautiful creations, Liz temporarily forgot her pain. She moved into the second room, and paused in front of a delicate bronze statue of a leggy Arabian colt with a daisy in his mouth. He held his short, baby tail at a sassy angle. Liz grinned, remembering how Karma had looked at three months–all legs and attitude. His personality had certainly changed recently. The mares were keeping him in line for the present, but before breeding season started, she'd need to separate him from the herd. He was approaching his second birthday, and would be capable of siring a foal, regardless of who the mare might be...including his own mother.

The blaring PA system interrupted her thoughts. Patrons were being asked to proceed to the auction area, the bidding was about to begin. She looked at her watch. Almost eight. *He's not coming.* Her throat tightened with disappointment, and she blinked back the threat of tears.

She moved into the third gallery, now deserted. For a moment, she pushed aside her sadness, overwhelmed by the beauty in the room. A large, dreamy watercolor caught her eye and, gazing into the luminous eyes of a white mare, Liz thought of Fair Lady.

"Beautiful."

Her heart leapt and she whirled around. Kurt's face beamed, warming her with his dazzling smile and deep brown eyes, a sight she'd missed more than she'd known.

He murmured softly, "And I don't mean the painting."

She felt warmth spring to her cheeks. *How could I ever have fooled myself into believing I didn't want this man?* Relief settled into her bones and she smiled, suddenly feeling shy.

"I'd given up on you."

"I'm really sorry. I worried that you'd leave before I got here. Traffic was horrible, and an accident at the Alameda exit really fouled things up."

"Ah, the famous Alameda exit. I went there once on my way to a horse show."

He looked at her curiously, and she smiled.

"Daydreaming instead of paying attention. Maybe someday I'll tell you about it."

He turned to the painting she'd been admiring.

"This one's great! Looks just like Fair Lady, doesn't it?" He offered his arm. "Shall we? I haven't had a chance to look at any of the others."

She slipped her hand into the crook of his elbow, thrilled by the chance to touch him again. A whiff of his scent tickled her nose, and she savored the familiar longings it stirred. While they strolled companionably through the rooms, she glanced sideways at him. A serene look softened his face, one she'd never seen before, an expression that bespoke inner peace. Every so often, he would stop to comment on a painting or sculpture. He surprised and delighted her with his excellent taste in art, and his knowledge of several of the artists.

His voice sparkled with enthusiasm. "I finally got my letter of reinstatement from the show commission."

"You must be thrilled."

"Yes, I'm a real person again."

He looked at her as though he wanted to say something else, but instead, slipped his arm around her shoulder and moved her forward.

She hated to break the spell of the delicious moment, but she had so many questions.

"What are you going to do now?"

He stopped and stood very still for a moment. When he answered, his tone sounded tentative.

"I have some money saved. I've always wanted to have my own place, be an independent trainer."

Alarm set off a thump in her chest. *He's planning to leave again.* She looked up at the face she adored, a face still shrouded by mystery.

Her voice cracked. "Where?"

He grinned down at her. "Right here where I belong."

They paused in front of a large oil painting of four mares with tiny foals at their sides. The small herd grazed through grass that the artist had tinged with pale colors, making it look as though it reflected the sunset. In the background, a small, rustic farmhouse lay nestled against a stand of evergreens, also touched with light. The windows of the house glowed, as though the people within basked in the warmth of firelight and love. She felt herself drifting into the field of mares, feeling the breeze that comes up at sunset. The breathtaking sensation tugged at her heart, and Kurt's arm tightened around her shoulder, as they stood together, bathed in the beauty of the scene.

An hour later, Liz walked beside Kurt through the cool night air. He helped her into his truck, climbed up behind the wheel, then pulled a package from under the seat.

"I brought you something."

She gazed at the man who'd consumed every waking thought, and long nights filled with dreams. His features were soft with emotion, a vivid contrast to the studied detachment he'd shown for months. She carefully unwrapped the layers of brown paper, then gasped with delight at the beautiful pot. She ran her fingers over the smooth surface, feeling the earth that had been molded beneath native fingers. The deep colors and burnished surface reflected the passion of its creator.

She gazed at the piece through a puddle of joy. "It's beautiful! Thank you."

Kurt lifted her chin and tenderly kissed away each tear. Her lips found his and her heart sang a new song.

A few minutes later, Liz turned the key in the ignition of her own truck, then smiled through the window. Kurt's wide smile and sparkling eyes filled her with joy.

"I'm happy you're back."

"Me, too. Now, you be careful goin' home." He reached in the window and squeezed her shoulder. "I'll see you next week."

On the drive back to Diamond Springs, Liz replayed the evening, recalling each sentence, every nuance. Kurt's trip to New

Mexico had been the key to his freedom. He was a new man, and she'd be starting over with him. The pain and disappointment of the summer could play no part in the new script. She'd need to put the past out of her mind, and trust him completely if she wanted to be part of his life.

Fifty-One

Kurt watched Liz's taillights dim and disappear down the long drive. *I don't deserve such forgiveness, but I damn sure appreciate it.* He turned and headed toward the entrance to the museum, a new spring in his step.

Bill Benton stepped into the lobby as Kurt entered.

"Hey, Kurt! Good to see you. I heard you took off for parts unknown."

Kurt shook Bill's hand. "I did, but I'm back. Listen, what's the status on Ebony? I understand there's a lawsuit going on."

Bill grimaced. "He's the blackest white elephant I've ever seen! Eve won't take him back, Celia doesn't want him around." His eyes narrowed. "Why do you ask?"

"He's a damned fine horse, and he got a raw deal. I want him, if he's available."

"Celia's in the patron's lounge. Let's go find out."

Digging through boxes in the attic, Liz found the one she wanted, then climbed down the ladder and carried it into the living room, where Colleen waited.

"You know, Colleen, I feel like this is my first real Christmas. It's been such a long time."

"I'm happy you've included me."

Liz picked through the box, and lovingly unwrapped the Christmas ornaments of her childhood.

She held up a tiny crystal angel. "My dad brought this to me from a horseshow one year."

Colleen picked up a delicately-etched gold sleigh and peered closely at the detail. "This is gorgeous. Where'd ya get this one?"

Liz thought for a moment. "I think I bought that my first year in vet school."

Her throat tightened as she gazed at a small silver frame that held her baby picture. Each memento filled her heart with both sadness and joy.

When they'd emptied the box, Colleen stood up and jingled her keys, a wicked twinkle in her eye.

"Let's go find ya the perfect tree. After all, ya can't entertain Kurt under--er, next to just any ol' thing!"

For the next week, Liz immersed herself in the spirit of the season. To make this special Christmas complete, she'd wanted to add something new. It had been years since she'd shopped for decorations. She enthusiastically whistled "Jingle Bells" as she headed home from a shopping spree in Placerville, the floor and passenger seat of her truck overflowing with all sorts of bright goodies. She grinned. There wouldn't be one spot on the farm that didn't reflect her happiness.

To add to that joy, Kurt called every night. He was staying with his mother in San Francisco, trying to right some past wrongs. The night of the auction, Liz had learned that after he'd lost his wife and son, he'd withdrawn from his own family because he'd felt unable to cope with their sympathy and pleas for him to come home. The Taos mess had further complicated his life, adding shame and humiliation to his sorrow.

Liz recalled the resolve in his voice when he'd told her of his plans to spend some time with his mother and sisters, see if he could make it up to them for casting aside their love. The small glimpses of the tender man inside the strong exterior made Liz's heartbeat chatter with excitement, knowing he was finally free to be himself.

~

Fifty-Two

Early on Christmas Eve, Liz chose a long, dark red silk caftan from her closet, and shimmied into the luxurious garment. She brushed her hair until it shone, dabbed a spot of perfume at her throat, then padded barefoot down the stairs and into the living room. She switched on the tree lights and gazed at the beautiful sight, her heart skipping in anticipation of sharing it with Kurt. A fire crackled in the fireplace, and champagne chilled in a bucket of ice. Through the window, she caught the flare of headlights turning into the driveway, and she drew in a long, deep breath. Tonight would be just the beginning.

Minutes later, she opened the door and smiled.

"Merry Christmas."

"Ho, ho, ho! Don't *you* look beautiful!" He stepped inside and pulled her into his arms, growling into her ear. "I've been away too long."

"Yes, you have," she breathed on a sigh, melting against the warmth of his chest.

"Won't happen again. I promise."

She tilted her head back and narrowed her eyes. "If it does, I'll hunt you down with dogs."

His answering kiss took her breath away.

When they came up for air, she giggled. "Are we going to spend Christmas Eve in the mud room?"

He grinned sheepishly and accepted her hand, following her down the hall to the living room.

Kurt poured the wine, then settled down beside her on the couch and raised his glass. "Here's to new beginnings."

"Amen. Let's start with yours. What are your plans?"

His excitement sent a boyish flush across his features.

"Well, I don't have much to get going. Just a little money, and a fantastic black colt."

She gasped. "Ebony?"

He chuckled. "The very same."

"But, I thought he was going back to Eve."

"Nope, he belongs to me now. He's a great horse, and I can't think of a better way to get my reputation back than to give him a chance to regain his crown."

"You really like him, don't you?"

An embarrassed smile played with the corners of his moustache, and he glanced down at his hands.

"Yeah. He and I have a lot in common."

Two champagnes later, Liz rose from the couch and smiled down at him.

"I need to get dinner going before I fall asleep!"

"Hmmm. I can think of other things to do besides eating."

She flushed with delight, then winked. "Maybe for dessert."

"Good. I'll save room."

Liz carried the dinner tray into the living room, and set it down on the coffee table, aware that Kurt watched every move she made.

"You have to stop staring at me like that–it makes me nervous!"

He grinned wickedly. "You'll have to get used to it, 'cause I'm not gonna stop!"

She shook her head and turned to stir up the fire. Stunned, she stared at the oil painting perched on the mantel. The beautiful pasture with mares and foals, the cabin in the background, the extraordinary light in the scene.

"Oh, my God, Kurt." She turned, wide-eyed to meet his pleased smile. "When did you..."

He moved to stand beside her. "After you left the auction, I went back inside. This one was just coming up for bid."

She gazed at the painting, overwhelmed by her love for the man beside her.

"Liz?"

She turned at the husky tone of his voice, and saw a mirror of her own emotions.

He took her hand. "I can't imagine my life without you."

He softly pressed a small box into her palm.

Shaking fingers fumbled with the gold ribbon. When she finally managed to open the box, a diamond flanked by two tiny gold horseshoes sparkled back at her from black velvet. Speechless, she raised her eyes to meet his.

The tenderness in his gaze enhanced his whisper.

"I love you, Liz. I always will."

His soft voice swirled around her, caressing her heart. From somewhere far away, her own response echoed.

"And I love *you*."

He slipped the beautiful ring onto her finger.

"Will you take a chance with me?"

She looked at the man who'd allowed her to finally feel alive. To feel the pain, the passion, the joy, and the sorrow–all the things her father had warned would come with taking chances. Her heart swelled with a deep love that had dwelt there for a long time, waiting to be acknowledged. She moved into his waiting arms, stepping over the edge of her cliff, and into his space.

Responding to the love in his dark eyes, she whispered her answer.

"Always."

She melted into Kurt's kiss, and from the painted field before them, heard soft nickers of welcome.

Printed in the United States
200401BV00006B/55-57/A